Draconian Symphony

Benjamin Dempsey

Tell-Tale Publishing Group, LLC   Stargazer Imprint

Tell-Tale Publishing Group, LLC
5714 Peri St
Swartz Creek, MI 48737

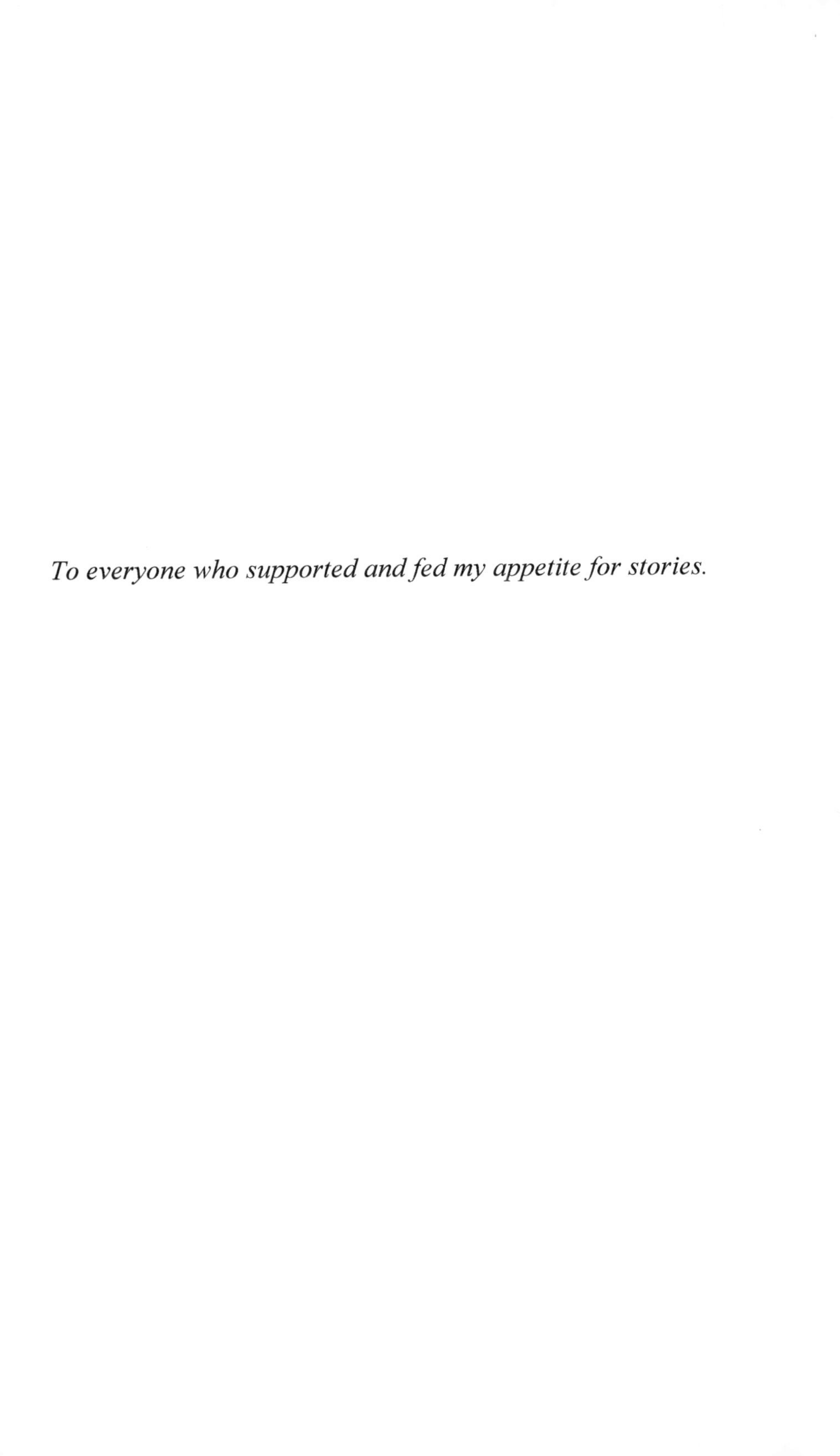

To everyone who supported and fed my appetite for stories.

OVERTURE

Chapter One

The She-Devil

On my bed, at the edge of sleep, I was not alone. The rhythmic racket of an open window could claim the credit of rousing me. As a self-trained mage of questionable rationality and uncertain origin it wasn't often I received visitors in the night.

From the dim shadows a silhouette sashayed toward me, sheathed from the intruding moonlight by storm clouds. My flesh turned goose and I moved to flee. Just then, the clouds parted, my room lit up.

I froze.

A curtain of coal cascaded down a slender neck and framed a corpse-pale face of most handsome visage. She opened her eyes and I plummeted into a pair of predatory pits, scarlet and terrible. Her mouth split open into a smile, each razor edge whispering for prey. She wore but a nightgown and heeled shoes.

I licked my night-chapped lips and gulped spittle. My left hand trembled.

She approached. Her hips swayed with each step. She looked into my eyes and, with such little encouragement, higher thinking faded into figments of free will, falling to less than a single thought. My left hand twitched.

A tantalizing hand reached for my face. She was closer now, and smelled of honey and alcohol. Her heart's a-rapid and a-rhythmic tone pounded in my head.

I latched onto her neck and a slow, throaty breath escaped my mouth as I rose from the bed. Her eyes widened, her brow furrowed, her mouth opened, distended wider than should be possible and she screeched. It was the sound of wind tearing apart metal. My knees buckled, and my hands flew to my ears. She slipped out of my reach, but I still smelled sweet liqueur.

The shock of her scream broke whatever reverie clouded my mind.

"You . . . reject me?" My dark visitor spoke. "ME?" She snarled, baring serpentine fangs. I reached for the sword-servant beside my bed, a blade over five feet long and half as wide as my forearm.

"Just who is this strange visitor, knocking in the night?" I said in merriment as I bought my sword to bear. "Drakkengard, we have a visitor!" The blade trembled to life. Incandescent red script lit up the length of the black blade, casting a supernal glow on my room.

"Well? Who do I owe the honor?" I ask, Drakkengard at the ready.

"You fucking jackal! A woman in your bed and *this* is how you react?" The intruder's arms tensed and her fingers dug into her palms.

"Strange kindness is too rare to expect." The stranger was slender, and common sense might suggest she's physically weak. But common sense is a liar and a gambler, so I kept my distance.

"You mangy, impotent dog!" She extended her arm and her hand griped an unseen handle. From innocuous space, she pulled a thin, curved blade that trailed smoke.

"I will have my feast!"

I doubted she had my best interests in mind.

The fiend lunged, thrusting at my flank. I stepped aside and slammed into her with my shoulder. She stumbled, tripped on a heap of discarded clothes and slumped against my closet. She took a moment to catch her breath and ducked. My blade tore through the cabinet, raining splinters everywhere. With luck, the noise wouldn't wake my sister.

Before I could defend, pain flared in my side where her sword pierced my flesh. She introduced me to the heel of her shoe and knocked me back. I now sported another puncture wound.

She might want to remove those heels before she breaks an ankle, I mused unkindly. The hand clutching my wound was sticky with blood. Could it get better? I could but hope.

I straightened myself and we locked eyes. She was smiling. Was it a smile? It must be! This was so much fun. Why wouldn't she smile? She faced me sideways, her sword at the ready, my broken closet beside her and a wall behind her. We shifted our stance to more evenly face each other, my sword to my side and the door to the hallway behind me. Her off-hand was hidden behind her. Delightful. She was full of surprises.

The first move was mine and I dashed to strike with the pummel of my sword. She ducked aside and my blow cracked the stone wall behind her. The impact rattled my arm and weakened my grip. I spun to find she'd backed away and now held something.

Strange. It glowed bright red. Was it burning? It looked to be the size of my head. It resembled flame, but the colors were wrong. I've never seen such a bright-red flame, and its heart was black. She wound up her arm and pitched it.

The blast launched me through the door and into the hallway. My nerves screamed of heat more ferocious than the surface of Sol and of coldness more savage than frozen seas of Neptune. Or did it tickle? The sensation wasn't something my brain could not comprehend or even contextualize. My foe sauntered toward me. Now I was sure she was smiling.

"Does it hurt? Is it greater than you've ever felt before in your entire peasant life?" She held another ball of pain-flame in her hand.

"If you beg, I'll put it out for you. No need to suffer overlong." She was taunting me. She thought she'd won. Who did she think she was? Who did she think I was? Ignorance is no excuse! This was slander! How *dare* she!

I coughed and rose to my feet. The unfamiliar not-fire had just reached my shoulder. There was a funny metallic tang in my mouth--not a good sign.

"Hm? This little sparkle here?" I waved my arm, agonized by the false blaze.

"Come now, come now, I've *eaten* worse than this!" I laughed. I couldn't see out of one eye from the pain. It was too funny to handle.

"But if you wish to invoke the arcane, allow me to acquiesce."

A simple principal: to use a living body as a crucible for refinement and reconstitution of ambient arcane energy. Crowley called it Magick. Turned called it Dark Energy.

"It feels good." I let out a heartfelt sigh, or was it a moan? No matter.

Inside me the infinite flows, shapeless and without direction or purpose. I give it shape, direction, purpose.

"Let it burn!" and my arm burst with conflagration. Not the sickly unnatural flames of my foe. True flame. Perfect flame.

Mine. My flames washed away the red scourge, purifying my limb and leaving it as it should be. This flame doesn't burn my arm. Just as it's difficult to bite through your own finger, so too does spell-casting err away from self-harm.

I vanished my flames from the world, leaving just a few trails of smoke drifting from my arm, but they are still there, beneath the flesh. The magick I took in is now flame, and even if I spend it, I can take in more magick to fuel my furnace. If you can use it, magick is infinite, unless the body breaks down first.

My foe was staring at me. She'd dropped her stance and had an odd expression on her face. Was she afraid? Was she shocked? No, it's something else. What?

"You're a mage." Her tongue swept across her lips. Weird. I steadied my grip on Drakkengard and embers flickered on my left hand. If I was lucky, she wouldn't catch on that fire is the only magick I know.

"I'm trying to sleep here and you just invade my home. If you want my life, I must demand you earn it," I fine-tuned my posture. Her face expression blanked for a moment and she grinned.

"You say the weirdest things, boy. Wager accepted." She retook her stance at last.

"The same applies to you, mind" I took a step to the right. She took a step to the left, now we both faced each other, standing in my hallway.

Out the corner of my eye, a young girl peeks around the corner of a doorway. Damn it all! I wasted too much time and now my sister's at risk.

"Diana, get away, now! We're under attack." I bellowed. My sister vanished into the gloom. I couldn't let her get caught up in this rubbish. I turned back to my foe once I no longer heard footsteps.

"Now come!"

She lunged for me and I blocked fast enough to avert my disembowelment. I shoved her sword away with mine and threw a jab with my off-hand. She batted it away and brought her sword across my chest. Blood splashed across the wall beside me. It was painful, but shallow. My body looks normal but it heals quickly. I should be fine.

I swung when she tried to advance but it was a feint, and I gouged a hole in floorboards, spraying woodchips and slinters at her face.

She reeled and I tackled her to the ground. She rolled away as I struck, and a few locks of her hair fell to the ground.

Still blinded by the debris in her eye, she drew back a fist. I ignored it and swung forward, arcing for her neck. Before my blade could reach her, she slammed her knuckle into the ground.

The floorboards exploded from the force and she pirouetted into the air, landing on the staircase at the end of the hallway. Blood dripped from her fist, and her chest heaved from the effort. A picture fell from its frame.

"Ha-ha, oh you are a treat!" My embers danced as I sized up the distance. The hall was aglow as my foe hurled another of those false balls of flame but it was easy to avoid as I charged head-on. It emitted no heat as it flew past, which was weirdly galling.

From the foot of the stairs I leapt, cutting through the base on my way. The staircase trembled as I landed, the first of its supports severed. I hacked away at her feet and forced her to the rooftop door.

Fire flowed into my left hand and formed a chuckling sphere. Before she could react, I hopped forward and hurled it to the ground.

A thunderous roar echoed, loud enough to hurt my ears. The world spins Arctic to Antarctic. Something hard and sharp struck my back and made something else go crunch. Winds blew past me for a moment, and something rigid smashed against my ribs.

"He he—Aha-ha-ha!" That was fun! I rose to my feet, and my joints cracked in a peculiar manner. Drakkengard was still in my hand, unharmed.

"Ah, good" I sighed in relief, and took in my surroundings.

It was the roof terrace of my house. From here, there was little chance of harming my precious sister if I let loose.

My foe had landed a short distance away from me and muttered curious curses. She was more harmed than I, and on her feet now. Her body was splattered with blood, but she didn't show any signs of harm. My blood, then?

The moon hung high and distant overhead. It illuminated this summer night's reverie. A gentle breeze carried dangerous silence. My left arm belched smoke.

"I ask of you," I shifted my weight to one foot. "Let's do this right. Hold nothing back." At my will, my entire body erupted in a cloak of flame. The smoke was thick and choking and so self-gratifying, this burning of mine.

"I can't win this way. Damn you to hell, human! Damned if I do and damned if I don't!" She stashed her sword back to whatever pocket she had.

"Burn the sight of me into your eyes, pig, then roll over and die," I mocked.

It started with something too-sweet in the air, reminiscent of decaying flowers and dead fruit. It was the sickly sweet of fermentation. My mouth salivated and my stomach turned in its cave.

It reached my skin, a myriad of molesting hands groping over my body, penetrating my skin and stroking my bones, probing my organs with slender fingers and rusty nails.

It continued into hearing, a sound on the edge of sound, an unknown word. A second word is spoken, a third, a fifth, a hundredth, a legion whisper at the edge of consciousness. They demand incomprehensible acts be done upon impossible things.

The phenomenon becomes visible as her body excretes a strange substance. Black and purple mists rise from her flesh and enshroud her entire body in an impenetrable fog. Those noxious vapors betrayed not an outline.

A new sound becomes audible. Paper is torn away, a thousand tiny sticks snap one after the other or are they bone? Or tree bark peels under the heat of the sun, or a cicada breaks out of its cocoon, having waited years to kiss the sun for just one day.

The mist of death subsides. The breath I held escapes.

She stands there, clad in black. No, not clad, her clothes have vanished from the world. Her skin is pitch as night, yet glistening like carapace under the lunar rays.

She leaned back and spread a pair of large wings, tufted with downy fur. They continued to stretch out behind her until reaching their full length. Each was longer than she was tall. A thin membrane of skin stretched across the three slender fingers of her wings, before coming down and anchoring them to her hips.

Her shoulders now sported two sockets each, one for her arms, now pushed forward, and another for her wings, which sat to the back of them.

She pulled back her wings and left them at rest upon her back, concealing just how large they were.

She stretched her long, thin limbs, and bared the six appendages taut before bringing them to rest. Her movements showed off the lean, powerful muscles across her chest and back. They spoke of the great strength needed to move her colossal wings. The muscles across her chest in particular pushed forward her modest bust, making it much more impressive than its actual size suggested. Her breasts heaved with her every breath.

Her wide torso tapered into a too-thin waist and narrow thighs. It was impossible to fit much of a stomach in there, let alone a digestive track. Didn't she eat much? Then I realized it was possible that she ate nothing.

Her long, thin legs ended in appendages closer resembling a raptor's talons than any human foot. The heel was held high off the ground and she balanced on five elongated toes, each ending in a deadly claw.

From the base of her spine swayed a prehensile tail, half a length longer than either leg. It swished back and forth in uneven strokes.

Her arms appeared the same, but with a changed color and texture. Large, thick fingers ended in curved claws double their length, which glistened with menace in the moonlight.

Her long black hair fluttered on absent wind, and on one side of her head protruded a small, dagger-like horn.

At a glance, her face is the same, but her eyes . . . what was once an odd shine is now a luminous carnelian glow.

This she-devil threw back her head and let out a cacophony of echoing laughter. She exposed a mouth full of long, sharp teeth. Her canines protruded past her lips when she closed her mouth. The contrast of black and white made the inside of her mouth look bloody, unless it was bloody and this creature was far stranger than I first supposed.

Old, no, ancient. When the old world broke apart, she was old, yet so young in the face of how old she yet would be. The ghosts of chains hung from her limbs, and her hands are soaked in betrayal's recompense. If she just asked, an empire would rise and fall for her entertainment. Lies, fire and fuel wrapped around a black, leaky heart. In her eyes, she was just a little horn, which saw destiny as a problem for others. Instead, she conjured up maelstroms of other people to stem the flow. A starving maw whose teeth couldn't let the food pass through its lips. Oceans of hunger. A second mouth split open across her chest, tongueless and filled with teeth. It was soon joined by another, and another. Her flesh was a maze of gibbering mouths that gaped and wailed and gnashed and drooled, desperate for something of sustenance. She stood, terrible and exquisite under the light of a thousand-thousand stars, despairing for prey.

"Feast your eyes, the least I can allow before feasting on you." Her voice rang with the sound of a thousand beasts howling a symphony of discord. It sent tingles along my spine. I never understood the term 'apex predator' until now.

"My dear, dark lady, you are more than I could have ever hoped for." My voice trembled. I readied my sword. My eyes burned with burgeoning tears and I stifled laughter. She stood naked, not in flesh, but in spirit.

"Aha AHAHA! You are a strange one. I must have you!" She pushed against the ground and rushed toward me.

No matter how fast, she avoided each swing of my blade. I brought Drakkengrd up to block, but found empty air. Pain lanced across my back. I jumped forward, spinning around to defend my blind spot.

Blood ran along my spine, drop by drop, to the open rooftop. She stood where I was a moment before, my blood on her claws and a grin on her face.

The flames enshrouding my body flicker, just for a moment. The woman blurred toward me. I parried two swipes for my chest, but I still ended up bleeding from the midsection. I caught a glimpse of her, standing to my side, tearing and piercing me with a wall of claws. She was one hundred knives in the shape of a woman, terror and splendor forged together.

I laughed and howled as my nerves screeched and my flesh was plundered. Defense didn't seem worth it. In fact, it wasn't.

Her claws sunk inch-deep into my back and scraped along three bones. Pain seeped from my spine, molten mercury dripping from my wounds. There would be no more delay.

I thrust Drakkengard into the ground in front of me and reached behind me with my free hand. I latched onto the demoness's wrist. With my blade as a brace, I heaved the woman over my shoulder and slammed her into the ground. Her wrist was still in my hand, but bent at an abnormal angle.

Before she could recover I slammed my foot against her arm, and she grunted in pain. What other sounds could she make? I adjusted my grip on her wrist, increased the pressure on her arm and heaved the other way.

Her arm makes a sordid, organic sound, far louder than it had any right to be. I could picture in my mind how it happened, the twisting and straining and eventual fracture, made worse as the bones ground against themselves. However, it happened, and I looked down upon the result.

I let go, then, allowing her arm to fall, hanging limp from the break. Her blackened skin was torn, allowing voyeuristic glimpses of bone and sinew as it twitched on itself.

She made no sound, just stared at her now useless arm. It wasn't healing the same as her other wounds. Why wasn't it healing?

I removed Drakkengard from the ground, stepped backward and waited for a response.

"It's just a break. Is it such an abnormal thing?" I asked. She laid against the ground and looked different, not the inhuman predator, just another frail creature with brittle bones and weak flesh. It put acid in my mouth.

"Come on, get up! Do something! You're alive aren't you? Burn me! Slice me! Rip into me! Come at me!" I shouted, and paced back and forth, flames licking my left arm in frustration.

"Or should I just end you now?" I spit, and glared at her.

The woman rose to her feet, glaring at me with seething eyes. Each simmering pit was a marble of jet, adorned by many carnelian rings. At last, she reacted!

"Your kind really pisses me off, you know," she growled. Her right arm hung limp and useless. I didn't think she was having as much fun as she should be. A pity.

"Then hate me. Just don't disappoint!" With a smile, I flipped Drakkengard around in a reverse grip, her blade facing away from the enemy.

The she-devil crouched, the muscles in her legs as tense as steel. Pylons should have creaked and groaned under the pressure. But no, nothing made a sound, but it was eerie for so much power not to quake the world.

I faced her side on, fists raised. Breathe in, breathe out.

She leapt! She wailed a protracted cry the dead would weep in fear of. I hopped to one side and landed a heavy blow to her stomach with Drakkengard's pommel. She landed on her feet and skidded backward before turning and leaping at me. Again. I stepped aside. Again. But then she wrapped her tail around my midsection, her momentum allowing her to swing behind me and latch onto my back. Her claws sunk into my sides and she tore into my flesh with her teeth. Blinding flashes of pain shot past with each bite, threatening my balance. I groaned and threw myself backward. I landed with my weight on my back, pinning her beneath me. There were several nauseating crunches as a few bones snapped under the strain. Cold, cold and hot, biting cold and searing hot temperatures assailed the nerves along my back, and forced me off her.

Aberrant translucent flame assailed my flesh. I drew in magick from around me and burst into flames, drowning out the atypical blaze assaulting my back. By the time I was done the She-devil charged toward me. Her right arm must have recovered as it now held her sabre. Her whole body was veiled in her too-red fire.

I brought up Drakkengard and met her blade with my own. Metal sparked against metal, her off hand tearing through my flaming shroud and raking across my chest. Our blades met again. I caught her off-hand. Her claws dug into the skin around my fingers. She reared her head back and smashed it into my own. Her small horn struck my crown, and it could well have been an icepick.

My vision swam and went dark. Temporary connection loss please contact my head! Pain is a concussion? I swung my sword with wild abandon, trying to keep away while I was not *in domina*— in control.

My face was wet. Blood? Tears? Pulp?

Something sunk into my chest. Was it a blade? It must have been. I was having trouble bleeding. No, breathing. My head was so light, everything was scooped out. Empty.

"You give up, brat?"

My vision returned in one eye. She was standing—was it a few meters or a few miles away? My perspective was horrible and skewed. An ocean of blood flowed from the blade by her side. The wound in my head, was it? No, it was not as dire as it felt. I could…

Although I can't see her, Drakkengard's weight tells me she's still in my hand. It's comforting. I struggled to raise my sword. My hands trembled with the effort. After a few moments, my arm gave out. I kept a loose grip on her hilt but couldn't stop her blade from hitting the ground with a clatter, for which I murmured apologies.

The woman's eyes widened for a moment, before narrowing, glaring at me.

"Then you can die."

My flames, which had dimmed, exploded with renewed vigor. I dragged myself toward her one foot at a time. Each step forced me to reassert my sense of balance from scratch. The sound of Drakkengard grinding against the granular ground beneath me grated against my ears. Still, I was smiling. This was good. All was well. This happiness was . . .

My body drew in more and more magick as I compensated for my wounds with raw power. Higher and higher my flames grew, a blazing torch in the night. I wondered how many would see should my flame be snuffed?

With a muttered curse the night stranger approached, sword in hand, her eyes glistening with pity, or was it loathing? I couldn't tell. I tried not to watch. The more I watched the more of her I saw. It was too distracting.

She thrust her blade into my gut, turning my insides into a spit roast. My flames flickered in fever. She grabbed the hilt with both hands and prepared to lift, to spill me over the ground.

"Farewell," she muttered, her voice more normal.

"You and me both," I tittered. Her eyes widened as my sword was impaled into her chest, and her stomach, and her arms and her legs. Her eyes swiveled to see Drakkengard still in my limp hand, but changed. What was once a rigid blade was now a swarm of metal tendrils burrowing into my foe's body.

"This will not be my end, demon," I whispered. Her legs gave way, forcing her to her knees and bringing me to the ground with her.

"I will not die from your hate. I will not die from your wounds. My end is not tonight, and not at your hands." I collapsed upon her sword. Blood and sweat saturate the air. Is this her death?

Another tendril rose from Drakkengard, positioning itself right against the woman's neck and pressed against the soft flesh.

I mustered my strength and lifted myself off her blade, a mistake for sure. My blood gushed onto the rooftop by the pint but I tried my best not to let its effects show. I tried to ignore the intestines poking out of the open wound.

"I should kill you. That would be so much better or at least simpler." My foe clung to consciousness as best she could, but was she really helpless? It would all be for naught if I died here too. "Alas, it would be such a waste to throw away a life I worked so hard to earn."

Her eyes widened, but she said nothing.

"I could kill you now, but if I don't I know you'll make sure you live. Therefore, you, who invaded my home and tried to slay me in my sleep, I will let you go, but know your life is indebted. You will go but-" I let out a weary chuckle. "Let's just say you owe me," and everything is done.

I pulled Drakkengard away, and hobbled to the stairway.

I didn't even turn to see the woman's response.

It did not matter.

If what I saw in was is true, our bargain would hold.

It was done.

***

I returned to the roof. I'd have returned sooner, but I had to reassure my sister first, and make sure she went back to sleep. I climbed over the parapet and sat on the roof's edge. My feet swung over the side. I took a deep breath of the night air and considered the twinge in my side caused by such action. Those stitches should be enough to keep my insides from being reintroduced to my outsides long enough for the wound to close. The blood on the roof was still wet and had attracted the flying vermin. The life-stuff of the demon and myself became foodstuff for flies and micro-fauna.

Ignoring the stench of blood, the chilly night air and my itching wounds, I stared out. I stared out past my illegitimate house, past the hungry fold of Waltham Forest to what lays on the horizon.

I drank with greed the sight of Great Londinium, of the Royal Palace and Fortress, of the High Apostle's Golden Throne, of its crystal castles and babel-towers. Its docks were filled with tankers from the offshore hydrogen farms and its hyper-metropolis boroughs teemed with fashion and quick fixes and free meals for loose fools without such troublesome scruples as ethics and even citizenship.

After a day or two's rest, I'd go and join them. Distraction and fun would lose distinction and losing track of time becomes the exact opposite of wasting it. Time is garbage, an ever-mounting vault of refuse that bogs the constant race against the lethal boredom. More than the paranoid monarchy, more than the corrupt ministers, London's greatest sickness was boredom. The city looks the same today as it did yesterday, last week, last year and last century. Plenty of buildings have come and gone, but nothing has changed for so long. Millions of people gnaw at the bones of a dead zeitgeist and wonder why their culture grows gaunt.

The news feeds might as well be silent. They don't talk about how civil unrest is oppressed by its own apathy, and they don't talk of how the warring states of America are too scared of the dark to stop the fighting. They don't talk of how people think the Japanese don't even exist anymore since no-one's seen past the Divine Winds for hundreds of years. Nor do they discuss how there hasn't been a meaningful scientific discovery since the twenty-second century. They don't explain how everyone's waiting for the end of a world that's never coming. There's nothing to say. It was like that when we got here. The energy crisis was solved centuries ago, but left the world living paycheck to paycheck, with no surplus to invest in making things better, or even different.

My thoughts return to the demon. Maybe it's time I looked to other worlds. I still have unfinished business. I can use her to finally get revenge.

FIRST MOVEMENT

Sonata

Chapter Two

The Red Queen

Diana

I gagged at the smell of sulphur tearing through my nose. Uneven stones crunch underfoot.

"This, is this the place?" My 'brother' stepped forward, his mouth covered by his hand. An odd lie for him to make

My 'brother', Draco. He says he doesn't know where the name came from. He adopted it before he became lucid.

"Hey, you wanted a way in, I brought you here. You can't blame me if you're too up your own head to give me proper direction!" The black-haired woman scowled. She calls herself Lascivus. No comment there.

Lascivus, a demon Draco fought and defeated. He exchanged her life for a single favor. Today, a favor he spent to have her bring us here. An unfair trade if you ask me.

"It stinks!" The third member of our entourage whined, voicing what everyone was thinking.

A curious creature, it is, clad in black robes, a red gem round its neck and physically rather mousy. It responds to the name

Drakkengard, and is a useful tool but obnoxious. If anyone is at fault, blame Draco for coddling it so much.

A vacant, lifeless wasteland consumed the horizons. The air was stale and thin, it carried the smell of infertile soil. This place is little more than the bleached bones of planetary roadkill.

A red sun hung in the sky, but its light was too weak to blot the stars. It could flicker out in just a moment's notice. This place was a dead rock with nothing to boast but a thinning atmosphere, a stony surface and a dying sun. Well, save for one other thing.

"I don't see anything." My brother gazed from one horizon to another.

"Thank you for sharing with us, I pray we never go without your insight in these matters!" Lascivus snapped. She hoped she didn't mess up and make a fool of herself.

"I'll cut your tongue off!" Drakkengard growled. Was it supposed to be bestial? I was watching a Chihuahua threaten an anaconda.

"Easy Drakkengard." Draco placed his hand on her shoulder. She froze at his touch for a moment before relaxing.

"Lascivus, can you scout overhead for me? I just want you to look for any sort of structure." He said, directing his gaze to the dark-haired woman.

"Certainly, the Royal Laze's Air Force will get right on that and—NO! Do your own scouting!" She spat at the ground and kicked a rock. It tumbled a few meters before being reunited with its better half, separated four thousand years ago when a stone was struck by lightning.

My 'brother' flexed his knuckles.

"In the contract, demon. 'Take me to Malign.' Now, I'm not sure about you, but I don't see her here. I don't consider your end of our deal kept, she-devil," He spoke. No one else noticed his left hand flinch.

"Give me a break. I brought you as close as I could at this conceptual range. I swear on my father's work, honor is a waste and a weakness. The things I do on pain of death," She grumbles. A moment passed, and the woman made no motion to move.

"So, will you do it?" I asked, more to speed things along than needing an answer.

"Ugh, no. Do you take me for a field-layer? Besides, I've a better method," She said.

The succubus narrowed her eyes, and a faint glow outlined her pupils. Like many of her kind, she could 'see' life, for the same purpose that sharks can feel bioelectricity. This I knew.

Draco could command flames, but I could know, provided it existed in the past. Any event, knowledge, insight, even a thought, if it occurred in the past I could know it. Post-cognition in its truest form.

A mortal brain is limited, mind, and there's always a risk of frying it. In my current state, the whole thing was too random. There's no telling how long it would take to find something. Such is why my 'brother' sought the aid of this infernal creature to find this location. Still, Alexander's library pales compared to the lost wisdom in my mind, and once I've learned something, it stays with me, forever.

Lascivus cast her supernal gaze across our surroundings, lingered for a moment over Draco and settled at a point in the distance.

"Right there. In this dead place she shines like a beacon, a pillar of—oh wow" Her mouth fell ajar and drool beaded over her lip. "I-I could gorge till I burst and barely drain a splatter!" Her hand flew to her throat. The stupid creature had to hold herself back from throwing herself at the source and suckling for all eternity.

"Then there I go." Draco said. A wisp of smoke trailed from his hand.

"Wait-wait-wait-wait! Are you planning on trying to kill *that*?"

"Yes."

"You—you're insane! I mean, you are anyway—but even so, this 'Malign', it's got a whole continent, no, a whole world of life-force!"

"You can kill a world. Just look at this place." Draco glanced at his left hand. "Planet, god, math, don't care. I can't stand her incessant torments any longer."

I flinched, but he didn't notice. This delusional fool really was hopeless. Still, I have to see this through. I have as much invested in the outcome as my dear 'brother.

"Are you some sort of new breed of idiot, or just wrong in the head?" Lascivus demanded, exasperated. "Ugh, don't answer. I'll do my part, but don't expect me to hang around once I'm done." She flicked her wrist, wrapping her thumb over her forefinger. To my surprise, I didn't know this gesture. Must be some recent demonic insult or something.

We got back to walking, unfortunate for my aching feet. I wish we could just take a shortcut.

"A heap of broken images where a star beats," Draco said aloud, staring across the barren wasteland. "And the dead trees give no shelter and the dry stone no sound of water. Only shadow under this red rock," He scooped up soil from the ground and tasted it. "And in a handful of dust I find fear." Great, he's quoting T.S Eliot now.

If Malign really was here, I didn't want to know how she's been sustaining herself all this time. No, I could guess. Draco will not be happy. Well, even less than normal. I couldn't really say he's been 'happy' since the last time he played the piano.

***

I lost track of how long we'd been walking. Time's not really something I could complain about. I've enough past in my head to make months pass without notice. Instead, my attention turned to the thing Draco dragged out of the abyss, a 'life'-eating creature of Hell. This one was wearing heels in a dead savannah. Appearance is one thing, but had she never heard of practical footwear? Yet there she strode with no concern for her ankles. Maybe it's just a matter of demon physiology? Somehow, I doubted it.

"So why are you here, girly?" The demoness must have noticed me looking at her.

"Everything concerning Brother concerns me" I replied. I would have rather she ignored me, but I wasn't about to stoop below some life-thief from the underworld.

"And what's your plan when you get there? Blush and hope whatever nasties leave you alone? Or just leave yourself for 'Big Brother' to protect?"

"Watch yourself demon" Draco muttered.

I drew a long, slender knife from my belt.

"I know how to take care of myself,"

"Oh looky, kitten brought a toothpick, how charming" She snickered, hand against her mouth in mock dignity. I could snap you like a twig tight now, can you take care of that?"

"She-devil." My 'brother' flashed a tight smile. "You will refrain from threatening my sister, or I will run you through with my bare hands, so help me."

"Oh, you done it now." Drakkengard giggles

"Trust me to land the guy with a little-sister complex." She grumbled.

27

Trust him to undermine me with over-protectiveness. He wouldn't have allowed me to come along at all if I hadn't implored him, which took exploiting every trick I know to convince him.

Our troupe fell silent for the remaining journey, left to our own thoughts towards the alien landscape and what befell it.

A structure emerged from behind a crestfallen mountain.

"Right there! That's the place," Lascivus slapped her hands together. Draco said nothing, but pulled Drakkengard closer to himself.

"This place will burn" The animate object giggled. "Master will burn it all away, and we can all go home. All-down, all-down away." The obnoxious sword continued tapping its finger to some unheard tune.

"Well I'll just be on my way now, I-" Lascivus tried to back away but Draco's hand fell on her shoulder.

"My dear despicable lady, you go nowhere till I say we're done, or I—no, just—we go!" He barked, stumbling over his own words.

As we drew closer, the imposing structure showed itself. Hewn from uneven stone, crude buildings encircled a tower rising from their center. Broken metal hung in painstaking arrangements from every crag—lightning rods to leach the storms and store the power for what few needs this place has. I knew. Just what uses the electricity though? My stomach lurched over itself.

Affixed to the face of this behemoth tower was a huge metal double door, taken from someplace else and forced into the rock. The rusty ring handles broke away when Draco touched them.

"Drakkengard," He grasped her by the neck. "Play time." It giggled, and transmogrified into its true shape—the black blade that is my 'Brother's' keeper.

He paused to caress its hilt, and delivered two swift slashes upon the double door.

As a doll, Drakkengard is a bad joke, but even I can't deny its impressiveness as a blade. Shape-shifting according to its Master's want at the molecular level allows a blade both sharper and denser than any mundane object the mind can imagine. Even better, when a sword it doesn't talk.

A pair of triangular-shaped door chunks fell to the ground with a resounding thud and raised a small cloud of dust.

"Show off." The succubus scoffed, and poked some debris with the toe of her heeled shoes. Then the smell hit us.

It billowed from the doorway, carrying with it the reek of death and decay— the rotting of fetid flesh, the pungent stink of filth—a myriad of things best left unmentioned by all but the most perverse of observers.

"By my father's throat, that smell! It's almost as bad as Glaysa-Labolas's room." The demon gagged. Funny, I'd have thought a demon would have a stronger stomach for this stuff. By the time I noticed he'd moved Draco was inside the building and vanishing into the darkness. I gave chase, following the steady trail of smoke flowing from his left hand.

"Slow down, would you," I called out, chasing after him. He spun around and glared at me, freezing me in my tracks as his hand erupted into flame. Several seconds passed as he studies me with unfocused eyes before he turned away. I let out a sigh of relief.

"It's just you." He muttered and extinguished the flame in his hand, or at least tried.

"Just, please stay behind me. The sleep, is, not good" He murmured, flexing his grip on his sword. Staying out of his sight a while sounded like a good idea. With any luck, this would be done soon. This place, the walls bore nothing but scratches and stains, and the air—just breathing might have been desecrating my lungs. The once short corridor reached out into forever before us, yet still we waded on through the unbearable atmosphere.

We reached another door. Smaller, less foreboding than the grand entrance but still sinister. With a trembling hand Draco threw the door open, revealing an intersection. A quick sideways glance showed both passageways had long since caved, but in the place where they met stood a spiral staircase, rusted and twisted, reaching out with gnarled metal for one more touch.

Draco placed a foot on the first expiring step. Its shriek of protest echoed above and below us. At the sound, my 'brother's' head snapped up.

"There she lays, thrust between the soil and the sky, wallowing in her sty." His gaze turned downwards, following the haphazard trail of the stairs.

"But below, crushed below the night-soil of the Abomination," His left hand trembled, and the age-old structure rattled in sympathy.

What lies in the pits, this too, I *know*.

"Please, leave it be." I whispered, taking a step towards him. If he goes down there, the one who came before might be who comes up.

"What are you whispering about? I don't get it, what's down there?" The demon demanded.

"*Carpe Noctum*. I fall!" Draco cried out and brought his blade across the battered spire he stood on. A resounding *clash* sounded, and was followed by a flash of sparks, and a sudden, unending creak as the structure let loose its death rattle. It all came crashing down, taking him with it.

"You—Is he insane?" Lascivus screamed, an unintelligible curse followed as my 'brother' vanished into the dark.

"By my mother's voice I must be too" She muttered under breath, before diving into the hole, the glimmer of miasma trailing behind.

"That they just killed themselves is too much to ask, isn't it?" I said aloud, and stared at the dark for several seconds before relenting.

"I guess I need to know how to fall" I closed my eyes, and with a lashing of mental effort I peered into the past.

Knowledge entered my mind, so much nonsense,

Quantity of dead vermin here.

The chemical make-up of the atmosphere

Names of servants who once lived here

What their final words were

How they—no! Focus!

Age of the staircase

How many feet have passed its steps

The weight it took to collapse

How the pieces fell

Which pieces got stuck in the wall

How deep the stairwell goes

What can be used as a handhold

How many things could kill a person falling down

Where they are

I kept my eyes closed, information still tumbling in my brain. I tried not to notice the horrible pain in my temple.

"Okay, I can do this." With a deep breath, I jumped into the hole.

Falling, spinning and twisting in the air, blind and wholly reliant on the new knowing. I kicked off a wall as it came to close, avoiding a jagged metal beam. I grabbed my legs with my arms, curling myself into a ball small enough to fit through a hole in the latticework. Once through, my hands slipped off smooth rock and less smooth railing, each touch slowing my descent by a fraction.

I quickly moved my legs to prevent them being sliced off by a rusty step and grabbed the pole below it with my hand, wrenching my shoulder out of its socket.

With a cry, I let go, but I was falling slower.

I thrust my feet against opposite walls, causing the friction to grind away at the soles of my shoes, slowing me further still before making myself as narrow as a tube to fit through an equally narrow hole, tearing away shreds of cloth and biting at flesh.

With one final kick, I spun myself onto my side before crashing into the ground. The force of the landing popped my shoulder back into place. I let out another scream of pain before gritting my teeth and ignored the taste of hot ash in my mouth. Thanks to my efforts, I might as well have fallen two meters rather than three stories.

I picked myself up and dust more ash off myself, leaving red stains on my clothes. My hands and side were bleeding, but not by much. I took a step and tried not to wince as pain shot through my arm. Steeling myself, I walked.

As my eyes adjusted to the gloom, I focused on my other senses.

There was breathing, shallow uneven breathing. I can't tell how many people.

Filth assailed my nose, every form of filth and blood and decay. My eyes watered and my throat gaged. Death slithered over and through my body, intangible, a myriad of sensations the body can't but find revolting.

The walls and floor and ceiling were dirt, with minimal support. The tunnel wasn't straight, but bent and turned and twisted around corners and bent back upon itself in an encircling labyrinth. If you lost your sense of direction, you could wander until you died.

Lining the walls of the labyrinth were cells, no, these were cages—each just large enough to fit a beast, and covered in a film of filth and grime and excrement, bare of furniture. To call those occupants people was too generous. Once they were people, now, now they were nothing. Eyes blind. Flesh covered in scabs and scars and boils and festering wounds. Skin so thin, if the bones weren't so soft they'd pierce through. None of them moved. At first, I suspected they were dead, but at least some were still breathing. I dreaded to know what they have suffered, and for how long.

One cage's occupant had dug their way into the next cell before dying. Their neighbor now rested on their hide, and gummed on their bones on reflex.

Covering my mouth, I ran toward the source of the light, fast as I can. Faster. Desperate to escape the unseeing gaze of these husks I can't call alive.

I stopped when I reached my 'brother' and the demon. The mysterious light source was a flame atop his left hand. His blade remained in his right. His clothing was ripped and torn, as was his skin though that quickly healed. I suppose he tried to slow himself with flame. It didn't work as he had intended, it seems. The demon is unharmed, she probably just flew.

"Just—just what are these things?" Lascivus choked, her eyes darting from one heap of misery to another.

"Leftovers. It hates to throw a toy away. It plays with them when there's nothing else." Draco said. There's no tone in his voice. No pitch. His speaks, lifeless and empty, from experience.

"These things, how? How are they still alive? There's nothing left! I, gods I'm gonna be sick!" The demon clutched her hands to her eyes, desperate to be rid of the sight.

"It takes everything, everything we have, everything we need to keep, everything we didn't want to admit was real, takes it all." Draco approached the nearest cell. The light from his flame flickered across his face but face and flame were both too lifeless.

He placed a hand against the bar.

"My brothers, my sisters, we born a second time, our sire is the same." He said, his voice rising. "I ask of you, WHAT? You who lost *every-thing* and gained *no-thing*! WHAT?"

I spied movement, those wretched husks wee rousing. A vacant hissing filled the air.

"There was no reason! No point! No excuse! Naught but naught itself!"

The hissing continued to grow—the desperate vocalizations of creatures who've long forgotten their own voice. The flame in Draco's hand grew with them, illuminating more and more of the vacant shadows.

"There is no hope for you! No despair! She took everything and left you nothing! Now what? What do you have? What do you want? What should I give? What should I take? What?"

He stumbled and shambled back and forth, his whole body wrapped in a blaze, and the noise! The hissing swelled louder and louder in a cacophonous chorus of anguish and unbridled horror.

"*Fit caedes omnibus locis! In girum imus nocte et consumimur igni!*" Draco bellowed, resounding through every cage, every tunnel.

He spread his arms and spewed forth a torrent of fire. Roaring, it circled then split, screaming up the wretched paths. I shielded my eyes and kept still, hoping he still retained enough sense to recognize me. One by one, the blaze sought the un-people in their desolate shells. One by one, it embraced their crumbling, misshapen forms. One by one, they shrieked relief from the hollowed-out pit of their being as the fire released them. Their cries become a new chorus, a final expression of self. As it chased crescendo, my 'brother' opened his mouth, and sung the tune to their final song. Ignorant of self and other, they sung as one.

They sung of the past, and how it shaped them. They used no words, if the words they desired existed they do not know them.

They sung of their fate, and how it chained them, using long inhuman sounds. The closest resemblance I could make is a sort of manic sobbing laughter.

They sung of silence, of the end. They ended.

One by one, they surrendered themselves to the flame, leaving naught but bones and ash. Even with my eyes clenched shut I could see every one as they passed from this world.

One by one the flames extinguished, until one was left, standing alone in the middle of the room.

I opened my eyes and look to my 'brother'. He let out a deep gasp and slumped to his knees, drained of body and mind.

"You shouldn't have done that," I said once I'm sure his wits are about him. "They would have died eventually. Now you've tired yourself out, and I'm sure she noticed the racket." I took a step back as he rises to his feet.

"They didn't deserve to die alone, not after everything, not alone. They deserved, no, I wanted to serve witness." He leaned on his sword for support.

"How, uh, sentimental of you." Lascivus said, fumbling for words.

"Forget it. We make haste," He heft his sword over his shoulder.

"Yeah, in case you forgot, you broke the stairs on your way down. Unless you plan on learning to fly, I don't see you getting out of here." Lascivus shrugged. Draco paused for a moment then shot her an expectant look.

"What? Oh no! No way. I'm not flying you all the way up there! I had barely enough room to dive down here, a complete mistake I might add. Besides, you're way too heavy! I'd never get off the ground!"

His gaze shifted to me.

"You bastard. You really expect me to!" I fumed, rubbing my temple. "Fine! But next time, how about *I* violate *your* head with boiling ice!" I swear it's all I can do to stop myself lobotomizing him while he sleeps.

I closed my eyes and clench. It took longer this time. My mortal brain still hadn't recovered from earlier.

It stampeded into my consciousness, words and thoughts and visions and meaningless feedback. The overwhelming force caused me to double over. Bit by bit I pieced together something useful from the torrent. Finally, I got what I needed and slammed the floodgate shut.

"Are you alright?" He asked. How nice to know he cares.

"You're a filthy dog-meat leper-queer, now give me a moment." I took breath and straightened my back, wiping the sweat from my forehead.

"Okay, okay, ugh. There are two other entrances besides what we just came down. Go, no forget it. Just follow me" I said, and turn around with a huff. Without checking if they're following or not I left, trying to ignore the smell of burnt flesh and filth.

Sure enough, there was the tell-tale tapping of footsteps behind me, one more rapid than the other. After just a few seconds, my 'brother' caught up.

"Are you, are you sure you're alright? I just . . ." He started, searching his self for the words.

"I'll be fine. Just don't ask for that again. Not for a few hours at the least." I tried not to let my exhaustion show. In truth I would have been less weary if I had just run a triathlon, but I wasn't about to admit it.

"I just—sorry." I didn't reply. Lascivus watched our little exchange from behind, no doubt looking for some way to make their little deal work to her benefit. He trusted hell-dwelling cave-spawn, how ridiculous. She's unreliable and whimsical, liable to turn on us at any second, and I wouldn't know until she decided to. People like that are the worst. You'd think, having spent the past several years in my 'brother's' company, I would be used to their sort by now but no such luck.

We'd wasted enough time. With a purposeful stride, I led the others through the dead maze, past scorched corpses and fetid soil. I located the staircase I knew was there and led them up it, pointing out which steps were little more than a delicate arrangement of rust and should be avoided.

From the top of the stairs, I led them to the foot of the twisted spire. In my searching, I gleamed more than I sought, instead of just the maze I learned of the entire structure. I got a pounding headache to show for it.

Behind a rotting wooden door was an erratic upwards path of steps and ramps and ladders and places that overlap by chance but didn't mere days ago.

"Watch your step, especially you Brother. No matter what happens, we can only take this route once," With that warning I took the first step onto the rickety tower of scrap.

From there, we climbed, and the slow pace was agonizing. Precocious moments spent sidling along a narrow wood beam, a sudden flash of adrenaline when it fell away just as the last person steps off it.

As I pulled myself up a ledge, I spied the sun setting through a hole in the latticework tower. Behind me my 'brother' chuckled.

"What's so funny?" Lascivus demanded from below him.

"Nothing, dear demon. Now's just a good time for a dirge."

"You can suit yourself," She grunted, hoisting herself up after him. "But I'm not going to snuff it yet"

"Chickens, eggs, what does it matter. The hour is good."

"Brother, please quit rambling" I grumbled, trying to keep balance on sloped metal. My footing gave way. For one brief, horrible moment, the entirety of the tower stretched out below me, beckoning me into its maw. I started to fall, but came to a jerky halt.

"Watch your step, especially you Sister" Draco chuckled. My arm was caught in his left hand, while his right holds onto his sword, which was impaled into the scaffolding for support.

"Anything to make me look like an idiot." I grumbled, grabbing his hand with my free arm. With a grunt he pulled me up. There's a faint tingle from beneath his skin. He's using magick to support his muscles.

The remaining journey skyward went without pause. The higher we got, the quieter my 'brother' falls. Even the demon quits her snide remarks.

Nearer the top, the chaotic mess gave way to sturdier architecture, untouched from whatever ravaged this castle. I could only guess what terrible event shredded the base. Of the things I learned about this place, what ruined it wasn't among them, and I dared not push myself for a third look. Either way, I was grateful to have solid stairs at my feet again, never-mind the sheer miracle this place still stood at all.

At the top of the spire, a battered and beaten door had been strewn from its frame. For a moment I feared something else beat us here, but a second glance said it was blown from its hinges a long time ago.

I moved to enter the doorway, but the edge of Draco's sword stops me. He took the lead himself and went through the broken hole. Keeping my annoyance to myself, I slipped in after him.

The room we found ourselves in is a large, round, and empty thing. The beaten and battered floor struggled to preserve checkered markings long ago stamped to dust. Whatever ceiling there once was had crumbled away long ago, leaving it exposed to what little elements still stirred on this dead world. A thick layer of dust coated every surface and the crumbling remains of pillars lay dissolving in the corners of the room. On the other side, two fallen stairways hugged the wall, and led up to a balcony overlooking the floor.

A ballroom. This was once a ballroom, but what could it be doing atop this spire?

An alien sensation crawled along my skin, biting at the soft flesh below and stabbing at my organs, tasting the fear that trickled from my lobes. I couldn't see it, but a predator lurked this room. It was an acidic, choking presence that cuts straight to the reptile brain, and I have to fight not to leap from this tower in irrational panic.

I risked a glance at the two by my side. The demon had drawn her blade from her own abyss and searched the room with eyes torn between possible hiding places. My 'brother' though, he stood in the middle of the room, still, distracted, staring into the shadows above the stairs. For a full minute, he remained motionless, and I did nothing but watch him. A full minute passed, and on the sixty-first second his left hand burst into flame as he readied his sword with his right.

An uncanny sound filled the room, fleeting past our ears and into the night sky, a sound I rationally cannot place, like the sound of a tree growing, or of an idea failing—Something inexplicable to my hearing but undeniable.

The sound dimmed, and was followed by a long, drawn out death rattle.

Something was flung to the floor in front of us. It landed with a *splat* and a *crunch*.

A body, the body of a young woman lay on the ground, her exact age indeterminable from her appearance. Long gashes marred her sides and chest, and upon her back and thighs the flesh had been branded in the shape of an open palm. One breast was torn off, her jaw was dislocated along with one arm and her spine bent impossibly.

My throat dried up. The sound from before was this girl dying. With us in the same room, whatever was in the shadows killed her.

I opened my mouth to speak, but the words fell short as flames enveloped the corpse. I turned and Draco's left hand was outstretched. Her dead body dispersed in a gust of ash.

Even after the carcass was gone, the flames stayed, burrowing into the battered ground as though to erase even their own stain.

"What. In the name of Hell. Was that?" The demon gulped, more from surprise than horror. It did appear this task was turning out hardly as she expected.

"Deserere, is that someone with my eyes I see down there?"

A languid voice spoke, but in a tongue few can recognize. Dead, but not quite extinct. Lascivus couldn't understand it, which must have been disturbing for a demon such as her.

"It walks in my door, dragging its claws and spitting its voice. It burns my crops and steals from my flesh! This *succulent* beast is home at last!"

The still burning flames hissed and flew back to Draco's trembling arm. He opened his mouth to speak and uttered in the same alien tongue as the shadows.

"Abomination." He accused.

"Heeeeee! You hear? He calls me such *slander*!" The voice shrieked the last word. Behind the shadow's cloak, I noticed more movement.

"Meaningless!" Draco bellowed. "Abomination, who bore Atrocity into this world!" He let out a blood-curdling scream and leapt up the banister, sword in hand, using magick to allow a jump beyond his reach.

He swung his sword at the shadow, and met the blade of another.

"So impatient to gorge—My darling longs for me even now."

"Destroyburnfeedlivedisappear!" Babbling madly, he turned the blade away with brute force, but was stopped by a second, and a third and a fourth blade that shot out from the darkness.

"Stop hiding!" The flames on his arm erupted to cover his entire body, illuminating the shadows above, revealing the target of his rage and anguish.

Long, narrow fingers reached out to cup his face, causing him to recoil in horror. Crestfallen, the hands slumped. Exposed by his flames, a woman in a wine-red gown stood and stared him in the eye. She was a mere few inches shorter than he is, no small task considering his height. At her side, a hooded figure in burgundy robes of velvet waited, immobile and silent.

"My son." The woman cooed. Draco flinched as though slapped.

"No! Not you! Never you! Whatever blood was between us you spilt long ago. Don't say words you forfeited long since whence!" He snarled and swung his sword, but her silent attendant blocked it with his bare hands. Draco forced the blade, causing it to dig into the person's palms. Drops of liquid metal fell from the wound.

"Why have you come, my child?" The woman tutted, and reached for my 'brother's' face again.

"Quiet! To kill you!" Draco barked. His whole body erupted in flames. The woman ignored them, reached through and placed an open palm against his cheek. Her flesh burned and she let out a long, ecstatic moan. Disgusted, Draco threw himself back over the balcony, landing on the ballroom floor in front of Lascivus and myself.

"Ooh! To feel your bite again, how I've longed for it." The red woman shuddered, and savored the taste of her own cooked meat on her tongue.

"Just who is this woman?" Lascivus asked, taking a step back.

"This . . . Abomination." Draco spat, readying Drakkengard. "This is Malign. *Aargh*!" He screamed, his voice muffled by the fire around him.

Malign stepped towards the broken stair railing and raised one arm.

"Soon, soon we will feast. We will taste everything my delectable son has become, but first, Deserere! Kill those two with him. This should special, private."

The hooded figure nodded once, and leapt off the balcony. Something threw me to the ground, and the sound of metal on metal rung in my ears. I looked up and saw Draco, blocking a blade aimed at my chest.

"Sister, flee!" He shouted.

"No! I need to see the end. I won't leave!" I replied, I scrabbled to my feet and drew my knife.

The one Malign calls Deserere let out a hiss, and spun around to lunge for Lascivus, who casts him aside with her sword. Their blades clashed against each other in a show of sparks and ferocity before each leapt back. Draco and I darted in opposite directions, and the three of us surrounded our would-be executioner.

His robes were torn and tattered, and covered in clumsy stitches. From each of his elongated sleeves emerged a red-stained blade, with glowing runic script down the center. The hood fell away when he clashed with the demon, exposing a smooth face with delicate, boyish features. His eyes, though, were sewn shut by thick metal threads which pierced the organs as well as lids. His mouth had the same kind of metal thread hanging loose from scarred lips.

He let out a hiss and lunged at Draco, revealing why his mouth no longer needed to be sewn shut. His mouth was empty—behind metal teeth lay nothing but a gaping cavern of a mouth. His tongue had been ripped out! Yet he's still weathered Malign's attention far better than most of her victims.

The battered creature revealed his lunge as a feint, dropped into a crouch and from there thrust out his leg at my face. I swerved away, but another blade from where a foot should be and grazed my shoulder. I drove my knife into his leg but several smaller blades stopped it. Strips of cloth fell aside, exposing not flesh, but metal emerging from flesh. No, imitating in a mockery of flesh.

"Brother, he's the same as Drakkengard!" I cried, ducking below a leg that became a club. Draco met this revelation with a roar and a heavy blow intent on taking off an arm, but the arm became a whip-like tentacle and caught Drakkengard in its grip. Lascivus came forward, her thin blade was not enough to sever the tendril, but still cut the false-living metal. Deserere let out a screaming hiss, and I lunged forward, sinking my knife into his back. As soon as I make contact, metal spikes emerge and grow out to skewer me, shredding his robes further and forcing me to abandon my knife to get away. However, it was enough to allow Draco to get Drakkengard free.

My 'talent', although exhausting to use with precision, is not wholly useless in the frantic pace of a fight. What I can *know* is restricted to the past. But just what is the past? The moment after a moment, that first moment is part of the past. It takes at least a moment for a decision made by the mind to be carried out by the body. In other words, I can react in battle before I've seen what I'm reacting too. By using post-cognition as pseudo—mind reading I can emulate precognition. I can't keep it up forever. Doing all of that is exhausting, but it does allow me to end most fights quickly.

My 'victim' shrugged off a blast of hellfire from Lascivus with little more than a sharp hiss and met her sword with a bladed arm. He keeps company with Malign—I'm surprised he is aware of pain at all—but either way it gave me a chance to retrieve my knife and wound him before rolling out of the way of a guillotine-like leg. From his other flank, Draco drove his sword right through our foe's arm, causing liquid metal to gush from the wound. Grinning, Draco twisted the blade. Deserere's arm split open like frayed wood and the golem screamed. At this, Lascivus turned aside his other arm and impaled his gut. Finally, I rushed around behind him and thrust my knife into his head, from the base of his skull right up to the peak of his cranium.

He shuddered as both Draco and Lascivus removed their weapons, and fell face-first to the ground, my knife still sticking out from his head. I *know* he's stopped thinking.

"Stupid boy," Lascivus said from behind a dark smile. "But he's better off dead"

"Come on Malign!" Draco bellowed in that alien tongue. "I've slain your pet! Come down and *die*!"

"Deserere!" The red woman shrieked in anguish and rage. "How *dare* you! How *dare* you shame your mistress like this! Get up! I demand you *get up*! You'll be the death of me at this rate!"

Deserere's body shuddered and, to my horror, rose to its feet. My knife still sticks out from its head, and metallic blood sloshed from its wounds, but it moved anyway.

"Yes, *yes*! My dear sweet Deserere will never die will never leave me." She cooed as though in a dream. "Even if I cut everything off, bleed everything out, cut everything, burn everything, you'll never leave me, will you my beloved Deserere" His shuddering form slithered over to her as it straightened itself out. The three of us sprung back, wary. Her servant was one thing, but I knew I was no match for this vile woman.

I rushed to hide myself behind a fallen pillar. Lascivus stared, sword held in trembling hands. Malign lifted her servant by his arms like a rag doll. I can only imagine what this creature must look like in the succubus's eyes, we both knew the 'person' that called itself Malign was nothing to take lightly. She may see her 'life-force' whatever sort of measure that is, but I was alongside that woman for two years.

I'd seen her force a small boy to kill and eat his fellow inmates for sustenance. Seen her stitch a quad amputee to an emaciated youth and force him to run an obstacle course. Watched her inject mercury into a slave's veins and force an ancient vampire into feeding off him just to survive a few more hours. Monsters with unpronounceable names have wept acid to be freed from her clutches. Mighty heroes has she hunted and slain just so she could self-flagellate with their legendary weapons. Not many gods can take down an entity like that. If my 'brother' proved to be something capable of taking down that level of power, I honestly can't think which I would be more afraid of should they be the one left standing.

Deserere melted in Malign's arms, his whole body shifted into a liquid state then reformed in her hands as a sword, not as long as Drakkengard but near twice as wide and single edged, almost like a meat cleaver but bearing similar glowing marks along its face. Although most of the sword is straight, the final third of the blade hooks around towards the blunt edge, like an enlarged sickle.

"Deserere my sweet, it is good to see you again. Come, let us discipline my filthy child and his insolent friends" She whispered, holding the blade up against her cheek.

"Las-Lascivus." Draco stuttered, his eyes never leaving Malign. "Our deal is done. There is now nothing between us" The demon made no motion to move.

"Don't you get it? Go!" He barked, erupting with flame.

"You backwards mongrel, you drag me all the way here and try to stand me up after just one dance? You and me, this party's going nowhere without us both!"

"Fine! Don't blame me if it's your last!" My 'brother' relented. From my vantage point in the shadows, I prepared myself. The outcome of this fight would decide who I have to hide from every day until the dawn of the new era.

Draco and Lascivus observed Malign as she bared her blade, each positioned at a ninety-degree angle from their foe and each other. If Malign is concerned she doesn't show it, instead a ludicrous, crooked grin is plastered across her face. A bead of sweat formed on my brow, and I retreated further into the shadows.

A tongue of flame flickered about Draco. Lascivus licked her lips in apprehension. I breathed in.

Draco swung his sword at Malign as hard as he could. Malign deflected, but Drakkengard left a deep, angry gash across Deserere's steel-flesh, and the blade oozed liquid metal over Malign's hands. Following up, Draco unleashed a torrent of flame, engulfing Malign and her sword in a blazing inferno. She screamed in both agony and bliss. From within the blaze shimmered a faint, unearthly glow. I shielded my eyes just as flash of dazzling violet light threatened to blind me.

A moment later, the light was gone, taking the flames with it. Draco staggered, clutching his head in his hand, but Lascivus appeared unaffected and leapt at malign before she could press the advantage. With a savage hiss, the demon unleashed a brilliant flurry of blows that forced Malign away from Draco's vulnerable form. She even landed a few swipes against flesh as she presses the attack, although they heal within moments. Cackling, the red woman disarmed Lascivus with ease then went for the face. Lascivus brought up her hand on reflex and Deserere's hook pierced straight through her palm and out the other side.

"You WHORE!" The demon cursed in her native tongue, and her hand changed into the wicked black claws of the real body behind her magick. With her new weapon, Lascivus gripped the blade and snapped off the hook with her supernatural strength. Now recovered, Draco rushed in, attacking with a series of speedy and heavy blows and making use of his now even greater reach.

Lascivus ripped the metal out of her hand with a grunt and tossed it away but Malign, spying her action, leapt back and raised Deserere and from his bleeding wound tendrils of metal flew out to latch onto the airborne piece, bringing it back and re-affixing it in place. Scowling, Lascivus spat, and her sword reappeared in her hand in a puff of smoke.

I breathed out. How long did that exchange last for? Moments? Minutes? I could have believed years.

Malign struck out with her sword with a sudden speed and ferocity. At first I thought it would fall short, but as it swung through the air, the blade stretched and elongated, giving it enough reach to whip across and gouge a chunk of flesh out of Draco's midsection before he could react. With no waste of momentum, she swung it around to divert an attack Lascivus attempted from behind. Draco snarled, fire erupting all around his body, and charged. He took another shot to the shoulder and slammed into Malign with the flat of his blade.

Malign tried to strike his shoulder with Deserere, but Lascivus caught her hand in her claw before she could bring it down, and with a flick of her wrist, broke Malign's arm. She tried to scream, but was cut short as Draco thrust Drakkengard into her chest, slicing through her lungs and heart and imbedding it to the hilt. Malign let out an airless gasp and shuddered, but didn't fall. Draco adjusted his grip on his blade and let out a bellow, twisting his body and ripping Drakkengard out through her side, slicing clean through her other arm in the process.

Blood, bone and flesh poured from the wound, sloshing out onto the ground, but Malign didn't fall. Frustrated, Lascivus cut across her ankles followed by the back of her legs, forcing her to her knees, but she still didn't fall.

Malign broke into laughter. She laughed with greater and greater force until tears streamed from her eyes. With her grievous wounds and a single lung in her chest she laughed her heart out.

Trembling, Draco moved behind her and kicked her in the back, forcing her head to the ground with a crack. Still she laughed. He repositioned himself by her side and readied Drakkengard in his hands, ignoring the blood flowing from his shoulder and stomach. Still she lived. He lifted his sword above his head and with a hideous scream, brought it against Malign's neck.

Malign still laughed.

Draco grunted and struggles as Drakkengard ground against an unseen force a hair's breadth above Malign's exposed neck. The blade twisted and toiled but failed to penetrate the barrier.

Malign's whole body glowed with violet light and exploded with enough force to send sending both Draco and Lascivus flying. Lascivus slammed headfirst into the base of the stairway while Draco crashed against one of the few remaining pillars with a painful crunch.

Malign stood, her legs were already healed and her chest not far behind. She picked up her sword and found her severed, still-warm arm. She jammed it into her bloody stump, and it too became whole again.

"Stupid boy! *Stupid boy*!" She screamed. Striding over to Draco as he tried to rise she lifted him up by the neck.

"Thankyou! Thank you *so much*! I haven't felt that good in YEARS!" She howled out a cacophonous laugh and hurled him into a wall. It collapsed where he struck, burying him in rubble and causing the tower to shudder.

"Please, please, please-please-please-please-please *let me return the favour*!" She tore him out and smashed his face into the ground.

"My beloved!"

Again, his face struck stone.

"My darling!"

Again, she brought him to the ground.

"My pet!"

Again and again and again she broke his face against the floor. Each impact sent blood flying, and from his battered, bleeding body smoke eked.

"My beautiful *child*!"

"*Don't say that word*!" Draco bellowed, erupting with fire and sending Malign reeling back. Her skin blistered and peeled. Her hands flew to her face, and when they drop again she was once more unscarred.

"My *son*!" She sang out, and the violet glow envelops the room.

My limbs might as well have been driftwood and even moving my eyelids was challenging. Just looking at her was killing me. My stomach filled with rotting flesh, maggots crawled through my veins, and a dark phantom clawed at the back of my brain into my lungs.

The light! That was it! That light was doing something. I averted my gaze, and while an immediate improvement was too much to ask for, my condition stopped getting any worse. Whatever that light was, it drained something, consumed something from anyone that looked at it. Did Draco understand this? Out of the corner of my eye I saw him charge, covered in flame and staring right at Malign.

Damn everything! I needed to, but I couldn't look away. I had a sworn duty to see the outcome of this fight, no matter the cost. I steeled myself and turned back to the conflict.

Their weapons clashed against each other, the force of impact knocking them back, but only for a second before they clashed again. Fire, light, and the sound of clashing blades drowned out all other sensation. No matter how determined he was even he must have felt the effects of Malign's power by now.

"Submit! *Submit*" Malign cackled, her face pushed into his.

"Die!" Draco slid Drakkengard up Deserere's length and, caught off-guard by the sudden slack in pressure, Malign couldn't stop him from sending her blade flying with a powerful heave. Caught without a weapon, Malign was forced onto the defensive.

No matter how much crazy strength she has, Malign was not an unarmed fighter. Fist after fist he beat her to the ground. She tried to summon her sword but it was too wounded and long-abused to do more than shift and roil where it fell.

Without it, Draco stood a fighting chance, but only if she was out of tricks. I could have post-cog'd her head as I did her servants but a mind as twisted and disgusting as that could devour mine at a touch, I didn't dare peer into that madness.

No, it was not my place to interfere. I slumped back with resignation. Besides after suffering so much of Malign's light it was a struggle to move. Even if I found the strength, I'd be culled in an instant.

Malign leapt away from Draco, fending of his assault, and darted for her servant. Just before Draco reaches her, she scooped Deserere up and he resumed the shape of a sword. She let out a chilling giggle and loosed another horrific burst of light. It washed over Draco like a storm, forcing him to one knee.

A pity I lacked his threshold for pain.

My heart burst into flames and melted. My left lung burst like a balloon while the other filled with corrosive gases. My stomach ripped open, allowing digestive acid to spill over my bowels, melting through the sensitive flesh. My skin froze, my eyes boiled and melted, and my teeth shot up into my skull, shredding my tongue with debris. My bones splintered and shattered in the space of moments, and all my nerves were devoured at once by a never-ending swarm of ants. That violet light—I shrieked in agony, the ground rushes my face as my senses were overloaded with phantom sensations. A second voice screamed besides mine. It sounded like the demon's but I couldn't care.

I laid there, shivering and sobbing as my mind refused to comprehend what just happened.

Thinking hurt.

Knowing hurt.

Being hurt.

Everything hurt from here to eternity.

"You. The little mouse that scampered away with my son!" Sound was painful. Why didn't it stop?

"How does it feel, my hunger? Does it hurt? Is it good? You don't deserve to feel my tongue devour you." . . .

I'd stopped whimpering. It didn't hurt anymore. I didn't feel anything but pain, and with nothing else to compare anymore even pain didn't feel, it just . . . was. Everything that was good had been stripped from me, devoured by her light. I couldn't even remember what a *good* feeling felt like.

"Vanish into dust!" Something icy pressed into my stomach. Looking down I saw Deserere's hooked tip. That's—that—what should I—Clawing through my foggy mind I grasped at rational thought. A part of me recognized I was danger, and the accompanying adrenaline surge washed away most of the numbness. Ye gods, is this how he felt all the time?

I struggled against her grip, but to no avail. Even at my best this woman was plain stronger than I.

Deserere's hook pierced my flesh, tore through the skin and into the soft meat within. No! Damn it all, I can't die yet! Not yet!

"BROTHER! HELP!" I screamed, even as the blade worked its way through my abdomen. Every moment she prolonged my suffering made her leer stretch wider.

Blood spattered across my face. At first I assumed it was mine, but Drakkengard had pierced Malign's chest.

"Do *not* harm my sister!" He growled, and with a heave lifted Malign up upon his sword. For a few, precarious moments she hung there, staring at the sword in her chest, then Draco swung the sword with all his might, and sent her sliding off to the middle of the floor. Disregarding her, Draco knelt to inspect my wound, brushing it with his finger.

"Thank everything." He sighed after a moment. 'It isn't bad. This will hurt, though." With no more warning, he dragged a burning finger across my stomach, and I hissed with pain.

"There. Now it won't bleed." He said, standing. I could see the mark where he clumsily cauterized my wound.

"I don't care what you say, if you can move, go wake the She-devil and get her to take you away. Otherwise, hide. Don't look up. Don't listen. Don't even move. I won't let you die."

Draco walked away, flicking the blood off his sword. His clothes were bloody and shredded, and there was a slight limb to his walk where Malign struck him in the knee earlier. One eye wasn't opening and his left hand kept twitching and sputtering out flame.

He intended to die—The realization struck me, he was willing to get himself killed to make sure she stays dead. Damn it all!

I smacked the ground with my fist. If they both died, nothing would happen. Nothing would change. Yet there was nothing I could do but leave it to fate. Whatever happened here happens.

Malign stood as Draco approached, her glow had returned, but with less vigor. Her face split open in a twisted grin. Any coherency she had was gone by this point.

They met each other swinging, and both their blades left shallow wounds in their wake. Again they cut, and again they bled. They weren't even trying to defend, instead trying to dodge and attack at the same time but couldn't manage to avoid the other's edge. With each swing, blood splattered around them. Faster and faster, they exchanged blows, spilling more blood in the search for a finishing blow. Draco's body glowed with ebbing flame, but Malign's light didn't wane. Draco screamed as he tries to cleave through her shoulder, but took off only a slip of skin as she twisted out of the way and dragged her hooked blade down his chest. He stuck for and missed her abdomen, and in return she sliced a shallow line across his face as he recoiled back. Sluggishly, he brought his sword up, but before he could bring it down she embedded her hook in his shoulder and dragged him down to his knees.

This was it. He was finished. Whatever fume he was running on had run out.

"So Malign can't be stopped" I muttered to myself. I knew this was the most likely outcome.

"Hush, my child" Malign cooed, leaning in close to him. "You disappointed me, but only a little. I'll let you die in your mother's arms" His arms dropped to his side, causing Drakkengard to hit the ground with a clang. He lifted his shaking left hand and spouted a feeble trickle of embers at Malign's face. If she felt it she didn't show, she just smiled.

"My little warrior, fighting to the end. You will die at the hands of what you took from me. Quickly now before I grow hungry." She pried Drakkengard from his clenched fingers.

As soon it rested in her hands, spikes erupted from Drakkengard's hilt, but Malign paid them no heed, letting her blood drip onto Draco's face.

Malign hummed an alien lullaby as she positioned his sword against his chest. When it touches his skin the blade recoiled. Before it could react proper Malign slid it in, forcing it through his flesh as easy as inserting a key.

Draco stared dumbfounded at his own blade sticking out of his chest.

"Now, sleep. Sleep, my child."

Draco's eyes widen as realization dawned.

His right hand reached out and touches the wound.

He pulled it away, and stared at the blood on his land.

His breathing became labored and uneven.

Tears welled in his eyes, and he looked up to stare at Malign.

"You. You did this?"

"Shhh, I have given you a gift. Take it."

"You break our word?" Even in the alien tongue, something sounded strange in his voice, an odd echo, two voices speaking in concert. How nostalgic.

"You harm us with ourselves." His gaze turned to where I laid. "You hurt those we swore to protect."

"Stop this! Go to sleep!" Malign demanded. She struggled to push Drakkengard deeper into Draco's chest, but his right hand shot out to stop her.

"No, not sleep. Now we wake!" He knocked Malign aside with a blast of flame and drew Drakkengard from his wound, rising to his feet.

"You once had a child." He uttered, ripping Deserere out from his shoulder and hurling it to the wall. Pungent black smoke rose from his body.

"You consumed that child with your lust, your gluttony . . ."

From Drakkengard's hilt, metal tendrils emerged and burrowed into his forearm. Long thick tongues of metal twisted and climbed his arm, inorganic vines that pierced the welcoming flesh—without resistance, without blood.

"You are an Abomination on this and every world you step upon,"

It was impossible to tell where Draco ended and Drakkengard begun. The tendrils reached into his shoulder. His body flickered with flame as he approached Malign.

"That child's corpse is the Atrocity you committed,"

The ground sizzled and burned as he walked, the air warped and distorted as he breathed. Malign floundered to her feet.

"We are that child's vanguard. He died, but we will not forget! We will ride forth and conquer, slaughter, reap and salt. We awoke with nothing, have nothing, suffer under nothing and we triumph over nothing."

Flames erupt around him, white, translucent flames, consuming everything their tongues lick. With no weapon, Malign stands before Draco as he walks towards her. Her vile light shone with renewed vigor, but if he felt it he didn't show. His towering silhouette eclipsed her.

"You, Abomination. are nothing!" He let out a great bellow, and swung his sword with all the power that flowed through him.

"My child, so beautiful." She whispered, adoration in her eyes.

His sword passed through her, and the light that surrounded her snuffed out.

He swung his sword again, and a thin, narrow line bisected her body.

He swung again, cutting that line in half.

Again and again, cutting both lines through the middle.

He swung again and again and again and again, until I can't even see his sword move, each cut slicing her finer and finer and finer.

The tower trembled. A chill of horror rose from the pit of my stomach. He wasn't just cutting Malign.

With each swing, everything along its path was cut. The floors, the walls, maybe even the air itself.

I couldn't even see Draco now, the light from his flames shone too bright, the center of the room was consumed in a featureless white haze that continues to grow, but still Draco cut.

I know because a sharp, pricking pain was spreading throughout my body.

I know because I could see thin red lines crisscrossing their way up my flesh.

"So-" Thirteen seconds had passed since the first cut. The flaming mass at the center of the room expanded violently. Everything was white and warm and grew even more so.

Chapter Three

The Void

Lascivus

The plentiful aches covered the full pain spectrum from dull to blazing, which my body informed me of as soon as I woke. Without opening my eyes I ran my hands over my body: a bomb went off in my head, but that was nothing new. My neck was stiff. I should find a better bed soon. Shoulders: fine. Chest: tender? Felt like a couple bruised ribs, nothing rest won't fix. Stomach: sore and rather hungry. When was the last time I'd eaten? There was a kink in my lower back, and one foot had gone to sleep but apart from that I supposed my body was fine. I opened my eyes and sat up.

"Damn all worlds!" I hissed to the stabbing pain now running laps around my body. On the second try I rose to one knee, using every bit of effort to stop myself flinching.

It's a specific pain, '*Magus Fury*' they call it. Magick burn. I jammed my scattered memories together until enough things stuck—Draco, that stupid idiot, he did *something*. Whatever it was, it exploded with enough force to crack a moon. It took way too much magick to keep myself from being dragged down with it. Ugh, now that I had a chance to think about it, I could have just done a hasty world-hop and been better off. Oh, what is it they say? 'Hindsight's the whore of a steer'. Either way, every cell in my body was stretched to its metaphysical limit, I didn't know where I was, and I badly needed a drink. I took a moment to look around and it really isn't anything I was expecting.

It really wasn't anything. Above and beyond anything else that can be said, this place was empty, just an infinite, featureless plain.

Each muscle contraction scalded like it could be my last but I made myself get up anyway. As far as the eye sees, I saw nothing. Not a building, not a hill. I saw less than that. I couldn't see a sky above my head or even ground beneath my feet. Maybe I was blind? Could that, uh, *whatever*, have ruined my eyes? No, that couldn't be right, I could still see myself. That was just bizarre. How could I see my feet but not the ground? By what light was I seeing myself? This place made no sense. I looked around again, this time I noticed a faint glimmer on the horizon. Life! Wherever I am, there was something alive in here with me! If it's that flame-spitting night-head I would beat him senseless for all the crap he'd put me through today, assuming it was still today. Anyone else, well, at least I wouldn't go hungry. Although I really didn't fancy my chances against that Malign creature. I'd say nothing could have survived that, but I did. Of course, I wasn't in the heart of it. If saving my hide wasn't such a pressing issue I might have been able to find out, not that I could see anything through that blaze.

I don't think I'd ever seen that much power in such a small place before, even when my father fights, although I'm sure dear old dad had more control that to just burn it away like that. Still, it was such a sight. Great, now I was aware of how hungry I am again.

The glimmer on the horizon could at least get closer faster. How long had I been walking? With no landmarks or stars measuring time was impossible. Maybe it had been minutes, maybe hours. It couldn't be much longer than that, I wasn't thirsty enough. I guess my stomach made as good a watch as any in a pinch.

The way this place screwed with my senses was throwing me for a loop. My body insisted there was magick about, but I couldn't tell where. I was a little concerned about what I was breathing too, for that matter. I could only hope I wasn't trapped in recursive space. Those're always a bitch to get out of. Lords below, how long had it been since I had a drink? Good thing I always kept a bottle in arm's reach. I flexed my fingers and reached out into the aether, trying to establish a connection to the pocket-scape I left my booze in. Nothing happened.

"What? Why?" I complained out loud, sparking what little magick I had left to try to force open a micro-portal. That I could expel magick at all meant I wasn't in an anti-magick dark spot, yet somehow I was cut off from the aether, the veil between worlds. I'd never heard of a place like this! A slight stomp entered my step, but quickly vanished as I cringed from the pain. Great, not only was I without refreshment, I was too sore to even throw a tantrum about it.

With nothing else I could do, I kept walking, fuming, and the distant glow drew closer.

***

I don't know how long I took to reach my beacon. Frankly I was too pissed off to care. Once I arrived, I was a bit taken aback.

The light I'd been following was Draco, I could have guessed that, but that's not what struck me. He stood still as a snapshot, his tattered clothes draped over him, his sword hanging out of his hand, a few small tendrils of metal penetrating his forearm and dull red flames making a cloak around his body. The marks along his sword let off faint, regular pulses—Two counts on, one count off, two counts on, one count off, like breathing, or a heartbeat, or an injured cat purring. I took a predator's look at him—he was running on next to nothing, less than fumes. Whatever it was he did gouged him for all he's worth. Fresh road kill had more vitality. So much for filling my belly while I was here, even a sip would probably have killed him.

"You really are a world-class fool, I just want you to know that" I said as I walked up next to him. If he noticed, he didn't show it. "Pulling a stunt like that, you nearly killed us all" He flinched. Weird, was it something I said? "You know, you'll recover faster if you turn off the heat, not that I'm complaining" I shrugged. The warmth did feel good against my skin. It wasn't cold, wherever we were, but it was by no means comfortable.

"So do you know how to get out of this place?" I asked. He made no response. "Well then, it's just you, me and the sword here, until we starve to death." I was just blurting my thoughts as they arrive. "Hang on, something's missin'. Wait, where's your sister?"

There's lots of different kinds of screams, you hear a lot of them in Hell. Almost every scream is trying to communicate something, usually 'danger', either towards or from the screamer. Then there's the ugly, wet screams made because inaction is suddenly the worse torture they can endure but there's just no actions they can take anymore. This was the latter kind. He screamed himself into the ground, till his voice cracked and stuttered and his lungs ran out of noise fuel.

"Diana. Diana. My sweet–ster–led her," he mumbled, hunched over and panting heavily.

I should have kept my mouth shut.

"Ki-d-I-I-I killed her, not right, not right!" he murmured, shaking his head from side to side in desperate denial. "Not me. Not her. Two things. Just two things, and now-gah!" Dim flames lashed out around him as he clutched his head with his free hand.

What should I do? What should I do? Should I comfort him? I can't do that! The only method I knew would make things worse. Maybe I should kill him and put him out of his misery? No, that'd be a senseless waste. He was *not* going to die until he was ripe again! What then? Bind him? With what? Whatever pseudo-magick I was feeling was beyond my reach, and my reserves were done for, everything I had was occupied keeping my skin on. I won't hold him down. Taking his sword away would be a *big* mistake. 'Never trust talking furniture', that's what my father always said. Ugh, on my first name, what to do? I didn't even know how safe we were here. Worse comes to worst, there was always the proud tradition of heartfelt slaughter.

Just had to find a way out before it was too late,

***

Sometimes he screamed, those were probably the worse times. Screams that never ended, that approached from every direction in the space without space. Other times he begged, pleaded to delusions to undo his actions, or make an exchange. If I ever got home maybe I could arrange a deal for him. No, I'm sure father could think of a better deal.

Sometimes he made threats, he threatened gods, he threatened time, he threatened himself and he threatened the place we were in. Occasionally, some phantom appeared before him, but whatever it might be it was gone when I looked again. I'd been here too long. A ranting madman just didn't work as company, and no matter what I tried I couldn't see home from here. I couldn't even find the aether.

Sometimes he just stood there, calm as the Dead Sea. I couldn't keep the false hope from swelling, but there was the hollow vacancy still in his eyes. He'd just stepped out for a while. He always came back though. Whatever was in the back of his mind mustn't be what he was after.

I'd still no luck with making a path home. No matter how I turned it I was doing something wrong but I couldn't for the life of me work out what. When it got too frustrating I joined in his screaming. It felt good, for a bit. How long had it been? I'd have to eat Draco soon if I didn't find the way out.

Then there was music. He was singing. It was a language I didn't know, and I'd no idea of the words but it sounded pretty, well, most of it. Some parts sounded like Lussuriosi at night, not bad but-

Much more of this and I'd be ranting right there with him. He'd stopped getting emotional, but he was still talking. I'd no clue what he thought he was seeing, but it was unnerving. He hadn't said a word to me the whole time. I'd tried getting his attention, but he just looked right through me. What was his problem anyway? He killed his sister, I get it, but couldn't it wait until I was out of earshot?

***

My eyes snapped open. I was asleep? How long? Bah, I didn't care. I didn't think time existed here anyway. My body was a bit more limber and my head was a bit clearer so it did something. I thumped the 'ground' with my fist and got up, and thumped my head. Feels like a chin.

"W-what? Damn everything, who?" I scowled and grumbled, but the sight of Draco staring down at me froze my expression. "What? Your imaginary friends get bored with you too?"

"I didn't realize you were thirsty" He said. What? What in all hells did that mean? I clenched my fist around a bottle and—wait, what bottle? Yup, that was a bottle of my best mead, still caught halfway through the aether.

"What? But how? I—wait!" Damn my eyes, I must have retrieved it while I slept! My body knew what to do all along! Mother was right, the flesh knows. "But just what did I do?" I wondered aloud, feeling around the gateway I'd formed. "This isn't right. Everything is there, but backwards? Everything is back to front. How does that work?"

"The back of something is always backwards, be it prop, song or stage," Draco shrugged. I guess a coherent answer was too much to ask.

"Still, I can't deny it worked" I said, and pulled the rest of the bottle into the real. Without another breath I ripped the cap off and thrust the neck down my throat, letting the burning liquid fill me.

"Oh sweet mystery of life, at last I found you!" I gasped, tearing the bottle away and choking on air. "Oh yes, I can think again" I let loose a grin and took another swig.

"Our cue is up, they're expecting us" The man in tatters said, a slight of urgency in his voice.

"What? Whatever. I think I got this. Between the nap and the booze I'm just about alive enough to do the ritual properly, and now that I know the method it should be a one way trip." I chuckled, and sprinkled hellfire on the 'ground' around me, making a crude circle. Fermentation adds new life to make liquor, and that's good enough for me to feed upon.

"We'd best get out, while you still know the way" Draco said, looking at his sword oddly.

"Yeah, yeah. If you want me to take you out of here, shut up and stand in the circle." With the desecration in place, I began the strange method that seemed to work in my sleep. I reached out, not to the aether but as though I was reaching from within, not forward but behind me, down not up, back to front and inside out.

"There! I see it now! Hah! Even in the arse-end of the universe, booze leads me right home!" Draco stepped into the circle and rubbed his temples.

"Something tells me I will not enjoy this. Well, maybe a little." He muttered, adjusting his hold on his sword. That's right, there was three of us, I had better compensate.

"Right, hold on, if I'm right, you're about to find out what the inside of the back of your own head tastes like." The desecrated circle flared to life around us, cutting a hole through the real.

"If you're wrong?"

"Imagine your brain being molested by Euclid's worst nightmare in a bunny suit!" I shouted over the flames.

"Again!?"

1. The Prisoner

Draco

Disorientation distorts the discernible direction of done deeds that darken the drive of the death-rope right, no, wrong! Inside is an empty urn that can't hold 'ny more, outside is a window stained with glass, also wrong. The stream has become a river that has broken its banks and threatens to bury the forest in a marsh, or perhaps not. I squeezed my hand and was overcome with relief as the texture of Drakkengard's grip rubbed against my palm.

I blinked thrice and saw the visions of nothing that those plagued by sight have seceded, an in their stead were visions of rock and mist and demoness. Off in the distance was the splashing of water and the buzzing of angry insects.

"Lascivus?" I asked. The she-devil turned and offered me a grin. A bottle of unknown liquid was in her hand, and a few other empty bottles lay on the surrounding ground.

"Oh? Back with us now, are you? And here was poor little me getting lonely." She said, and flicked her head in slight. I shifted my weight, feeling hard rock beneath each step.

"Your ego is enough that you could keep yourself company, surely!" I laughed, twisting around to look myself over. My clothes were tattered. I was covered in dust, debris and ash. One shoe was about to fall in half, I was missing a sleeve, and one pant was just strips waving in the wind, not to mention the various rips, tears, and missing chunks of fabric here there and everywhere. Yet even this much clothing was a gift from the fates better than none.

"Really, I don't suppose there's a tailor around here? I think I'm having a textile tragedy here." I made a vain attempt to brush some of the dirt from my dress.

"Really? After all that your clothing is all you can worry about? I don't believe you." She shook her head. Not only was *her* clothing unscathed, both her heels were still present and in pristine condition, a critical hippo indeed.

"Clothes are what separate folk from beast, after all."

"I've seen too many monkeys in suits to buy that."

Feeling better than I was, I stuck Drakkengard blade-first into the ground.

"Drakkengard, time to wake up" I sung out, giving her pommel a scratch. The sword bulged and expanded, living metal cascading over itself as it reformed into the shape of a young woman dressed in robes.

"Master!" My sword squealed and latched onto my arm. Out the corner of my eye Lascivus shook her head.

"Look, Drakkengard, our new acquaintance is here too" I gestured to the succubus.

"Hi old lady!" Drakkengard cried out, flapping her arm in wave. Lascivus's brow twitched, forcing me to stifle a smirk.

"What did you just call me?"

A sudden sound drew my attention away from our congress. The three of us were not alone. Through the mist that edged my vision I spied ephemeral figures in communion with one another, mostly in groups of two or three but sometimes more. They were gathered in the light of a somber castle that stood behind them. The sound of voices filled my ears. No, it was always there, but with so many talking it had just faded into a dull drone, like hornets or wasps all abuzz. I was battered by voices speaking various tongues, alien languages outcry in protest, accents of anger, voices deep and hoarse. It was deafening, yet I couldn't understand any of it.

There was no commonality to their appearances, their apparel and appropriates, their mannerisms and minutiae, all stood in stark contrast from one another. Some were presented in finery, some in fetters and others in skins of setters.

"Who are these people?" I asked. "And what are they doing here? For that matter, where is here?"

"'Here' is called Limbo, and those things? They are the poor saps that think they can bargain with the best of them. Maybe they owe a debt they can't pay, maybe they want a job done, and some are just tourists. Every way, they come down here, and the third bolgia comes up here and they trade words till their tongues bleed. Oh, they plead, and beg and barter and bribe, and more often than not they walk away thinking they came ahead. If their opponent was good enough, they never catch on.

"You brought me to a house of deals?" I asked, "I wouldn't have guessed you a broker."

"*We* made a deal, didn't we? One trip to repay a blood debt."

"A bargain for you, I'd say. I'm sure your neck is worth more."

"Could be, could be. Walk with me" She said, making her way into the throng of veiled figures. I followed, while Drakkengard walked ahead.

"Why is there so much mist? I can't see." Drakkengard waved her arms to shoo away the vapor.

"We promise customer anonymity. It's bad for business if people know who else we've served." Lascivus explained, and indeed although I could easily make out each figure, their faces stayed naught but a dark blur.

"A bemusing trick, I suppose it works." I shrugged.

"Although Limbo is technically our territory, a while ago we declared it neutral ground and moved the border back. Got a bit of a squatter problem now but that's nothing. Now, through here . . ." Her words trailed off as we approached a large stone gate hewn into the cave wall. Over the gate's arch were the words '*Lasciate ogni speranza voi ch'entrate*' and on the ground below, more recently, someone had carved out 'WELCOME'. With a chuckle I stepped through the gateway.

***

The change of atmosphere was abrupt, something crawled along my skin, something slid down my throat with every breath— An odd sensation, but not unpleasant. The few figures I saw were heading to or from the gate, and none stayed to mill around or anything.

"Something feels strange." I muttered as the gooseflesh rose on my arm.

"You're probably feeling the miasma. Tickles, don't it? You shouldn't drink it though."

"How do you drink a feeling?"

"It's magick. Well, a form of magick. Different to the stuff you find on the surface. Goes down real smooth and gives you an extra edge. 'Demon Juice' some call it. I prefer alcohol myself, not that I haven't, ah, 'partaken' when the need arises" She said, continuing to walk ahead.

"If I recall, when we fought, after a point your image tasted purple in my eyes. Once that happened, you became . . . better,"

"That's the stuff. Course if you grow up round these parts you get used to it. Otherwise it packs a real kick in the teeth."

"It stinks! Like rotting grapes, and dead people's clothes" Drakkengard complained, covering her nose with her hands.

"Yeah, well for some of us it smells like the best bloody flowers ever, brat!" Lascivus snapped. She took a swig from the bottle in her hand then resumed her amiable demeanor, well, by comparison at any rate.

"Come on, we've got a long walk ahead." She said, walking off into the mist.

"Remind me again why I'm following you." I chased after her.

"You don't know where you are."

"Well, all things considered, I'd say I'm in Hell." I snipped.

"You don't know *where* in Hell you are." She replied, stern, and took another swig of her drink. "You don't know how to get out. You can't trust anyone here."

"Except you, of course."

"Yeah, uh, sure, except me. Are you finally *loathe* to spend any time away from me?" She smirked.

"Ah. Of course, how could I have forgotten such a fundamental matter?" I sneered.

"Besides, not like you've anything better to do"

"I take offence to that assumption. Besides, I'd have better things to do if I wasn't stuck down here. Your fault, I recall."

"Hey! If it weren't for me, we'd all be stuck down the deep end of that empty hole. Be grateful"

"Mayhap I liked the hole. Did you consider that?"

"The whole time you were in the hole, you were a gibbering vegetable."

"I'll give you that. I'm still not sure what happened back there."

The mist thinned to expose a staircase no doubt leading deeper down to some such damned destination or another.

"Come on, you empty-headed ape" She called, darting down the steps. With a shrug I followed after her.

As soon as I stepped off the short set of stairs, I was struck by a second sensation—the conjunction of cold and sharp that clears the sky and skirts the seas—none other than a cyclone.

"Why is it so horribly windy?" Drakkengard yelled out.

"And why so abrupt?" I continued. I was surprised grass grew from the ground here, bent and mattered from the constant winds but nonetheless present. How curious.

"It helps stop fighting over territory. The influence of any given territory is cut off at its edge." Lascivus explained.

"So 'wind' owns this land?" I asked, drawing closer so as not to hoarse my voice.

"Sort of. Look up!" She commanded, pointing.

Throughout the 'sky' of this place semi-human figures flitted, carrying the wind behind them as they flew. Most were amazingly thin while others had no body at all. Some flew upon wings larger than they were, and others propelled by the wind, others couldn't be told from the winds themselves.

"They're naked!" Drakkengard proclaimed in wide-eyed astonishment. None of them had so much as a glove adorning them, their raw, windswept flesh exposed for all to see, those of them that have flesh, at any rate. They tangled and entwined in the air, curving through the sky in a cascade of carnal communion. Hands and mouths and feet and face all pressed up against one another and everything else

"Keep walking. You *really* don't want to stay in this place too often." Lascivus laughed as we continue our trek.

"This is Lussuriosi, ruled by wind and desires, the two most fickle things in existence. At least, that's what mother says." My guide cast a sideways glance as two of the fleshless flew alongside us.

They chittered in hushed whispers to each other, their voices nothing more than a trick of the wind on any other day. They appeared genderless and almost featureless, little more than an outline in the shape of a person. The two of them flittered around me, ignoring both Lascivus and Drakkengard.

Lascivus growled something at them, speaking the guttural tongue of demons. The two winds hissed and flitted away, but the noise drew out several more, both with and without flesh. Those without flesh hissed and murmured in growing volume while I was able to catch just a mote of what the bodied once said.

"Tasty . . ."

"We want it!"

"So good . . ."

"New plaything."

"Still warm . . ."

More and more flying things gathered around us until it becomes impossible to walk onward. The fleshless ones had no discernible sex, but the rest displayed their characteristics proudly, thrusting them forward to draw attention to them and away from their brethren. They reached out with thin limbs and slender tongues in desperate need for any contact. My left hand twitched.

Lascivus let out an infernal bellow, displaying her fangs, and fired off a burst of hellfire The flock scattered away.

"Disgusting things. These are the worst filth." Lascivus scowled, pushing forward with irate vigor. "Flesh is a tool, not a purpose. They lose themselves in the act and forget why they do it. Eventually, they forget everything else and just rut without end. When that happens we throw them out here to wallow in their own sensations," Lascivus spat, bristling. The flock returned, or another cloud, but this instance they kept their distance, hanging a stone's throw away.

"Mind you, the wind sprites are all right. Mostly they just hang around other flying things and play games. Can't actually touch anything, you see." She rambled. We walked past a rock incline and Lascivus stopped and groaned.

"There's the worst of the worst." She said, pointing over to a nearby plateau. Spread out atop of it was a blue skinned creature. Her hair was ragged and slick with an unknown substance, her lips swollen, her bust engorged, and torso flesh torn. Her waist tapered to horrific thinness, barely containing her bizarre curved spine as it sat atop her bloated thighs. She flashed a bloody, broken grin that showed how few of her teeth were left. She made to move towards us, but her body was too deformed to even lift her off the ground.

"That's the thing about miasma. It does what you want it to, just keeps doing it. I suppose that woman wanted to be beautiful. Now look at her."

"She'll die like that?"

"Yup. We call them field-layers, since lying in a field is all they're good for. Not even the filth-lickers will touch them." Lascivus explained, then turned aside and continued on without a second glance.

"Should I put her to sleep?" Drakkengard asked, staring with candid fascination.

"Don't bother. A field-layer doesn't suffer. They don't even realize what's happening. Leave them be, and they'll starve to death with the same stupid grin on their face as when they lost themselves. Now come on."

***

Through the stormy fields we pressed on, leaving the carnal maelstrom behind us and moving further down into the pit. After a time I beheld before us a perfectly flat pane of ice water. The foamy brine crashed against an unseen barrier that separated it from where we stood.

"Eh, right. I should have brought an umbrella, yeah" Lascivus grumbled. Unbidden, Drakkengard bound into the frozen rain and frolicked about, laughing and giggling as it washed over her.

"It's cold!" She shouted in a shrieking giggle, spinning and jumping and causing frigid mud to splash over her sandaled feet.

"Rain, really?" I glowered. A slight shiver ran through my body.

"Oh, Golosi isn't *that* bad." Lascivus muttered, although whether to she or me I couldn't say.

Hunched over and with great haste we barreled through the fields of slush, with shards of ice pelting against our backs as we ran. Out of my eye's edge I caught faint glimpses of our surroundings—of beings wrapped in cloth working the sodden soil with crude implements of labor, of creatures of water diving into the slush and flying high into the air, of a woman bathed in frost that rode in a canopy atop the back of a great three-headed beast, and of others in rags tearing gourds and vines from the ground to toss into the back of metal carts pulled by indefinable creatures made of water and dirt.

It took a short run to make it through the drowning plains but it dragged out for far too long for anyone's liking. Once in the dry, we sat on the edge of its curtain.

"If I never even look at that place in a million years, it'll be too soon." Lascivus panted. Her whole body was drenched, her hair was a mess and her skin was pale and goose-fleshed. Steam rose from my own body as it tries to warm itself on instinct, and Drakkengard looked not even damp beneath her ever-present grin. Not for the first time I couldn't help but envy her metal body.

"You must admit, that's was a bit fun" I chuckled, leaning back on my arms. The hard ground pressing my soaked clothes into my back was nothing short of dreadful, forcing me upright in an instant. Lascivus laughed but was struck by a shiver.

"Damn this cloth, and all its makers" I scowled, tearing off the decrepit garb that covered my torso and throwing on the ground. I placed my left hand against it and after sputtering for a few moments it bursts into flames.

"And thus, there was fire" I said as both Lascivus and myself sidle closer to the source of warmth.

"So what is the instance behind the rain, such an odd place for an isolated monsoon" I queried, looking over at Lascivus. She didn't bother to remove her outer layer of clothing to dry it off. I suppose demons aren't bothered by such things as much.

She stared at me for a few silent seconds before shrugging and turning to the fire.

"As strange as it might sound, it's actually really hard to grow food down in Hell."

"No! Really?"

"Oh yeah. Our little set-up gets around that though. The soil's worthless, but the ice has lots of nutrients and stuff to make the crops grow good. We grow stuff that can take the heavy rain, and what's left behind becomes fertilizer, which the water eidolons carry back up to be rained down on the next rotation. At least, that's how it was explained to me. I'm not big on agriculture" She shrugged before wrapping her arms around her legs for insulation.

"And are all your crops grown there?"

"Nah. From Golosi, we get vegetables for food, materials and recreation, and we trade that and other stuff for meat from other places. We can't raise any decent animals here, well, nothing you'd want to eat anyway. Beasts in Hell tend to get weird, with a capital Y." She shivered, rubbing her hands together and holding them against the flame. Funny, I don't think I'd ever seen someone actually do that until now.

"I must admit, you're quite the wellspring of information," I said, rolling my shoulders back and scratching my neck as my body relaxes.

"Hey, a girl's got to have some class, right?" She smirked, and her chest puffed up with pride.

After resting for a while, we continued on. After a time, I came across a slightly more welcoming sign of civilization. I saw multitudes of people, if 'people' is not too strong a word. We approached them and soon enough they were upon my every side. They stood behind and before makeshift stalls, with supplies and services out on display. Voices rose in discordant chorus, and they cried out—

"MORE!"

"LESS!"

"NOW!"

"NEVER!"

"LOWER!"

"HIGHER!"

"SOLD!"

Coin and accountability exchanged hands, and half the party were rearranged only to begin anew the eternal joust of commerce. Back and forth, back and force, they dueled with deals in a dervish of capitalist desires.

While I was still taking in the sight, a small haggard woman with grey skin approached.

"Greetings and salutations kind patron. This your first time here yes?"

"Well I-"

"Of course, of course. By all means, where else would you be? For that matter, where have you been until now?"

"What you say?"

"But that's not important! Mayhap, perchance, you might accept the services of a poor, humble tour guide?" She grins, exposing a solid gold grin.

"Peon, get out of my sight before I melt that metal mouth of yours. Be gone!" I scowled, waving the woman away with my arm. She hunched over and grumbled but nonetheless scurried away.

"Tour guides" I shuddered.

"Oh never mind that. Hey, as long as we're here we might as well take a look around, yeah? Come on, let's go" Lascivus let out a chuckle and darted over to the nearest stall to purvey their wares.

"Yay shopping!" Drakkengard squealed, tugging on my arm and chasing after her. With a shrug of defeat I followed.

The first stall we approached was loaded to the head with all sorts of exotic looking fruits, gourds and preserved flesh, in a dazzling variety of colors and shapes, unlike anything I'd seen in London. Far too many, I noticed, bore the exaggerated brightness of something best left untasted.

"Hungry?" Lascivus asked, taking what looked like a purple crab-apple and dropping a pair of coins in its place, although I was unsure from whence they came. One of the coins lands crookedly, causing it to roll off the counter and onto the ground. The merchant behind the stall fell to his crooked knees and scrambled for the lost currency. Lascivus cawed with laughter, which Drakkengard was quick to imitate. Her lips still crooked, the demoness tossed the 'fruit' towards me, which I deftly caught. A sickly-sweet scent filled my senses, not unlike over-ripe melon, or perhaps fermented peaches. My mouth watered in anticipation, yet I made no attempt at eating the food.

"Won't you be eating any?" I asked, glancing towards the she-devil's vacant hands.

"Don't worry about me, I don't eat . . . fruit." She replied.

"Yet you bite the low hanging quote apple. I think I'll pass. Persephone warned me what happens to fools who eat the fruit of underworld" I shrugged and toss the morsel aside.

A warm, wet liquid flowed unbidden down my throat. I coughed and gagged, but swallowed the juice regardless. I cough again, and extracted the fruit from its brief lodgings in my mouth, only to see Lascivus's scowling face. Her speed truly is frightening.

"I show you some hospitality, the least you could do is eat the damn fruit, you ungrateful bastard." She muttered some unheard curse under her breath as she turned to leave. Drakkengard moved to attack, but I stopped her with a gesture.

"Its fine, not actually that bad." I said, taking a proper bite of the fruit.

"Of course not. If I would try something, don't you think I'd have done it back at the entrance? Stupid son of a she-goat." Lascivus spat. My left hand twitched, but I took another bite out of the fruit instead.

Disregarding her peculiar mood, I continued to follow Lascivus through the marketplace. More than a few times an unscrupulous merchant tried to peddle some bizarre or downright alien ware for what I could only assume was an outrageous price. Each one was turned away by cruel words and more than a few harsh threats. One over-eager artisan, with an oversized belly and a neck full of gold just didn't get the hint. Instead he got a bruised larynx and a heel through his foot. That cheered the demoness up.

"The currency in these parts-" I fingered a coin Drakkengard had just slipped into my palm. The coin held little luster, and on one side was an odd insignia while a symbol of a serpent was on the other

"What about it?" Lascivus replied curtly, glancing over at a stall selling pictures.

"What standard is it? The material is nothing special so what determines the value?"

"A slave, at least it used to until a couple hundred years ago when the market collapsed. An economy that can die from overwork is not a very good one it turns out. Now a coin buys labor. Everyone has something they want done. A single coin can buy what a fit, healthy adult can do in an hour. How long they took to learn to do . . . whatever, that makes things more expensive as well but I never cared much. Leave it to the economists."

"That seems awfully vague . . . who decides how much that is?" I handed the coin back to Drakkengard who slipped it up the sleeve of her robe.

"Plutus does all that. He works out how many 'laborers' are in service, how quick they work and how good they are. Tells the big-shot merchants if they should raise or lower their prices, not that most of them listen. That's his seal on every coin"

"The king of coin can't coerce his kindred of commerce, interesting, and what of the flip side of the coin? Whose hand made that mark, and why?"

Madman may be, but not a fool. The more I learn about this place the better chance I'll live to see outside of it. I didn't know why this she-devil was leading me deeper into the pit, but I doubt she'd let me return to my home if I just asked. Besides which, I could stand to be away from that empty house on the hill for a while longer.

"That, you naive mid-worlder, is the crest of the House of the Serpent. Every man, woman, child and *thing* that lives in the underworld is ruled by the Serpent, and His house. They swear fealty to His name and banner. His rule is Just and Kind, and He has led the Underworld through millennia and into a Golden Age of prosperity." Lascivus enthused. That I could hear the poorly placed proper nouns in her speech was more than a little unnerving.

"Quite the special place in your heart he's got." Drakkengard stifled a giggle

"Of course" Lascivus snorts.

With an unerring path, Lascivus led us through the marketplace, glancing at wares and ignoring passer-by's. Once or twice she stopped to exchange a few coins for something that caught her eye. As we moved deeper through the circle of peddlers, I noticed that fewer and fewer miscreants dared to approach, and none of the merchant's even try to haggle when the demoness makes a purchase. An idea formed in my head.

"They know you here?" I asked, more of a statement than a real question. Glancing back at me, Lascivus grinned.

"I swing by now and again."

"And let them know you pay your own price, no doubt."

"A good policy for anyone round-"

"Ha-ha! The mean old lady scares the shops" Drakkengard sung out, cutting Lascivus off mid-sentence as she skipped ahead.

"Hey, kid, wanna see how pretty you'll look with that necklace shoved up your ass?" The She-Devil spat. Drakkengard darted off ahead and poked her tongue at her.

***

Lascivus must have noted my earlier complaint, as our next stop was a tailor.

"Go on, I'm sick of looking at your drowned rat impression" She said, scowling as she gestured towards a rack of clothing, oblivious to the typical shop-owner's inquisition being rattled off beside her. I moved towards a rack, but the demoness stopped me.

"On second thoughts, maybe *I* should pick. I really doubt you know what 'tasteful' means when it comes to clothing.

"This is coming from a woman who I've yet to see out of heels . . . including when I was trying to kill her. Why do you indulge such a pointlessly risky habit anyway? Or to be more specific, why hasn't it gotten you killed?"

"Years of practice, you poor naive surface-dweller." I raised an eyebrow in response.

"Okay, okay, when you've spent fif— a few good years as a kid learning a pointless trick, it tends to stick with you. I learnt how to do anything in heels."

"But why? I mean heels, really? Figuratively no-one wears heels anymore. Not for centuries"

"Hey, shut up. I had a weird experience in Albania. High heels were one of the least weird things to come out of there." She harrumphed, and picked out more of the tailor's wares. A tall pile had grown on the counter and I should have noticed sooner. Well, it wasn't like I was paying for any of it. Was I?

"I can't help but notice you're being, uh, rather generous of late, that is to say . . . " I fumbled to edit my words as un-incriminatingly as possible. Lascivus just quirked her brow.

"What? I've got to make you look at least half-decent."

". . . Why?" My legs tensed up.

"Surprise."

Lascivus dropped a few more of those outlandish coins on the counter and handed me the pile of clothes. They were soft to the touch and smelled faintly of cinnamon, or at least something similar to cinnamon. How curious.

"Well?" I looked up and saw Lascivus staring expectantly at me.

"What?"

"Are you going to put them on, or just fondle them all day?"

"What, here? Right now?"

"No, on the eve of the winter solstice, yes right now." She said, throwing her arms up in the air.

"I refuse." I said flatly.

"Why? Don't tell me you actually enjoy wearing a monsoon on your back' She asked, raising her eyebrows at me. I pretended not to notice Drakkengard stifling a giggle beside me.

"I'm not stripping naked, right here in the middle of a crowded street"

"Oh, come on. Look at that guy. He's naked. So are those two. No one cares. 'Naked' doesn't even refer to the same thing here. Just do it, you big baby."

"Drakkengard." The grinning girl perked up at her name and threw herself at me, hurling her arms around me in an awkward embrace. An opaque metal curtain enclosed around me, formed from the sword-maiden's flesh. An oddly tinted shaft of light shone down the open top of my impromptu changing room.

"Prude" The demon tutted from outside my 'cubicle'.

"No peeking, now" I warned, and ignored the protests of my dejected companion. The metal that surrounded me says nothing.

Without further waste, I changed out of the sopping and quite frankly disgusting remains of my clothes, and put upon myself the new attire that the She-devil had selected for me.

Once finished, I tapped the walls of my confine thrice, causing Drakkengard to reform her feminine form beside me. As soon as I had air to breathe, I turned around and ignited the remains of my old clothes with a snap.

"Was that really necessary?" Lascivus asked skeptically.

"I don't like leaving my laundry lying around. Any old who-knows could find it" I replied.

"Don't question Master's wisdom, hag" Drakkengard chirped and pulled a face. I breathed a sigh of exasperation as I pulled my servant away before Lascivus could attack her.

"Play nice you two or I'll march right back to Limbo and stay there for the next thousand years." I turned away from the two of them.

"That's not so bad" Drakkengard said, wide eyes in puzzlement.

"Perhaps I could take up clock-making." Drakkengard flinched like she was slapped.

"I'llbegood" She spouted, trembling and rigid where she stood. Lascivus raised a finger in several objections and opened her mouth, but no sound came out as the syntax drained away from her mind and spilled onto her ankles, staining them in ink . . . I mean she was at lost for words.

I shook my head, dispelling the fault and taking the opportunity to actually take a look at the clothes the succubus so graciously selected for me.

It was a rather striking waistcoat ensemble, with ruffles and knee-high riding boots.

"My dear Lascivus, I could spontaneously express affection towards you right now. I won't, but I could." I twisted my waist to try to see how my back looked.

"What do you think Drakkengard?"

"You look like a big idiot fop, it's perfect."

Lascivus gave a triumphant *'humph'*, her arms folded across her chest and sporting a self-satisfied smirk.

"Now that one issue has been addressed, what now, oh guide to the abyss?" I sent an expectant glance the succubus's way.

"Oh, I've got a few more places to take you."

"And if I refuse, you leave me here to fend for myself in a realm what's rules I do not even begin to grasp, forced to fight every day for the next, etcetera, etcetera. Very well. Lead the way, temptress" I extended my arm, gesturing for the she-devil to step ahead of me.

"Oh come on! You make it sound like I'm forcing you" She complained. I elevated an eyebrow.

"Why do you always have to be so cynical? It makes it so hard to exploit you" She said in a half-whine, and hoisted her nose as she walked past. No, that's wrong. Perhaps a quarter-whine is more accurate. I just hope Pi isn't involved again. That always ends badly.

The three of us crossed another threshold and the market place was left behind us in favor of a most repugnant bog. At the first step my feet sunk into the moist ground. At the second step a horribly repugnant scent assailed my nose with a full battalion of bilious odors. At the third step I stopped to gather my bearings. The swampy wetlands stretched out in all directions, coating the landscape in murky browns and greys. I noted with idle dissatisfaction that the sopping marshland had already soaked my boots up to the ankle. Here and there slight weeds struggled to rise above the waterlogged soil, gnarled and pathetic looking scraps of green in otherwise barren mire. Somewhere in the distance humanoid figures engaged in some sort of activity together, beyond that was a rather uninteresting wall. At least it was neither raining nor turbulent. For that alone I was grateful.

"You really know how to impress a person" I idly wiped away a bit of mud splatter from my new waistcoat.

"Hey, shut up. Do I look like a landscaper? The underworld isn't here to look pretty." Lascivus said, prodding me in the chest.

"No really, this is may indeed be *the* most breathtaking scenery I have ever had the good fortune to rest my eyes upon."

"You want me to leave you face down in the goop?"

"Yes! I can venerate the truly ground-breaking mud work your people have done here."

"Just shut up and keep moving. I could've left you back at Limbo you know. Then what would you have done?" Lascivus said, leading the way ahead.

"Master would have been fine!" Drakkengard piped up, bounding up to Lascivus and matching pace, her hazel eyes ablaze with excitement. "He would have been all *'kshaa!'*, *'uuɔoou!'*, *'the stab*!' and we go for cake and find a new mansion and I don't know, but you can go fall in a ravine, 'kay."

"What my companion means to say is I'm sure we would have managed somehow" I say, cutting Lascivus off before she can complain.

"So why are you following?"

"I am following because, to be blunt, you are leading me somewhere. I want to see where, and find out to what end. That and I needed new clothes. I *really* didn't want to track down a tailor on my own spurious merits."

"You claim the strangest priorities." She said, unconvinced.

As we moved through the marsh, the figures began to shift into focus. At first I thought they were performing some kind of tribal dance, at least until I noticed a jaw get dislodged by a large hairy fist. Then again, I only knew two dances.

All around, people of varying degrees of humanity engaged in brutal blood-sport— beating and breaking and branding with their fists, feet and whatever alien appendages or available tools they could acquire. Mud and blood caked their skin, and their clothing seemed little more than an ascetic curiosity rather than an effort of modesty as these people of either and neither sex ripped and teared with broken nails and sanguineous smiles, stained by their over-sustained efforts of mutually assured suicide.

Nearest to myself, two such people engaged each other in such a fashion. One was a large woman wearing scars and holding a thick tree branch, her flesh so engorged with muscle her skin tore with each movement. Her opponent was a less defined, but no-less opposing entity with a long, dripping mane adorned with water weeds and skin smooth like a seal or an orca. The woman brought her makeshift club against the creature's neck, but it passed right through with a splash as though attacking a reflection cast on a waterfall. The apparition shimmered, and from behind the illusion came a two-fold mule kick that sent the woman crashing into the ground beside me. A steep groan issues from a collapsed face as she fell into unconsciousness. Moments later, her body began to steadily sink below the waterlogged ground.

"This is Styx, the mire of *Adirato*," Lascivus went right into explaining without my asking. "another possible fate for those who can't show a bit of self-restraint when it comes to miasma. They fight anything they lay eyes on, and keep on fighting until they can't get up, so we just throw them in the bog"

The last of the woman's form disappeared below the surface, and I was suddenly struck with an unsettling sensation of vertigo as I spy through the clear water in her wake. For just a few brief moments I caught a glimpse at what lay beneath the surface— hundreds, hundreds upon thousands of comatose figures lay at rest in the deep. Their bodies were falling apart after centuries of giving and taking untold abuse for the sake of the fleeting thrill of the fight, yet an unseen force knitted the pieces together bit by bit.

"So when they can't get up," Lascivus continued, the mud and blood once more concealing the tomb below the water. "They go down, taken by Styx for their bodies to be repaired. They rise once again, stronger and more experienced, and they fight some more.

The water creature, its foe now dealt with, turned its attention to me. It regarded me with bulbous, piscine eyes for a few moments before grinning, exposing a mouth filled with tombstone teeth then melting into the marsh below, vanishing without a trace.

"Of course, after a while some get too strong for the others to take care of, so it's up to the kelpies, nymphs, kappa and merfolk to beat them down. This way, they don't disrupt civilization and we don't have to do much to keep it that way. Keep walking" She said, taking the lead again.

"Why keep them around at all? Why not execute them, or drop them on the moon or some such inhospitable grave?" A horse-headed kelpie leapt from the water to snatch an over-muscled woman and dragged her back down before she could make it to shore.

"And give away an undying army? When push comes to shove, Stygians goes to the front lines. They don't follow orders, so you just drop them where they can see what you want flattened and let them run wild. Most of them are so waterlogged they can keep fighting for ten years straight before someone gets a lucky hit and takes out their legs." She casually explained, giving most of those around us a wide berth as she walked.

If she was trying not to draw attention to ourselves, she failed miserably, as a rather roily looking rabble approached our entourage with as much grandeur as they could muster. The group numbered no more than three, although I suspected their collective worth fell somewhere less than that. Two of them still had a mock semblance of clothing, although whatever their original state was, their cloth has been reduced to uniform ruddy mud dyed rags and reeds draped across shoulders and around waists, more as an afterthought than for any semblance of modesty.

They approached wordlessly, holding their heads high and stamping the ground with every step, taunting the waters to even try to take them. I already had mud on my new clothes so I was far from enraptured to entertain these derelict souls, but I doubted they'd come to shine my shoes.

The center figure, perhaps the leader I supposed, being the most muscular, opened his mouth to speak and issued forth an unintelligible drawl accompanied by a stench of seaweed and decomposing fish.

"Back off, scum-sucker! Don't make me rip you a new feeding hole!" Lascivus barked, staring the trio down.

"Don't be that way sis, we're friendly sort, we just want back in the city." The one to the left said, spreading his palms in compliance. He was a thin, gnarly man and rather unassuming looking, but the effect was ruined by his entire left side being a twisted and misshaped mess, doing a rather good impression of a scorpion's tail if anything, which made the gesture tantamount to baring fangs in threat. Drakkengard moved in front of me, matched his wiry gaze and stood coiled.

The third figure, a rather short woman with a pair of broken swords and badly braided hair, had evidently had enough as she lets out an ululating cry and rushed towards Lascivus, her weapons brought to bear. The other two matched her aggression and made their move as well, both barreled towards me, sending water splashing up with every step.

I had a few brief moments to ponder if, because I didn't smell of miasma, I seemed weaker to them. Or was it because I was the best dressed in the group? Well, it was irrelevant regardless. Drakkengard moved between both of them, blades extended from each of her sleeves, and buried her weaponized arm into their flesh. Murky blood sloshed onto the marsh below. The scorpion man was stopped in his tracks, but the leader kept moving, tearing a chunk of flesh and bone from his side in the process.

Before he made it three steps he came to a sudden stop. A long, thin blade emerged from one eye and he slumped but didn't fall, his entire weight supported on Drakkengard's elongated arm. He let out an indecipherable gurgle as he spasmed on his stake. In reply Drakkengard flicked her wrist, sending the top of his head flying and allowing his decapitated corpse to sink into the Styx. I looked up and saw Lascivus remove a demonic claw from the sword-woman's chest, taking out her heart along with it. The she-devil stared hungrily at the organ, still in motion from its own muscular impulses, coated in sickly-black stains, and far too yellow than seemed natural.

A few seconds passed, and she reluctantly crushed the organ in hand, letting the flesh and juice spill out into the bog. She flicked her wrist a couple times to get rid of the gore then allowed it to resume its 'normal' hand-ness.

I turned to the third assailant, alive but wounded and still held in place by Drakkengard's arm-blade. Approaching the man, I took note of his hurried panting and distant expression. I briefly considered if perhaps I was wrong about his arm being from miasma abuse.

"I say to you, friend" I leaned down to look him in the eye, only courteous after all. "I currently hold your life in my hands. I can throw it away right now, and you sink into the Styx. You've never drowned in the river before, have you?" My captive made no sound, but his eyes latched on to me with an unreadable focus, his breath still coming in rapid bursts. "Below the Styx, you'll lose your mind and replace it with power, become just another dumb brute. Alternatively, I can give your life back to you, but it won't be free. You'll need to-" Before I can finish speaking, his stinger arm whipped up. A moment later, it was impeded by Drakkengard's back as she throws herself over me, stopping the limb from tearing into my spine.

I slammed my fist into his face, smashing the teeth from his mouth, rammed my hand deep into his throat and shoved his head to the ground. How dare he? Vile! Insolent! Despicable! Flame spilled out from my hand and down his throat, into his belly. His eyes widened in terror and he tried to scream, but was muffled by my deeply lodged fist. I didn't see the river, I didn't see the sky, I didn't hear the voices and I didn't know of the world. This *filth* hurt Drakkengard. The flame rushed forth, burning with the impetus to end him right now. In just a few moments he became naught but ash and slag and a memory. The slag sank into the bog water. I dismissed it in favor of inspecting Drakkengard. Her wound was already gone, even the damage to her clothing was no-where to be seen. I sighed in relief, and she gave me a worried smile.

"I'm fine, Master. A wound like that can't hurt a sword" I sat for a minute, holding her shoulders as I composed myself.

"Feeling better?" Lascivus asked as I rose to my feet. I said nothing.

"I don't think I've ever seen anyone so overprotective of a construct before," She chuckled at my expense. "She's living metal, most planets are more fragile than she is, and you go get all teary-eyed over a flesh wound?"

"She'll be fine. That doesn't mean I don't care if she gets hurt."

"She can't even feel pain on a physical level, she's just a golem. You're worse than those people in love with their cars"

"Kindly stop this topic before I set you on fire" I said, as civilly as I could muster. "Please."

"You're such a child. Fine, be that way. Let's get out of here before more hooligans slow us down."

The three of us continued across the river's surface. For whatever reason no more Stygians bothered to approach, something I was grateful for. The less goop splashed at me the better. After a small time's travel, we came upon a great blackstone wall, stretching out for the horizon in either direction. Walking atop the wall were the countless visages of human-shaped figures. Some gazed out onto the mire while others idly paced from one end to the other.

"And this is?" I wonder aloud.

"This is Dis, or at least her walls." Lascivus explained. "We should find an entrance one way or another. Left or right?"

"Left" I replied after a moment's thought

"Right it is"

"Now that's just petty." I complained.

Soon enough we reached a heavy iron portcullis, adorned by gargoyles and an impractical number of spiky protrusions. With some discomfort I noticed that the gargoyles made no attempt to conceal their gaze as they stared at us. Rude. At the foot of the gate stood a masculine figure, slouched against the wall and with an air of content boredom. Shimmering green scales adorned his bare chest, and upon his brow untold dozens of serpentine appendages lazily shifted and coiled. A long, smoky stick protruded from his mouth, as well as the mouths upon his hair-snakes, which created an impressive halo of presumably narcotic smoke.

The gorgon lazily lifted his hundred-fold gaze until it rested upon us, and slowly took in our visage without comment. A few moments of this passed and when it became clear he would not speak, Lascivus stepped forward.

"Hey, hard-skin, open the gate." She demanded in an obnoxiously assuming tone. Uncounted mouths deeply inhaled in an ambisonic hiss.

"Ffffuck off" He drawled, then took the stick from his main mouth and flicked it to the marsh.

"Look mall-cop, don't make this painful. You open the gate, and we never see each other again, or do you want to learn what it's like to suffocate five-hundred times at once?"

With slow, exaggerated movement, the colubrid snake-man produced another stick from a pouch around his waist and ignited it with a touch. A forked tongue flicked from his mouth to drag the stick in. He took another hissing breath and blew smoke in

Lascivus's face. Her immediate and not-at-all unwarranted reaction was to punch him in the snout, dropping him on his ass with one blow.

"Ffffuck you, fffowl ffeaster." He wiped the blood from his mouth and he picked himself up. A small audience had gathered at the top of the gate, all watching silently.

"I'm sorry, that didn't sound like 'I'll get the gate, madam'. Did I mishear you?"

"Ssssuck me, iiitch-sscratcher." He tried to lunge for her, but vanished before moving even an inch. The snake-man reappeared a few meters to the right of us, trapped in a headlock by a shapely woman with strong red hair and stained black eyes, draped in the cloth of Rome.

"Kievan, seriously, shut your mouths before I seal them with wax. Lascivus, sorry you had to put up with this idiot."

"I'm sorry my fist had to put up with his ugly face. Can you get the door, Mary?"

"You heard the lady!" The woman called Mary shouted. No physical cause made itself evident, yet the portcullis smoothly slid open.

"There you go, if you'll excuse me, I've a few words to have with this big-mouthed buffoon. Really, Kievan, you have no idea who you're messing with." The snake made no comment, his body limp with apparent unconsciousness. With a smile and a wave, the red-head vanished.

"At least there are some people here that aren't an asshole." Lascivus muttered.

"Look who's talking"

The three of us entered the city, and for the first time I beheld Dis.

"The burning city of Dis—the more 'civil' center of hell, I presume," I said aloud, and took in the sight as I entered the iron gates. Indeed, on either side of the wide, cobbled streets stood buildings like tombs, of all shapes and sizes, and upon the edifices of the intricate masonry of these tombs spouted gouts of flame at a-periodical intervals. The air wafted past with the comforting scent of fresh smoke and clean stone. Upon a slight of thought, I looked up, both expecting and not to see a sky of some sort. Indeed, my suspicions were correct, as within my gaze I spied not a sky of any sort, but the faint shadowy crags of a cavernous ceiling. What this meant, and the suspicion that provoked the examination, was that the flames of this city-torch are what lit up this whole starless pseudo-natural world.

"What a self-sufficient society" I said aloud, neither receiving nor wanting response, and got lost puzzling the motive behind it.

At the behest of my demonic escort, the three of us checked in for the night at a local inn, or at least a close approximation. The structure and décor of the building seemed religious in design, but I could find no sure-fire evidence one way or another.

The Inn-keeper, or at least the person manning the desk, was an amber-colored woman of mature stature and appearance yet possessing the most unusual quality of a translucent complexion. I could actually make out the pattern of the ornament on the wall behind her, an angular flower design hewn of iron and silver.

"I know what you're thinking" The translucent woman spoke, her voice like a babbling brook, and not metaphorically. "Imagine a living waterbed, without the bed." She winked.

"Hey! Stop flirting and just hand over the keys."

"If you ever get tired of riding a bicycle, a meliae would never be that possessive" The amber creature chortled and tossed a long black spike. Lascivus caughts it off-hand, and made haste for the stairwell and I, weary after the 'day's' journey, followed.

As I entered our room, Drakkengard leapt from my side and dove upon the bedding laid out for us, tittering gleefully as its coils tried vainly to repel her before conceding to simply support her weight with a groan. Lascivus shut the door behind us with a quiet *click*.

"Speak to me, dear captor" I leveled my gaze at the she-devil. "Will you now finally reveal your intentions, or must I spend another fitful bout scrutinizing your every err?" I crossed my arms. Her step paused in a moment of consideration. She matched my gaze, lowering her arms to her side. The black spike that sealed the door was still in her hand.

"This routine again?" She sighed. An edge of frustration seeps into her voice.

"A person prepared beforehand is better than after reflection. I do not intend to walk into whatever trap you're laying for me with thanks upon my lips."

"You still think I'm trying to set you up for something? We've been over this!" She slapped her hand against the stone wall with a growl.

"That's a funny way of saying 'you can trust me', She-devil. I assure you, the reputation of your kind has been written, unchanging, for seven-thousand years."

"Reputation? According to what? Would you judge humans by their reputation among housecats? Is a flower in any position to call a gardener good or bad? You are living in a big blue ball of blindness, and you walked in there yourself. You think anyone on your streets have insight into the daemonic? Look out the window, go on, look" She pointed a rigid finger at the open frame in the wall, and I complied.

"I see the city of Dis, and its walls. I see the Styx, I see the outer circles, I see the gates of hell, and I see the misty forest of limbo where we emerged. What of it?" I turned to question the Succubus, but as I pull my gaze from the window, a metallic black object fills my vision. The next moment, my head exploded.

"This doesn't hurt, see? Your servant hasn't moved. She knows this isn't an attack. You know it too, this is just a feeling you can't compare."

"What . . .what are you doing?" I snarled. My hands rose to the object lodged in my eye, but were forcefully slapped away.

"Don't touch. I'm breaking your eyes from your mind. You will see my world without your delusions of normalcy." With that, she gave the black spike a twist and yanked it out of my head. Cold fluid ran down my face but when I touched it my hand came away dry.

"Now, once more, gaze upon my world and tell me what you see." She commanded. Dumbstruck, I complied. I turned back to the window and opened my eye, and tried to ignore the flowing sensation against my cheek.

Colors! My vision was awash with colors! Red, blue, green, violet, indigo, aqua, cream, infrared, ultraviolet, delta, gamma, micro, aether, magick, miasma—concepts and rules and laws and forces all exploded into my vision in ways I could not even begin to define.

"What do you see?"

"Everything, or is it, how can I say, a lack of nothing?"

"What do you see?"

"It makes no sense. I see where we emerged, and here, and a distance of ten-thousand years. We walked a day with each step, but not in the same direction. Each circle is exactly that, perfect, yet marred by the next circle invading its space. We walked a parallel path and intersected every ninetieth step. I spilled a drop of blood and am owed four shekels to my soul as accorded by the dynamical system—what does that even mean? I see written law shaping the coupled map lattice of the unreal and nonsensical numbers of people with a zero sum account. I see . . .see . . .” The vainglorious spectacle faded from my eye as Euclidean space reasserted itself upon my comprehension. The walls, rivers and structures became definable once again.

I slumped to the floor, released from unseen strings. My breathing came labored and a horrendous ache bore through in my skull.

“You are a drawing that has exceeded the boundaries of their paper. You have not changed, the world has not changed but how you interact will never be the same. You will forget what you just saw, as though a dream, but the understanding will never leave you”

“I, what? A Cartesian plane, XYZ, but that’s not enough. There is a fourth axis of space, at least a fourth, maybe more. If Earth is where all axes are zero, I am where XYZ are zero and the fourth is minus one. By traversing the fourth axis, one can reach extraplanar space, which is what you do. Where I am standing now corresponds to a real place on Earth, but whatever is there is completely unaware of my own existence, and I of it. Wait, I-” I scowled, tried to stand. My vision swam and remained swimming and vanished all at once.

“Why can’t I see?” I tried not to let the panic leak into my voice.

“The sight in your brain just turned off. As far as your body is concerned, that was a hallucination, which means you’re sick. It’ll come back after you’ve rested”

"Drakkengard, help me to the bed" I pawed blindly for her hand.

"Yes, Master" I found it, and following its guidance found the bed with my other. Double-checking its location, I gently lowered myself upon it.

"Is that how you—with your sword and the mead?" I tried to shift my focus from my sensory deprivation. One fifth of my senses flooded me with darkness. The bed was soft, but disturbingly cold. The whistle of a discomforting breeze slipped past. Like being held blindfolded in a cage*don'tthinkthatdon't*

"The same sort of deal. I have a bunch of stuff bound to my exact location, just on a different plane, one that's all empty space. At any time, I can make a 'bridge' and pull them through or send them back."

"Okay, I get it . . ." I took a deep breath, and exhaled. What was this feeling on my hand? Metal spiders with rust for hair made a nest in my skin. Light-eating bars pressed against my face, back, neck and thighs, in a cube smaller than I.

"You're as good as ineffable, and I'm never going to get a straight answer from you without bleeding. At least, that's what you want me to think. I'm onto your games."

"What's that supposed to mean?" She huffed. She spoke like a dragon and her firebreath set ablaze my neck. I reached out until I find the comforting cold-warmth of Drakkengard's grip and drew her close to me.

"Stabbing me in the eye and mind-fucking me will not make me trust you. Showing me a visage, all you've proven is that I can't trust my senses. You've yet to do anything to demonstrate that I can trust you."

"Look, go to sleep. You're just freaked out a little. You'll feel better when you wake up. Trust me."

"Bad choice of words." I muttered, and the room succumbed to unsettled silence.

***

I jolted awake to something wet falling on my skin, and an impassioned fire flowing through my blood. My eyes snapped open, and the first glimpse of my newly returned sight was Lascivus's face, contorted in pain and rage. My attention snapped downward, to where Drakkengard was holding Lascivus aloft upon a blade, expressionless. What had happened was obvious.

"Despicable" I struck her with my foot as Drakkengard yanked back her blade. The she-devil crashed into the floor.

"Wait! Just, just one bite! I wasn't-" The succubus cried out. My gaze hardened.

"Yours truly is the Mother of Harlots." I snapped. "Am I just another fig to you?" I drew Drakkengard up to myself, her form resumed that of a sword, and I made my way to the door.

"You are filth, however lustrous. Your mud would just stain my sword. Do you hear? I'd rather let you live than dirty ourselves spilling you onto this floor." I gripped Drakkengard tightly and cut down the door's lock.

The door fell with it, and I rushed past, ignoring all else as I ran out onto the streets. My feet hit the cobblestones of Dis, and I kept running, no destination in mind.

Where could I go? Anywhere, as long as I kept running, it would be fine.

Was the fire in my blood, or was it in the air that I gulp down with every hurried step? Was it in the muscles that knew not rest, or the mind that cried out for sleep? If I kept running, would the flame go out, or would it consume me whole?

How long did I run? How long had I been running?

I turned into an alleyway and slammed against a wall, forcing my stop. This was a dangerous place. I needed to be prepared for anything. I would be fine. This was no different to eternal London, proudly barbaric with its copper-men and urban tribes and night-stalkers. I survived there I can survive here. The only difference was I now dealt with bigger fish. Fish that hid behind flesh made of ruse-mail, fish that could surrender their mind for limitless power, but fish nonetheless. They could be cooked and eaten if piranha, bass, or shark. I had Drakkengard. I had fire. I was, and won't let that change.

Chapter Four

Escort

Lascivus

Stupid, rock-sucking, knee-bending, ass-munching, red-worshiping-argh. A burst dam of expletives crowded my head as I raced out of the tavern.

Stupid man for running alone into the streets of Dis. Stupid me for letting him get the drop on me like that. Any normal person would have been dead on their feet after being dragged half-way across hell.

I knew I should have grabbed a sleep draught back at the market. Hindsight was a mocking bitch.

I looked up and down the street, but there was no sign of him.

He wasn't that, so he must have hit the alleys, great. Hopefully I could track him down before a grue got its slavering fangs into him.

My stomach wound closed with a twinge of pain and suddenly the thought of letting him fend for himself a night or two didn't seem so bad. No, I'd be biting myself later if I did that. I'd just have to beat him up instead.

I might even strong-arm him into consenting to a fluid donation in repayment. For a brief moment, a grin flickered across my scowl, but it vanished just as quickly.

My skin crawled and itched from how hot the night was, as much as there could be a night down here, or weather for that matter. I'd been spending too much time in midworld. There was no sun, moon, or even orbit involved in this place, just fucked up space. To anyone not used to it, the underworld seemed like the inside of a sphere, except heading to the bottom took you to the center, heading towards the center leads you around the circumference, and all sorts of funky little disturbances happened along the way. An accurate map of Hell would be bigger than Hell itself. The only one that wasn't needed a crazy strong microscope to read. That was the directional mess that my investment had gone and fled into.

I ran up and down the twisting, winding alleys, crossing my own path repeatedly enough that I sometimes spotted myself in the distance, in glimpses of my back or side as the light bounced its weird path. I knew these alleys like the path of my own thoughts, but that didn't make it any quicker to navigate, let alone find one measly person. I couldn't even use my hungry sight to spot him, thanks to how much noise seeps in from ever other living thing down here. Get a bunch of bright lights together, and you can't tell what color each one is until you're right up close.

My surroundings changed. While Ereteci was styled after 12th century Europe, I found myself in the more Victorian styles that characterized Violenti. That Minotaur didn't stop me first was a bit worrying, he's meant to be watching all traffic in and out of central Dis.

An ill-placed step sent a loose chunk of stone into my heel, nearly making me fall over.

"Gah! Bear-cracked, feculent, never-blessed cobblestones!" I stomped the vagrant rock with my heel. I put a bit too much force into it than I should, and the heel of my shoe refused to leave the new hole in the ground. I tugged harder, and my foot came free, taking the strap of the shoe—and no other part with it. I grinded my teeth and glared angrily at the heeled-shoe. I hadn't expected to be running tonight, so I'd gone and bought a nice pair, rather than some more practical boots. I doused the offending footwear with hellfire and skulked off, a headache starting in my head—A rhythmic *thump-thump-thump* slightly out of sync with my heartbeat. I was about to go back to keep searching Ereteci for Draco when I notice the sound is not just in my head.

I growled in frustration and looked to the end of the current way. The alleys opened up to the riverside of burning Phlegethon, and all about the place unmoving bodies had been strewn, some with great gashes, some in pieces, and others suffering drastic burns. At the center of this carnage stood four figures—a centauroi and centauride couple, a satyr and a lamia —all crowded around something, laughing like jackals.

Something shouted, and the centauride ducked just as a ball of fire got flung at her head. She brought her hands together in a mocking clap, reared up on her hind legs and with a yell brought her full weight crashing down. Even from where I was, I could hear the crunch, and when the horse-woman stepped back, there was blood dripping from her hooves. The Satyr stepped forward before I could make out their victim. With held breath, I slunk to the edge of the alleyway. The Satyr yanked their victim up by the hair. In his other hand, he gathered a putrid cloud of swirling miasma.

"What sort of freak do you suppose this one will turn into? A field-layer? Another Stygian oaf? Or maybe a laughing marotte like the last one?" He sneered and brought the roiling addiction closer to his victims head.

"I don't care as long as I get to eat it afterwards. I haven't had a man inside me for weeks." The lamia dragged an elongated tongue down the victim's cheek, and stroked his dark hair with her hand. I could see his face now. A pricking, burning sensation filled my body. That was mine they had there. My food they talked of eating. My toy they planned on breaking.

The Satyr forced Draco's head down into the miasma, ignoring his struggles and laughing, never stopping the laughing.

"Thrice-damned cuckolding—DROWN IN WASTE WATER!" I screamed and the satyr's back exploded with hellfire. He let out a bleating, desperate cry as the unburning flame wrapped around him and he dropped Draco from the pain. Miasma licked my muscles. I reached him in a single bound and put all that momentum into his face via my fist. There was a satisfying crack and he launched into burning Phlegethon beside him.

I looked down at my prey, his body beaten and robbed of strength by superior numbers but his eyes gleamed with impotent rage. He glared and opened his mouth to speak but instead descended into a fit of coughing and spluttering, gagging up stains of red upon his ruined clothing.

"Look at you, who knows how long it'll take for you to be ripe again. I'm hungry but you go and act like a jackass. "I forced my face into a scowl but it didn't last. I turned to his other assailants, all of them wary but not afraid.

"I don't think you understand what I am. You call me a whore, say I'm filth, you mock this monstrous body of mine in doing so."

With a mental command, I reversed the spell that held my body in shape. Bone, muscle and flesh relaxed from n-dimensional contortions and settled back into their natural place. Pale skin resumed a more healthy reddish-black tone, and my small horn jutted out from the side of my head. My waist narrowed as false organs vanished. Crude, stubby fingers and toes melted away into precise claws and talons. My mouths gasped for air. My tail flicked out from its string-tight curl. Taut muscles bound around my chest bulged under my skin and my wings came to rest upon my back, naked for all to see.

I stared at my foes with hungry eyes, seeing their fear and revulsion at my exposure, every little twitch of their growing uneasiness, and measured just how much their life would feed me. They were not a bunch of baby deer, more a pack of savage hyena that needed to be taught their place in the food-chain. They might even have been formidable if they weren't so feebly killable. I flexed my claws as my body's tension unraveled. Time to kill.

He watched me, focused and unwavering as I made mincemeat of the beastfolk's flesh. Claws and fangs drew blood from even the cruelly gentlest touch and my hungry mouths gulped the fluid down— the delectable ecstasy of their life filled my sensations with sweet rapture. I gouged, cut, gulped, swallowed and wallowed in my blatant exhibition. Warm blood and cold blood mingled on my lips, as fur and scale stained my hands. I let myself go in the violent sensations, not caring who or what cared to see, until I was left, panting but satisfied, in a pile of bloody mess. I folded my body back into a human shape and plucked a pair of heeled boots from the aether.

"You think me something lewd and pitiful. Maybe next time you'll think twice before talking shit" I flicked the gore from my claws and wiped my mouth clean.

"Now come on, since you're so desperate to keep moving I'll march you the whole way there."

My companion begrudgingly complied and fell into step beside me, his irritating sword brought up the rear with a skipping hop and a barrage of pointless questions.

"Why was the river on fire?"

"I don't know. It was something a previous owner had installed and no-one's got rid of."

"Who was that previous owner?"

"Yama Raja did it, back when things were less organized and more depressing"

"Why was it sad?"

"Nothing to do, everyone just sat around moping, waiting for someone to pass through."

"Who passed through?"

"Self-titled 'heroes', usually people who wanted to break someone out."

"Why would they want to go away?"

"Because not many people come here willingly, and most want out as soon as they realise just what they signed up for."

"Why do people come here?"

"They make a contract. Usually help with some problem, 'kill my hated enemy', 'save my dying wife', 'may I be free from disease', 'give me power to smite my blah-blah-blah'. In exchange we take either the contract holder, or an agreed upon proxy to come here and work off the debt. Sometimes we get lucky with a two for one special—'take this person, and you can have me'— those are always good.

"Why do you wear high-heels?"

"Something that happened in Albania, I told you."

"How do people get out?"

"Do you ever shut up? They perform various labors—masonry, serving the army, cooking, cleaning, fluffing pillows. Their supervisor keeps track, and once they've done their quota they're free to go. Or stay, for that matter. Usually by that point they can't stand the thought of going back to whatever they left."

"Why?"

"Sooner or later, they try miasma. They either get hooked on the sensation or the power, or some other thing."

"Why?"

"I don't know. Because it's the human condition to be ambitious?"

"Why?"

"What do I look like, an anthropologist?"

"Why isn't your hair longer?"

"What? My hair is plenty long you little shrimp. What's that supposed to-?"

"Why are those people looking at us like roast beef?"

"What does that even—wait, what?"

As casually as pointing out an odd bird, the metal girl singled out a group of people, one of several that litter the streets and back-alleys of Violenti. In the middle of this group is a handsome young ghillie dhu—dark haired and with moss for clothes—sitting on a barrel with a bored look. Accompanying him was a fox-tailed huldra with a back of bark leaning against a wall, and beside her an epimeliad with hair like undyed wool, lying against a sack of apples. All three of them had bands of weeds tightly bound around their wrists and necks, with thistles and thorns drawing sap with every movement, yet the embodied plants paid no attention as the amber fluid dripped down their skin.

"This is the middle ring, where trees and flowers stake their claim." I explained to Draco. It was sometimes uncanny how easily

I fell back into tour guide mode. Too many diplomatic lessons as a kid.

"They're pompous and choking on their own stamen, but at least they've half a brain more than the beasts that run and rut in the first ring." I shrugged. The ghillie dhu's eyes never leave me, issuing a challenge that I accept without thinking. I walked towards him and met his stare.

"Alright soil-sucker, thanks to a hot-headed idiot, I can't just walk the middle road. You'd rather not get more blood on my hand, to be sure, but just to hear it from you I have to ask, will you let us pass?"

"Well here's a pleasance," He drawled, arching his back in a lethargic stretch. "The only-born childe, Little Horn herself, come to grace my mortar w'er presence. How bless'd are we, on this fine curse'd day, to warrant gift from her? Or should I say, curse'd on this bless'd day to be made tolerate this poseur?"

"Oh what's that? Talking back to the Serpent House? Are your last moments really best spent doing that? Wouldn't you rather spend those two-hundred years from now, rather than in ten moments with my foot up your ass?"

"To be sure, messing with you is the folly 'o fools, but this day and age, we all be kings and tools. Statues above, and filth below, while the middle keeps turning back and forth the same sad puppet show. Each dawn is the same spiritless bouquet, so go ahead bitch, make my day."

I scoffed, pacing back and forth before him.

"You've nothing to do, would you like a salutation? At what point in your sad tale should I give half a damnation? It's you who lacks motivation. Don't blame the administration with your shallow condensation and your ignoble misinformation. You don't like your station? Do something about the situation. Revolutionize a nation or just sunder a great creation, don't bore me with your annotation, else I'll remove you from this equation." He locked gaze once more and lingered for several seconds before throwing up his arms and reclining back against the wall.

"Alright, I see your point. The nihil embrace won't spare me your wroth and viler men than I have fallen to your bile. You can pass through my space without further trial. Just try not to step on the lisle"

"No promises, beatnik"

The leafy killers let us pass, and once they were out of earshot, Draco spoke up for the first time in a while.

"I didn't know you spoke beat." He said, his voice quivering with curiosity.

"Fah. I hate it, but I can't just pluck their petals until they wilt. If they started whispering of mistreatment, the whole bouquet of them would go on strike, and it'll be my head ground for tea."

"You had no qualms about killing those beasts."

"They speak violence as a first language, it's the only way to get any respect from them, besides that, they couldn't keep from attacking an army if their soul depended on it. The dirt-munchers, conversely, have a little more tact. A bull can knock down a wall, but nightshade can vacate the throne." I coughed. "That actually sounds clever in our tongue."

" . . . "

"But yeah, their job is less 'kill everybody' and more 'kill that one guy, he pisses me off' thing." I scratched at my throat. I hadn't noticed the dry, clammy itch of thirst festering inside my mouth, but there it was. It was a little surprising, considering how recently I drank some meat. My mind and body performed the tried and true motions and a moment later, I thrust a bottle of mead into my mouth.

The maze of alleys and back-roads seemed like it would never end, however after a while's more walking it underwent a drastic shift. The first thing noticeable is a rapid spike in heat. This was the warning before the grime-filled cobblestones give way to blistering sand, all aflame from the fire raining from the sky. A pelt of fire fell onto my top, where it sizzled and went out.

"Good thing non-flammable is in fashion this aeon. Still, this ring badly needs a footpath" I complained aloud, slipping my shoes from my feet before dropping them into my other space. I wiggled my toes for a moment, testing the feeling then let my feet snap back to their natural talons. Only the feet, mind, no need to be indecent."

"I don't suppose that sand is anything like walking on a foot massage" Draco said, gazing across the burning streets with weary eyes.

"A little. Ah, wait, your skin isn't flame retardant. No, it is nothing like a foot massage."

"Would master like a massage right now?" That annoying little slip piped up.

"No, I was—never mind. Who in whatever passes for city hall down here thought this would be a good renovation?" Draco demanded, kicking a lose stone onto the burning sand where it turned red.

"The occupants don't complain, they like the weather. "

Draco didn't reply he just stared at the burning alley before us. In front of him, the flames pitched to the side in an unnatural manner, leaving a patch of sand exposed for just a second, before more fire spread to cover it. That fire was also turned away, only for more flame to encroach from a third direction. When that got turned aside, the first bit of flame had snuck back in.

"Thrice-damn it!" He scowled, his brow knotted in concentration and a bead of sweat dripped down his cheek.

"That's what happens when you take your gifts for granted, you stay right where you are and never get anywhere. Besides, the sand would still be too hot to walk on."

"Any bright ideas?"

I pointed my finger up.

"We take to the roof-tops.

The three of us gathered up various crates and barrels people had left lying around and set about constructing a crude set of steps.

"People do live in these houses, correct?" Draco asked suddenly. He was oddly untouched despite the fire-rain, but it hardly mattered.

"To a certain meaning of 'live' and not all of them by choice, but yes why?"

"We've been passing through an endless corridor of backways and side-paths, I've yet to see a single door or window and I've not caught sight of the main road since we first arrived in this circle."

"You're still thinking literally. Just because the entrance isn't on any of the four sides of a house doesn't mean there isn't one. You don't need to know the details to manage it, but basically, it's an N-dimensional door lock. Keeps the riff-raff on the streets and out of homes."

"And we are among that riff-raff?"

"No, but they tend to concentrate on the main roads. They think they own anything that isn't behind a lock, including people. Having to stop because of a riot really pisses me off, so we're going the back way."

"To a certain definition of 'back'" he muttered as he pulled himself onto the roof. The slanted shingles offered little foothold, and he staggered dangerously before finding his balance.

"Will these hold? I'd had to gate-crash what goes on behind *your* closed doors." He asked off-handed as he pulled up his metal servant.

"Sure, it would take a behemkin to damage this architecture" I reassured him as I slipped my shoes back on. Warily, he took a step forward. There was a quiet *crack* and Draco was flipped onto his back with a *crash* as the shingle he'd just stepped on got launched flying from the roof by the misplaced step.

"Not that some renovation couldn't help"

***

The three of us stepped lightly as we made our way unseen across the rooftops. The streets and skies both filled with beings of living flame over time, clothed in rock and metal, their presence forcing us to stop and go frantically trying to avoid their gaze. These things of fire didn't take too kindly to trespassers . . . few things in Hell did, but the things of flame had the double irritation being unreasonable, and hard to keep down.

A particularly large shayatin flew lazily overhead, forcing Draco and me to press our bodies against the shingles to avoid its gaze, while the sword simply melted into a slightly shiny puddle. I could feel the heated air from its flight beat down against my back as I riled at how shameful it was to hide like this, but I had to hurry. Every minute I dragged Draco around unsecured was another chance something could go horribly wrong. A little shame was worth the effort.

The shayatin passed by, and I gestured for us to keep moving. This happened three more times before we finally reached the edge of the ring, which doubled the edge of this circle of Hell.

A steep cliff extended before us—at least a few hundred meters down to look at— and at the bottom lay a sprawling network of stone ditches which bustled with people and commotion.

"Now *this* is the real marketplace. Millions of deals a day, as the posters claim" I explained, hopping down from the rooftop to ground, which was now just bare stone. A white picket fence was poorly arranged around the cliff edge, already on the verge of falling in itself.

"I hate your architect. I really do." Draco frowned as he peered down the almost flat rock face.

"Afraid of heights? I'm sure someone like you wouldn't die from a little face-plant"

"Worse, I fear I'd suddenly and intimately know how it feels to put up with your excuse for a wit with 206 broken bones."

"Oh, you'll be fine." I assured him, and leapt over the fence.

The wind pushed and struggled against my face, unable to get out of my way fast enough. I counted to three and channeled a blast of hellfire straight down, slowing my fall by just a little. I quickly fired off five more, and reinforced my body before striking the ground in a heavy impact, sending dust and dirt into the air.

I rose from my crouched position to see Draco sliding down the cliff-face, his sword thrust into the rock and his weight dragging it down, at good speed too. I'd forgotten how sharp he could make that thing. A few more seconds passed, and he came slowly stopping to the foot of the cliff.

"Forgive me for using you in such a way" He mumbled as he puts his sword down. The girl leapt from it and latched onto his arm, but if she heard him she didn't reply. Ignoring both of them, I checked myself over for any sign of harm. Nope, all good.

"Let's keep moving, the Malebolge wait for no-one."

I sigheded with relief as we stepped into the crowd. There was less chance of being randomly accosted from here on. Not that I didn't enjoy beating people up, but it's only fun when not beating them up is an option.

"So are you going to buy anything here, too?" Drakkengard asked, Draco pushed through the crowd to keep beside me and she followed in his wake.

"I would suppose the quality of stock is much better" He commented, glancing anxiously at the crowd. If it bothered him, he didn't say anything.

"Vastly better stuff. For one thing, you'll almost never find anything immaterial outside of Dis."

"And what will you be purchasing today?"

"For one thing, we got to improve your tongue-wagglin', boy"

I waved down a passing Sedan Chair, carried by two burly looking giants with blue skin. A few coins to the front chairman bought us a ride, and I clambered into the litter, pulling Draco up after me and leaving that bothersome sword to get in of her own accord.

"Take me straight to the fifth bolgia, and make it quick." I demanded, and pulled the velvet curtain across the door for what little privacy it afforded. On command, the litter rose and the rhythmic jostle told me we were moving.

"What's in the fifth bolgia?" Draco asked. He was already reclining against the couch, his servant resting her head on his lap.

"Someone who can make you less useless" I folded my arms and peered out the gap in the curtain, watching the same-shaped buildings of the bolgia drift past, some were sideways, some upside-down, some below and some above as we passed through the non-Euclidian routes. As complicated as it was at first, the convenience made it worthwhile. If you knew the right path you could get from any bolgia to any other bolgia, everything was next to everything else at the same time. That said the rest of Hell was arranged so that you had to pass through every circle to get this far into the city proper. Some said it was a test of character, others said it was to keep the riff-raff out.

I continued staring outside and not at my travelling companion, or his companion.

Nothing got said for the rest of the trip. Any clever quips died in my throat before I could break the silence. It was unnerving that he hadn't brought up my foiled attempt to feed on him. Could this in itself be his tactic? I didn't suffer too long, however, as the litter soon came to an abrupt stop.

"Here we are, ma'am. Bolgia V" The chairmen declared in unison. I stepped out and started to walk away without a second glance behind me. I only got a few paces forward before Draco followed.

"Oh look, we even have a welcoming party."

"What ho, what ho, the little whore's come home!" A brightly dressed harlequin in an obnoxious iron mask dropped down from a banner and landed before us in a handstand.

"Can it, Alichino. I'm here for business, not your displeasure."

"Oh, but I do so like it when you piss me off, you are your mother's daughter after all."

"And you're the spawn of a clownfish, what of it Malebranche?"

"Oh fine. As soon as a new plaything shines in your eye, you've no time for a down-on-his-luck larrikin like me. Fine . . ." He scowled, but flips himself upright.

" . . .I, Alichino vi Malebebranche do invite you to swim in Burning Pitch, you flaming bitch."

With that, I strolled straight past him, in no mood for more of his petty games. Beyond the unmarked banner and down an unlighted staircase, a journey of some twenty minutes, I stepped into the lake of Burning Pitch.

A four person brass band played some weird jazz on the stage, and a number of fancy pushers sat around in circular chairs pretending to appreciate the finer points of things they thought would make them appear superior. Last time I was here, they were discussing the nuances of a man's ritual suicide. I held back a cough as smoky air filled my lungs, and made my way to the bar, only to find the barkeep mysteriously absent—probably a poorly thought-out statement on futility or some such garbage. I gave in, and turned to my companions.

"Yes?" Draco asked. His posture was only half-relaxed and his red eyes glanced about every odd second.

I stood there, silent, as I recalled how I'd intended to explain this part.

"As far as clubs go, I can appreciate the atmosphere, I suppose." He began. "Still, all this hullabaloo wasn't just for you to take me to a bar, now, surely? I fear I may have gravely misjudged your character."

"We're not here for drinks, you dolt, I'm looking for someone."

"That's good. I'm too young to get drunk." Drakkengard chimed in.

"What? You're a sword, how does that . . . wait, how old are you anyway?"

"Younger than you, old lady."

"Forget it. I'll just do it the old fashioned way." I grabbed a mini-pitcher of soy sauce off the bar counter and carefully poured it in the pattern of a sigil. A few crescent lines down the bottom, sort of rising thing up the top, funky cross in the middle, two circles around it with his name enclosed between them. I'd always thought the seal of Agares just looked like a steamy cup of coffee. It never had any sense of menace about it like most others in the Goetia.

"Can I help you, little miss?" A pale, old man suddenly occupied a formerly empty stool. His right arm was covered in feathers, and had a beak for a hand, while his exposed legs were covered in thick, green scales.

"I'm here on business, Agares, so yes." I jerked my thumb at Draco.

"This guy has a useless tongue. I'm willing to pay to get him a new one."

"You want language lessons? How adorable. Which ones?"

"All of them."

"You say that, but do we have time for me to learn how to speak Dalmatian?" Draco asked an uncertain smile on his face.

"Oh, no time at all. Costly, but efficient, that's my motto." Agares said, puffing out his bony chest with pride.

"What an unscrupulous practice." Draco muttered.

"And what price do you want?" I reached through dimensions for my money-pouch.

"No coin, I've enough of that."

"Well what?" I thumped the pouch onto the counter. Always with the bartering.

"What indeed. Your dignity?"

"No dice."

"How about I make a certain runaway come back?" I brought my hand up, but he easily caught it. My claws were not quite long enough to scrape out his eyes from there.

"You don't get to talk about her."

"No? How about a name?"

"One of my names?"

"Not to own of course, just to know. Something with at least a little power over you."

I narrow my eyes.

"Just what are you planning?"

"I plan nothing, I just like to keep my options open."

"*Tch*, fine. Give us silence so no-one else hears."

"That's fine, but the price for that is your friend here gets to hear your name too." I nearly lost balance on my heels, but steadied myself.

"Fucking—fine. For all the good it will do him." I scowled, my face flush.

"Let no-one hear our discourse." He raised his right hand, and the beak opened to let out an ear-splitting cry. As the sound fades from my ears, so did every other sound—the voices, the music, the movement—leaving only the rhythmic puffs of three people breathing.

"A crack separates the Earth we are on from the rest of its self. You may speak freely."

"*Tch*, you drive a bloody bargain. Blah blah blah, I am known by many names, some call me 'לילין'" The sounds slipped out of my mouth, easy enough to say but depending on how they get used, they could have a not too light influence on my fate.

"Bah, I might have guessed that, still hearing it from your own lips makes it pricy enough. Give me your tongue, boy."

"I never did consent to this deal, just so you know." Draco complained.

"That has nothing to do with me." Agares said flippantly, and then seized Draco's tongue with his beaked fist.

Draco let out a muffled sound of alarm. He tried to push Agares away, but the deal maker had already stepped back. Draco coughed into his hand. It came away bloody.

"How do you feel?" I asked, more curious than concerned.

"I feel like a part of my tongue that doesn't exist just got nailed to a table."

"Well, that's not entirely an untrue way of looking at it, but completely wrong in every sense of the word." Agares said.

"Did it work? Say something foreign." Draco asked, rubbing his jaw.

"I want to ride the moon like the filthy bitch she is" I said in flawless Sumerian.

"I highly doubt Luna would appreciate the sentiment." He replied in kind.

"Not too bad, but you've got a pretty noticeable English accent. Well, I guess that's all I can expect from a blood-thirsty Briton like you."

"Go swivel on a spike, you callous barbarian."

"Well, it seems my work is done. Do let me know if you've any other dogs that need to be tricked." Agares excused himself and walks away.

Chapter Five

Tongues

Draco

I walked without a word behind the woman that held me captive. That was perhaps too powerful of a term, but true nonetheless. Without her guidance, I was as sure as never existing. As much as I loathed it, I was at her mercy for the time. She had made all too clear that I was just a pig she was fattening up for slaughter come autumn. She'd already tried to eat me twice now.

I resisted the urge to touch my tongue. Not twenty minutes earlier the daemon that called himself Agares made a deal with my leash-holder, one of her names in exchange for knowledge of languages. A blessing of Xenoglossia. At the time, her sounds meant nothing to me, but in my recollection, they might as well have been the King's English. 'Lilim'. Just one of her names, and I was all the more enlightened for knowing it. At first, I supposed it an accident that I walked away with a small measure of unwarranted power thanks to her deal, but in retrospect, it was probably foolhardy to consider anything an accident in such a predatory world as this. I presumed nothing about who knew or didn't know about the morsel in my mind, but I considered it nonetheless.

"What do you think?" I asked Drakkengard.

"Not much of a treat, don't you think? I think I'd prefer some sweets or something."

"Quite right, immeasurable value does hardly imply value after all."

"What are you two talking about?" Lascivus demanded.

"I'm just contemplating the status quo, nothing more." I replied.

After departing the odd nightclub, the three of us took another cot deeper through the Bolgia, and after leaving the ring's influence, I found myself in what Lascivus referred to as Traditori. On either side, I was confronted by a lake of ice, divided into four rounds which stretched beyond my perception. We three journeyed across a poorly marked road down the middle of the lake, and what I supposed was our destination lay at a great black castle at what was perhaps the center of the lake.

"Alright, you can no longer swear in your native tongue without my appreciation, but surely there's more to your nefarious plans for me."

"Look, shut up, follow my lead and stop asking so many questions. You'll save yourself a lot of hassle, and we can get through this much quicker that way."

Lascivus, Drakkengard and I reached a long, narrow bridge. Behind us were the secluded trenches of the Bolgias. Before us was a great castle of glistening black ice. A frozen lake surrounded it, and I could see people and monsters trapped within the ice. Their bodies remained motionless but their eyes . . . every eye followed our movements. Perhaps even those I couldn't see were watching us just as intently.

I shivered and tug on my clothes. I wasn't sure how long we'd spent walking this stony bridge, but long enough for the coldness of the air to sneak under my shirt, at least.

"Hey Master, why don't you warm up with some fire?" Drakkengard tugged on my sleeve.

"I'd hate to burn these new clothes of mine, I only got them today."

"But they're so dirty already." She was right. My earlier scuffles had left my clothes torn and muddied.

"That's not important. Just because a book-cover is scuffed doesn't been you should tear it off"

I noticed a small figure approaching from the bridges end. Once it got closer, I saw that it's a child, a little boy in bright overalls, and muttering to himself at that.

"Of all the times to start shit. Stupid blood-doves don't know when they're not welcome. If I had my way, I rip they're stupid fluffy wings off and beat them with the tickly end."

He kept walking, caught up in his violent musings, until he slammed into me, and only then did he acknowledge my presence.

"You filthy peasant, watch it! I ought to break your knees into your face! "

"Oh, hey Bub." Lascivus didn't break her stride as she stepped around the child.

"My lady. Still ignoring me? What is your problem, anyway?" He turned away from me, no longer interested.

"You're a boring old geezer and good for nothing."

"That's rich coming from an uppity bitch like you. Going to see Old Scratch?"

"I couldn't avoid it if I tried."

"Tell him to stop slacking off and do something about those arrogant upstairs lots." The child pointed his finger straight up.

"If he won't listen to you, I won't even bother." She crossed her arms. "That kind of stuff doesn't concern me."

"Oh no, the princess just has to keep herself entertained. Never mind the difference you could make, there's a festival somewhere in the world that you're late to."

"Spin on it, deadweight." She flipped him off. His face turned red and he spun to face me.

"And who are you, her new toy? At least you're not a filthy bird like the last one." He sneered. There was a wet crunch as Drakkengard's fist slams into his nose.

"Thank-you Drakkengard. He was starting to piss me off."

"Yes Master."

"You miserable little shit" The boy glowered, clutching his bloody nose. Lascivus watched from a distance, bored.

"'I'll kill you, I'll kill you', blah. Blah. Blah! You're this deep in Hell, so you're important, right? You gonna tear that kid off and show you're a huge, ugly fly or something, right?" I leered. My heart pounded in my ears. My left hand twitched and spasmed and the flames spilled out.

"I'm sick of all these rules, all these words, drop the pretensions, let your hair down and punch me! Come on!"

There was a burst of pain, and I couldn't see anything but my balance said I was flying backwards. A moment later the rough stone of the bridge grazed across my chest. I pushed myself up and opened my eye. Half my sight came back. The right side of my face felt like a cannonball just shaved it.

I looked around until I found the boy and charged. I found myself staring straight up, and something like a boat crashed into my chest. I started to lift myself up again but I lost all feeling in my legs, one after the other. The boy was staring down at me, his face twisted and taut with wide, black eyes and bared teeth. He raised a fist. I caught the blow with my right arm. Something snapped. In that moment I thrust my left hand into his mouth and as far down his throat as I could, and let out all the fire I had.

The boy vanished—Lascivus, and the bridge too.

I wa sitting on a chair. When did that happen?

Drakkengard knelt on the floor beside me, embracing my right arm. The room I was in appeared to be some sort of lounge, the sort you might find in a manor or mansion.

"I hope you don't mind, but I took the liberty of cutting ahead." The voice came from directly in my head and from every direction all at once. This man was not there a moment ago.

His face is of blackest shadow. I can't even begin to comprehend his stature, but it is surely of the scale of celestial bodies. His body is covered in eyes from the top of his head to the base of his feet. I am beholden in their gaze, and know death

His face is of golden light. His body is immaculate, and there is no shame in his nakedness. He is more beautiful than all the stars in the sky. I would not be blamed for loving him, and I know my love would not be unrequited.

His face is of crimson flame. His body is a terrible serpent, and his frozen wings are chained to the deepest reaches of an infinite pit. The frigid air from his wrathfully beating wings teaches me the coldness of true judgement.

The man was dressed in a red tuxedo with cream pants. His strawberry-blonde hair fell in curls about his head. He smiled warmly at me.

I couldn't look away.

Beautiful.

I had read the written words of some of the greatest minds of all time, gazed upon pictures of graphite, oil and pixels, yet until now, I had never comprehended what was meant by immaculate beauty.   Every feature, every minute detail gave itself into what could only be described as Perfect. Nevertheless, true perfection does not exist. His features, perfectly symmetrical, perfectly proportioned, perfectly toned—they disgusted me as much as they enthralled me. My vision wavered, rotten flesh falling into an empty stomach, palpitations of an organ far exceeding its regular pace.

If he gave the word, I honestly felt I might give my life for him-

The world unpaused.

Gooseflesh covered my skin and I really wanted a bath. My hands were clammy and sweat ran down my face. Beside me, Drakkengard's skin was a rolling tapestry of blades. She slowly raised a sword-shaped arm.

"Let me begin by swearing I will allow no harm to come to you during this meeting. As a token of goodwill, I will heal your wounds." I shuddered at the sound of his voice. Sure enough, all my injuries vanished without even a tickle. It felt wrong in a way, like an unwelcome intimate touch brushing dust off a stone effigy of myself. Even my clothes were clean and whole again.

"Feeling better?"

I struggled to find my voice. After what feels like a lifetime, I managed to speak.

"What-?" I faltered. His presence was so imposing, so *defined*. I could have easily lost myself in his identity. "No, first . . ."

"You want to know who I am."

I nodded. "Are you the Adversary?"

"It is as you say." He answered merrily. "I am the ruler and prisoner of the abyss. I am the pride and the fall. I am deceit and death. I am freedom and temptation. I am judgement and forgiveness. I am the light bringer and the destroyer. I am."

"Then why have I been brought here?"

"It was the will of my child. The name Lascivus is known to you, as is the name Lilim."

"But why?"

"That child of mine did try to feed upon you. You bested her in combat, and let her go free in exchange for a debt. She repaid that debt, and the account was balanced, but you became indebted to her, when she let you out from the void where you trapped yourself."

"Now, now you own me? Is that it?" I clenched my teeth. My left hand twitched.

"To put it simply, yes. You are her ward and prisoner until the debt is paid off."

"No."

"Slavery can be a terrible burden. I know. There is always choice, however." He leaned forward. "I will now offer you a deal."

"What?"

"I become your sponsor and patron. In return you do work for me when called upon."

"No."

"Please, reconsider. This is no arrangement of formalities. In exchange for services rendered, you are given power, training, resources and guidance. Outside of what is asked of you, you are free to do with these boons as you see fit, provided you do not use them to oppose me. You won't just be some caged beast I set free." I flinched. "Your work will be open to negotiation. You will be provided for."

"And if I refuse?" It was becoming a little easier to maintain myself. My legs had almost stopped shaking.

"I will set some tasks for you to perform. They will repay your debt to Lascivus, and afterward I will make this offer again. If you refuse again, you will be returned to your home and you'll never hear from the underworld again."

"Isn't it obvious?" I laughed. "I refuse."

Chapter Six

The Doctor

Draco

I looked, drearily, about the hotel room I'd been deposited in. A tacky replica Botticelli hung upon a duck-print wall and the scent of curry-mint jam wafted from somewhere suspicious.

"So I'm a slave now? How about I just cut out my tongue and leave it by the boot polish, save you the trouble."

I plucked a tissue from its box and held it in my left hand. It browned, blackened and burned. The smoke was foul. Lascivus peered out the window across from me with an odd smirk on her face. Turned out these places did have windows. You just couldn't tell from outside. Drakkengard was sitting on the yellow-stained bed, hugging her legs and scowling at Lascivus. I plucked and burned another tissue.

"Oh, can't have that. You're on the clock, and we can't have our loyal workers getting injured on the job. Part of your job is amusing me—says so right in the contract."

"I don't believe you. No, you would, wouldn't you? How about I impale my tongue on a spike, put it in a red gingham dress and gurgle a sonnet? You can keep yourself occupied, and I'll be on my way."

"I'm legally entitled to a quart and 3/8ths of flesh, yes, but if you leave I'll just sic the hell-hamsters on you."

"That's also in the contract?"

"There's a loophole that allows it. Technically, it would fall under 'private Olympic sport'."

"When I do these tasks, and earn my freedom, I'll force hell-hamsters down your throat until you bloat to the size of a Volkswagen."

"Kinky, but I'll pass, and stop wasting those tissues." She pointed at the growing pile of ash at my feet, her voice high with mocking.

I placed the box with exaggerated precision upon a table beside me. My fingerprints burned into the corner. Smoke continued to listlessly drift from my fingertips.

"So what's stopping me? From running away, I mean."

"What do you know about names?"

"Names?"

"A name is a label. It defines what you are. Who you are. It influences what you can and can't do."

"I don't see the relevance."

"Right now, among what little names you've earned yourself, one of them is that you are my prisoner. It's a part of your concept. Moreover, that puts you squarely in my metaphysical domain. I know where you are, I know what you're doing, I can force you to my side and I can restrict your actions any way I please. My dominion of you is carved right into your soul, as plain to see as a pair of handcuffs with my name on them. You run, you wake up right where I left you."

"But you'll let me?"

"What?"

"If you're not lying, you can just forbid me from running away, and that's the end of the matter. You can even just forbid me from disobeying, and be done with this farce. Why don't you do me a favor and forbid me from remembering all this nonsense, so I wake up free and unresentful?"

"Where's the point? It's not just about getting these things done, it's about you doing them. If you don't remember doing the stuff there's no point to it."

"So you mock my free will. Cornering me into doing what you want anyway, and Old Scratch still thinks I'll *want* to join your horde of meat slaves after this debacle?"

"Well, time to go." Lascivus rubbed her hands together. My question floundered in the air for a bit before choking to death on the floor.

"Am I at least going to be told where we're going?" I dragged myself to my feet.

"Not until we get there, no." She flicked an ember of hellfire at the greasy carpet, and began directing the flames with her finger.

"At least you're open about inflicting petty cruelties upon me."

"You know, it's no fun if you don't put up a bit more of a struggle. I haven't even had a chance to use the shock collar."

"Trust me, on the inside there is a great wailing and gnashing of teeth."

"I'll take your word for it. Stand in that circle. Sword too."

"My name is Drakkengard, you miserable old hag."

"See? It's no fun when that complains. Show a little livelihood."

The window behind Lascivus exploded outward, sending shards and splinters across the room.

"Oh look, this room has developed a bad case of spontaneous combustion. Let's hurry up," I dryly declared.

"Sure thing, *minion.*" She stepped into the circle, muttered a few words, and tore space-time a new hole.

***

I gagged on liquid vertigo. What an unpleasant way to travel. We appeared to have arrived in a spacious and rustic alleyway. Something small and fuzzy scampered beneath a broken rickshaw looking thing. Large stone buildings stood either side of us and the sky was an odd green with few clouds.

"Bluh, it stinks of fish!" Drakkengard flailed her arms around and bared her teeth.

"Oh come on. That city I found you in smelled six times worse than this." Lascivus wiped her brow, took off her jacket and dropped it. It vanished into whatever n-dimensional nonsense she used as a purse. I straightened my coat. Drakkengard caught the fuzzy thing I saw earlier and stuffed it down the sleeve of her robes with a giggle.

Outside the alleyway, the streets were bare and quiet. An overly large sun crawled below the horizon, casting its light across the ocean and a nearby beach.

"A quiet town. Do you suppose they heard we were coming and went for the hills?"

"More likely they heard your mousetrap was coming, and fled the inevitable diabetes pandemic"

"Go burn in a pyre, hag," Drakkengard hissed.

"Stop that! Both of you." I grabbed her by the hood of her robes and pulled her away before she could take a swing at Lascivus. "So we're here at a lovely little beach town. What now?"

"We find an inn, and get ourselves a good drink." Lascivus spun on her high heels and headed straight for one of the buildings.

The signpost was marked with some weird writings. My new evil tongue was supposed to work on written words, but this sign was still illegible. These demonic shenanigans made no sense to me, and I just chalked it up to bad penmanship.

"You were drinking at the bed and breakfast we left not two minutes ago, and then there are the oceans of liquor I'm sure you have sealed away in whatever unfathomable dimension you're carrying."

"Even oceans run dry."

"Have you run dry?"

"No, but the further away that day stays the better it is for everyone." She disappeared inside the building. I glanced up and down the empty street once more before following.

"Hey maid, two bottles of your best plonk and today's special" Lascivus barked at the inn keep. He scowled and slowly walked into a back room behind the counter. Trying to listen for the actual sounds behind the arcane translation was harder than I thought, but it didn't sound like anything familiar. The inn itself was bland. Most of the furniture was wood, and looked to be somewhat warped by the oddly fragrant ocean air.

At Lascivus' lead, the three of us sat down at a crooked table. It had a faint smell of apples. I hoped that was apples.

"So where are we?" I idly rocked my chair back and forth on its uneven legs.

"Al'Juran. Nice planet, good for swimming. Not so good for other things. It's one of those bland places you go when you don't want to put up with anything."

"Okay, it's a bore. Why are we here?"

"Collecting payment, a certain someone's past due, and we tracked him back here."

"Who?"

"A local by the name of Vengai-Ra. He bargained for an undying body and the secrets of medicine. To pay for it, he sold his magick and the rest of the cost in manual labor. We're here to collect on that second part."

"An undying body? How's that work?"

"Complex stuff I'm sure you wouldn't understand, but basically his body always goes back to the point when he made the deal."

"Not like me, then. Wouldn't that erase his memories too?"

"Nah. His body goes back, but his soul doesn't."

"The dualists were right?"

"'Fraid so."

"Huh. John Stewart is going to be pissed"

"He is, trust me."

The innkeeper came out carrying two unlabeled bottles shaped like pepper grinders. Balanced on his arm was a plate covered in brown, green, and slightly paler brown. All three objects got placed gracelessly on the table. Lascivus broke the top off one of the bottles and took a long swig.

"Here, eat this" She pushed the plate of questionable mush to my side of the table.

"Am I happier not knowing what that is?"

"Relax, it's mostly fish." I scooped out some of the slop with a wooden spoon and pointed it at Drakkengard.

"Is this stuff safe?"

"*Ah~m*" She bit down on the spoon and chewed, a thoughtful look on her face. "Yup! Won't make you bleed or burn or anything." She pulled the spoon out of her mouth and the end had been bitten clean off.

"How do you talk so clearly with your mouth full?" Lasivus picked up the spoon handle and looked from it to Drakkengard.

"You ever see a parrot talk? Her range is limitless. Sing a line from Mark-Quinney"

"Yes, Master." Drakkengard cleared her throat and placed her hand against her chest. Mark's rendition of Maurice Chevalier's *You Brought a New Kind of Love to Me* warbled from her throat in all its rustic glory. Lascivus threw her head back and slammed back the rest of her bottle.

"Never do that again." The Succubus cracked open the lid of the second bottle.

"Oh come now. M-Q was perhaps the last great Neo-Crooner of the twenty-third century. People wouldn't hear music like that again until the end of the war."

"That was terrible and you should hate yourself for liking it."

"So what sort of melodies do you enjoy?"

"Huh? Well, I don't listen to much nowadays, but I grew up on the cacophonous chorus of the screaming souls of the damned. You ever heard them?"

"No. Are they mayhap still touring?"

"Nah, but they have a regular spot at the local pub back home every Sunday."

"Curious. I guess I'll check them out when I'm down there next. Alright, where's this Vengal we're snatching?" I pushed aside the plate of what I now suspect to be pure condiment, and stood   up.

        "Vengai-Ra, and no idea. He can't be too far though, my magick's top of the line."

"'Somewhere around here' is the top of the line?" We left the tavern behind us.

"Hey! A lesser mage wouldn't have even known what planet he was on."

"Yes, but that doesn't stop me doubting there's more than maybe thirteen casters in the galaxy that aren't better than you." It occurred to me that she'd never actually paid for that meal we just had.

"I'll have you know I'm one of the ten most powerful demons in all of Hell." That raised an eyebrow.

"*You* are in the same league as Light Bringer?"

"He doesn't count. He's not even on the charts here. You don't count people who are off the charts. It just isn't done."

"And how many people are off the charts?"

"Just three."

"You know, you're making Hell sound a lot easier to take over than seems reasonable. I beat you, didn't I?"

"That was- Ugh, perfectly understandable reasons for that aside, that was just a stupid flex off. You need more than muscle to take on a big leaguer, and if you've got enough other stuff, you might not even need muscle. That's just how it goes."

"I should remember to collect as much stuff as possible."

"Are you honestly plotting to take over my home? Right in front of me?"

"Why, I would never dream of betraying my nice and friendly and dare I say generous leash holders. Maybe I'll just take over the Earth. You know what, no. You can have the Earth. I'll just go up to whatever smug god put me in this ludicrous situation and bite their damned eyes out."

"You're delightful when you're angry. Don't worry. I'm sure you can rough up our good doctor until you feel better. Maybe throw him to the ground and show him who's boss."

"Madame, you disgust me. "

"If I don't, who will?"

A scream rung out. Lascivus rushed toward it and, with a shrug, I followed.

Just a few streets away a man was crying in the middle of the road, a younger man's body in his arms. A few scared faces peeked out from the surrounding windows, but no one came to help.

"What happened?" Lascivus asked him.

As he was babbling and moaning his story, I looked over the body. While the man looked about thirty or so, the cadaver looked a couple years younger than me. His hair was bleached white, and his eyes, mouth and throat were swollen blue while his eyes and finger tips had turned black. Some sort of blood poisoning, perhaps? The body stank terribly either way, like a burnt pie of beef and mercury.

Lascivus finished up talking to the man.

"Well, what did you get from all that?" I pondered the body. Maybe if I burned it I wouldn't have to smell it. No, that would smell even worse. Unless I burned it hot enough it just dusted in an instant, although if I did do that I'd probably waste these clothes for the second time.

"He went to see the town doctor a while ago about some bad headaches. Apparently, the doctor shone some odd lamp on his head and sent him on his way. Things deteriorated, and here he is, doing a genius impression of a doorstop. "

"That's nice. Did you find out where the doctor is, because I think that's our pickup?"

"Beaumont Castle, up on Tin Star Orphan Hill."

"Beaumont?"

"Well, it's pronounced Bearman but the locals have this really weird accent."

***

The castle turned out to be only an hour up a steep hill. The gathering clouds over the sea warn that it might rain soon. As for the castle itself, frankly it was a little disappointing in appearance. It was too intact to be considered ominous ruins, too poorly kept to be proud or majestic, and its walls were too bare to even seem distinctive. I don't think I'd ever seen such a hopelessly lackluster castle in my life.

"What poor excuse for nobility commissioned this piece of filth?" I strolled up to the three meter wooden door and wiped my finger along it.

"Al'Juran is ruled by an aristocracy. This is probably some idiot inbred cousin's old beach house that never got paid for."

"This thing gives a bad name to castles everywhere. Drakkengard!" The girl ran up over the hill crescent and leapt at the door, foot outstretched. Spikes and blades speared from her leg and tore the door to splinters as she shot through it. Once she's made a person sized hole placed her foot down and bounced over to my side.

"Good job." I rustled her hair. "Alright, let's find this fool."

Lascivus ducked in through the jagged hole, and I followed.

"This place doesn't need to be standing by the time we leave, does it?"

"No, why?" I flicked my wrist at what was left of the ruined door. It glowed red for a second and burst into flames.

"It's an eyesore."

Lascivus rolled her eyes, but made no comment.

The inside of the castle was, at least, a little more distinctive than the outside, but for all the wrong reasons. Everywhere strange mechanical pods had been erected on the floor, each filled with a spectrum of peculiar fluids. Some held whole specimens, other just bones or an assorted organ or two, and all bubbled, churned or stewed slowly in their isolation. A slew of paper notes were strewn about the floor and pinned to every available surface. I plucked one off a tube as I pass it. It was covered in more scribbles I couldn't read, and a few incomprehensible diagrams of lumps and lines. I dropped it, and out of the corner of my eye, the fire has started to spread from the door to the carpet of paper sheets. Drakkengard stared down an odd, clockwork apparatus and kicked it over.

"Who do these pretentious tools think they are? No one needs that many moving parts." She punched a clock.

"Hey doctor!" I yelled into the irritating castle. "Satan's little tax-boy is here to take you in. Make haste would you." I scuffed some papers with my feet and made my way down the hall.

"What is your problem? We could have beaten him over the back of the head or something. Now he knows we're here." Lascivus growled at me. I ignored her and let a few embers drip from my fingertips, causing the paper below me to smolder.

"I know you can't die! So get out here before I drag your flame-bleached naked ass out of the twenty ton pile of ash your castle is about to become!" I brushed my hair out of my face and boiled the insides of a nearby tube until it shattered, spilling purple goo all over the floor. Off to my side, Drakkengard pushed over a table of contraptions.

"You've gone mad." Lascivus shook her head. I looked up and saw another tank, bigger than the others, displayed rather prominently.

"And what do we have here? Some horrible monstrosity man?" I ran up and pressed my face against the glass. The tar fluid inside sloshed about like the midnight tide.

"Aaaaaaahh!!" A sudden yell turned my attention upward, where a man with an axe leapt for me from the balcony. I stepped aside, and he crashed into the floor, blade first, in a show of sparks.

"Doctor?"

"What are you doing here, you *idiot*? You'll ruin everything. What did you do to Henrietta?" He yanked up the axe while looking to the giant vat.

"Please tell me that isn't your wife in there." I scratched my head and gestured for Drakkengard to come over. Vengai-Ra, I presumed, sported an unkempt head of brown hair, lightly tanned skin, and a stained lab-coat.

"Thirteen-thousand flaming filigree pheasants, what are you wearing?" I screeched. Beneath the lab coat, the doctor wore the most garish Hawaiian shirt and board shorts combination I had ever laid eyes on. A vomit of clashing bright colors swirled around his garments in a way that I could swear might reveal the hidden mysteries of the universe if I stared long enough, or possibly even a clever depiction of a magic duck.

The doctor yelled again and attacked but Drakkengard stepped in and backhanded the blade into the giant vat. Viscous black fluid sprayed out the spreading cracks and the whole castle rumbled beneath my feet.

"*Please* tell me that isn't your wife in there." I started backing from the tank.

"No, you ignorant idiot. Argh, if you'd just been a few days longer I wouldn't even need you anymore. With Henrietta, I was on the verge of safely breaking the Hayflick limit. You could take your deathless magick and shove where the rains don't fall, and I'd be free." Vengai-Ra clawed at his hair, grit his teeth and ran for the door. Lascivus stepped out and slammed her arm into his neck, knocking him down.

Drakkengard, undisturbed by all this, gave the cracked glass an experimental tap. Her finger passed right through and left a small hole.

"Drakkengard!" I pushed her to the ground and threw myself over her. Before either of us has landed, the rest of the tank gave way. A colossal torrent of black liquid gushed over us and stampeded through the castle in a horrible stinking wave of fluid, foam and flesh. Oceans beat my back and plundered the air around us.

After twenty-four seconds it finally passed. I picked my waterlogged-self off the ground and helped Drakkengard to her feet. Something loud and angry growled from behind me. We turned.

In the ruins of the tank stood an enormous, humanoid shape, crafted from roiling flesh and muscle. Its featureless head almost scraped the chandelier making me wonder how it fit inside the tank.

Three holes split down the middle of its face as it turned to me. I reached out and Drakkengard formed into a sword in my hand. Henrietta folded back on itself in a way no spine should be able to and leaned forward to bring its head right in front of me. The space above the pulsing holes bubbled and tore and from that spot emerged fourteen eyes, irregularly arranged on its forehead. They blinked in rapid succession, and the brilliant blue pupils dilated. The bottom half of its head split open, and a graveyard of tombstone teeth ruptured forward like so many surfacing submarines. Henrietta shrieked.

"A mummy again endued with animation could not be so hideous as that wretch." I paid no attention to the words slipping my lips. A manic grin painted my face and Drakkengard felt so comfortable in my hand that this just might be a dream.

I had gazed on him while unfinished. The creature swung a lumpish limb at me, its end splitting and forking into branch-like fingers mid motion. I darted under its arm and drove Drakkengard into its shoulder. The castle windows trembled as it bellowed in pain.

He was ugly, but when those muscles and joints were rendered capable of motion, I wrenched my sword out, and idly noted how the flesh rolled over the wound, mixing up a well in mud until it vanished. A mouth split open in the creature's flank and tried to bite me.

"It became a thing such as even Dante could not conceive." I thrust my fist into the gaping maw and painted the creature's insides a mural of fire. It screamed in wretched agony. All across its body more mouths split open and added their voices to the mind-numbing wail. I pushed out fire as hard as I could, and from each mouth gouts of flame devoured its voice. I yanked out my hand, and it collapsed against the ground, sending one last tremble throughout the castle walls.

"Good doctor, your opus magnum was as lasting as a mayfly to the gods, barely a sport." I wiped Drakkengard's blade on my wet sleeve.

"You unthinking idiot! I wasn't trying to create a killer. Don't you know anything about science?" Vengai-Ra yelled, covered in black gunk and leaning on Lascivus for support.

"What are you--

"Duck, fuckhead!" I dropped down, just as a pillar of flesh swung overhead. Lascivus let the doctor drop to the ground and ran forward. She drew her blade from wherever and sliced right through the creature's limb, left it hanging by a thread of muscle and skin. Her sword vanished, and she leapt up onto the creature's head.

"This is gonna taste like shit!" Trails of miasma helixed around her. Her fangs lengthened and her horn sprouted amidst her hair. She slammed her head down and pierced the creature's skull with her fangs. It bellowed and flailed, but before it could even raise a limb it was already collapsing upon itself. Its scream changed into a grating death rattle as its body fell apart, whole chunks of flesh and bone falling from its hulking frame. After six full seconds, the creature was nothing but goo mixing with goo.

"Let's see you revive from *that*." Lascivus laughed, and sauntered over.

"Are you o . . .?" She fell on her hands and knees and dry retched twice, then vomited in earnest. Glowing red mist spilled from her mouth with every heave and faded away into the air above her. I walked toward her, and caught her in time to stop her collapsing face first into the liquid flesh. I made sure she was still breathing and glared at the doctor. He turned to run again, but Drakkengard dashed over and pinned him to the ground.

"Here's what's going to happen. I am going to burn the rest of this miserable castle to the ground. We are going to go back to that pissant village, and as soon as my ticket out of this mess has recovered you are coming straight to hell with us, in peace, or on a fucking pike. *Capiche*?"

***

A cathartic fire, a short walk, an angry mob and a demonic circle later I found myself once more in the presence of that smug perforate Lucifer.

"You did well on your first trial. I believe congratulations are in order." He poured a martini glass of something green and offered it to me, but I pushed it away.

"I'm not getting roped into any more bindings if I can help it." It was a lot easier to keep my composure this time around. I could only assume that horrific presence last time was intentional on his part. For now, he just seemed like an unassuming man in a suit.

143

"Can you help it?" He swirled the drink around before taking a sip.

"What's that supposed to mean?"

"Would you really rather be back in your big, empty house? Nothing but the ancient history to keep you company, wasting your days reading books and picking fights, is that what you want?"

"I was just another petty vagrant. It suited me. Now I'm just some lapdog you like to put your collective fires out on."

"Well, two more tasks and you can go back to your London hollow."

"That reminds me, would Vengai-Ra's plan have worked?"

"It would, but not how he hoped. He could indeed have sold his immortal body to pay off his remaining debt, but he wouldn't have the chance to capitalize on his research."

"Why's that?"

"He mistakenly assumed we gave his body immortality, when in fact we gave him an immortal body. His original body is long since gone, and if he made this new deal, he would have found himself a disembodied mind, a ghost quickly fading away. "

"You're trying to make it sound like you saved him. You could have just had your agent explain why that wouldn't work."

"But you didn't. Lascivus knew, and said nothing. You didn't point out his naiveté."

"You could have told us to."

"I could have laid out every little detail and forced you to follow it to the letter. Instead, I let you retain as much autonomy as possible, while still getting the job done. Which would you prefer?"

"I guess that depends on the importance of the task."

"Assume this is a cold, uncaring universe, and all things are equal."

"I guess your way pisses me off less." I tsked.

"Precisely. I am not He who demands we have free will but don't exercise it."

"You mean the maker?"

"I mean YHWH."

"Is that what all *this* is?" I swept my arm around the room. "The circles, the demons, the tasks and the deals, are all these just to prove YHVH wrong?"

"You're pronouncing it wrong, and no. *Well*, not completely. I fought the Demiurge once, and lost, yes. However, no one has seen or heard from Him for a thousand years. Some might consider our match forfeit. So now I focus my efforts on improving the life of my fellows."

"You mean the demons?"

"I mean all those that call Earth home, on any plane. We are all bound here, one way or another, and I'd rather not be surrounded by mindless drones that can only speak in words of prayer." He clenched his hand around his glass. It shrunk away and vanished in a black speck.

"And where do I fit in this whole stupid scheme? Why are you even taking the time to talk to me? Surely you don't explain yourself to every damned soul that passes through here."

"More than you might think, but in your case it was a request from my daughter."

"You mean Lascivus? Aren't all demons your children?"

"Most, not all, at least of those native to Earth, and some more than others. Lascivus is different though."

I thought about that for a few moments.

"She carries the name Lilim. That makes Lilith her mother, correct? Is that why she's special?"

"Hmm? And how did you find that out, again?"

"She told some vendor in exchange for getting me a weird translating tongue. At the time, I didn't know what it meant, but the sounds it was built with linger in my mind. When I mimicked the sound, my tongue made me hear 'Lilim'. I'm still not sure how that works." I frowned. I could have sworn I meant to dodge the question.

"The mark on your tongue is just a sign of contract. Really, it could be anywhere, but people do like to be symbolic. To answer your question, she is indeed a demon born of Lilith, one of many, but again different."

"What's so different?"

"There are many ways to become a parent, many methods besides the mixing of seeds. Among the many punishments placed on me and my wife for our rebellion, we were each cursed that no children could be born from a union with another." He looked down and closed his eyes.

"So where did she come from?"

"From a union between Lilith and myself." He looked back up and beamed at me.

"But you just said you couldn't."

"That's right."

"How does that even work?"

"People always underestimate what it means to be omnipotent. Can the Lord make a rock so heavy that He cannot lift it? The answer is yes. He could also lift said rock. Omnipotence means paradox doesn't matter. YHVH is always making prophecies. His word is law after all. It strokes His pride to explain everything that will happen. Lascivus proves that at some point he contradicted himself, and somewhere in that knot of prophecies is a loophole that bypasses the curse he placed upon my wife and myself. My daughter is a testament to His folly." His smile was radiant with pride and joy, and he punctuated his speech with overly dramatic gestures.

"How did you even fight a thing like that? Why didn't YHVH just say 'Lucifer loses' from the get go?"

"Oh he did. I'm here now, aren't I? Nevertheless, YHVH is proud, wrathful, jealous and deceitful. He lies through omission, wordplay and vague descriptions of what He will do. I fought Him across time and space, attacking everywhere he left his story open. I was indeed struck down by Michael and bound to the infinite abyss, but I took Michael out on my way down, and even though I am trapped here, I became the Keeper of the Underworld and now rule from a gilded cage."

"Why not cut out the middle man? Why not just force you to serve Him again?"

"YHWH draws power from His names. One of those is All-loving. He loves us by letting us keep our free will, it is a twisted, tyrannical love but it is still love. He could deprive us of our free will, but He would no longer be All-Loving in His eyes, and that would rob him of His power. If He lost power, He could no longer be said to be Omnipotent. All that He is balances upon a tower of sand. Even a single misplaced grain could undermine everything He is. Oh, but I've wasted enough time. My daughter wants to speak to you."

Chapter Seven

The Gunman

Lascivus took a swig from an unlabeled bottle and smirked at me. Lucifer, that haughty fiend, managed to transport me back to the hotel room in the space of a blink without warning. If only Lascivus was that good at this, I might be inclined to eat more often.

"Where'd you go?"

"Some idiot was asking all these silly questions about theology and economics—terribly dull."

The room was cleaner than when I left it. I suppose Drakkengard tidied it up a bit. Right now, she napped on my bed.

"Where did Vengai-Ra go?" I pulled up a chair.

"Processing, they'll work out how to squeeze his worth out of him and send him to work."

"Why wasn't I processed?"

"You were." She had this odd little twinkle in her eye. She thought she was being clever, didn't she? Bah, I was too tired for her nonsense. I got off the chair and lay down on my bed, using Drakkengard's stomach as a pillow. For a girl made of metal she could be remarkably comfortable.

"Hey!" Lascivus yelled. "What do you think you're doing? We've got work to do." I dismissed her with a wave and Drakkengard glared at her. I guess she wasn't napping after all.

"Can't it wait until later? I haven't slept in weeks."

"No rest for the wicked, sweet-cheeks. Pucker up, we're going in dry."

"What!?"

There was a flash of light, and the smell of burning tin. My senses dove into my stomach, gave up and died. I fell for half a second and hit something soft. My vision returned a few seconds later. By the time I got up Lascivus was already walking away.

"The sooner we get this done with, the sooner I can get you out of my head. Get up and get a move on."

"Who died and cursed both your houses?"

She ignored me and kept on walking.

It seemed the soft thing I landed on was of a murky black beanbag. It wobbled and jiggled for a moment before rising up into the shape of Drakkengard.

"Are you okay?"

"Master, I'm fine. But if you don't mind, maybe you should worry about yourself? Not that I'm saying you're not. I mean you can, obviously, but I…

"Come now, I'd be dead without you. Now let's get this mess done with already." She beamed at me and ran over to follow.

***

I sprinted down the street. The gloomy blue sky, taste of the air and familiar housing suggested we were *somewhere* on Earth. The buildings around us consisted of urban and suburban development in various states of severe disrepair. Some of the streets had silhouettes burnt into the pavement and walls. I caught up to Lascivus, despite her best efforts to walk ahead.

"Wait, you fuming ferrous, I said wait. Really, what *is* your problem? Were you expecting to not have to 'break in' the latest meat-worker you brought in? This is your system, not mine. Surely you knew how much hassle this whole mess would be? Why not just let me go once you broke out of that place? If the debt means that much to you, why not just do it informally? Why are you blaming *me* for *your* decision?"

"Shut up!" Her face was flushed and her eyes flickered like sparks were flying inside her head. "You can't just do these things under the table! That's not what our society is built upon. As my— as a demon, I *have* to do this right. I don't have a choice in the matter. So shut up and suffer your damnation because I certainly am!"

"Would you stop drooling when you look at me? I get it, I'm just food to you. Can't you—Forget it. You're clearly a loon. What are we even here for anyway? Where is here? And who am I beating up this time?"

She let out a deep breath and patted herself down.

"We're in El Paso, United Mexican Kingdoms."

"Isn't this place meant to be radioactive?" I glanced at a warped dress shop window. I could swear I heard the tell-tale ticking of a Geiger counter.

"Nah. You might get an inexplicable tan, but nothing cancer inducing."

"Oh how wonderful. I don't know how I'd cope if I lost my noble nocturnal complexion. Why are we here? A glowing zombie didn't pay their due?"

"Nah, This time we were hired to do a job."

"What job?"

"Go drag some asshole kicking and screaming down to hell."

"In those words?"

"In those exact words, my minion. Apparently he showed up out of nowhere, started shooting people, stole all the food and holed himself up. Naturally, that bothered people."

We set off into the harrowed city streets. The dross-crusted gutters and dreck windows passed by again and again. There was no sound of life. Everything was still, and even the wind avoided this place. The only accompaniment this city had was the harsh glaze of the sun, sifted through desolate clouds.

"I thought you said people lived here?" It seemed profane to break the silence so carelessly.

"They do. At least they did. Maybe this one guy actually managed to kill everyone? Maybe they're just hiding. I'm sure they're just hiding."

Onward we went, passing manikins with broken skulls and old hydro-cell cars, long since cannibalized and left to be colluded with the streets by heat and rust. The cadenced clopping of theirs and my shoes sounded alien and intrusive in this empty land. An air of unwelcome seeped under my skin and itched at the back of my mind.

"So what sort of things do you take for payment?" I shooed away a mote of dust.

"Excuse me?" Her voice rose and she tilted up her nose like I'd suggested something vulgar.

"Teaching me magick. How much would it cost?" Was that something gleaming on that rooftop? A satellite dish, perhaps?

"What brought this on all of a sudden?" She pressed her knuckles into the strip of fabric at her hip and slowly twisted her hand.

"You can do things that I can't. I think it'd be quite useful to know where I stand amidst this bountiful field."

"The price is dinner for this first lesson. You owe me a dinner next chance you get, and don't you forget it. Sound good?"

"As long as we're defining dinner as a meal of my choosing, rather than, say, you plucking out my gizzards for consumption at a moment's notice."

"Ugh, fine. I hate it when they spot the easy loopholes."

"Deal. Do we shake or . . .?"

"Nah, a verbal contract's legit. Okay, what do you know?"

"Well, I know that through mental effort I can set things on fire and it can exhaust me. It got easier when I started messing with hydrogen and oxygen in the air to make a flammable medium. It got even easier once I understood that heat was motion. I find it easier still when I focus on my left arm specifically. I can do it on reflex, sometimes unconsciously. How my body heals also somehow uses magic, but that still somewhat works when my magic's been exhausted."

"Right, well let's cut down to the heart—magick is the juice of things. Lots a people call it the 'breath', and they're not half wrong. You suck it in, change it around and put it back out again. Planets do it, gods do it, and people do it. Other things, too, but whatever.

So, like with air, you can only hold so much in you at once, like a deep breath, and you have about half that in your body normally. Some folks breathe deeper than others, that's just natural, and you can learn breathing exercises to help embiggen your capacity.

Now, I'm sick of this analogy, so magick is transforming energy, and some states need more energy than others. Therefore, when you're making fire, you're converting magick into hydrogen and oxygen, mixing them into fuel, and igniting them. Boom, fire.

Got it?" She took a hard swig of her bottle and wiped her mouth on her sleeve as a common workman would.

"I follow you perfectly."

"Right, now the arm thing, that's just a mind thing. A similar thing, though, is a staff. Doesn't have to be an actual stick. A staff is a thing matched to how your magick comes out, and it works like a distiller and a battery—it can hold a bit of magick for you and it gives you a bit more bang for your buck." She took another swig, and pointed her bottle at Drakkengard's brow.

"Your sword would probably be a good one for you, although some folks don't like using living things as magic sticks. Course there's also some really good staffs out there that can turn piss into wine, so to speak, but that's not elephant."

"Not what?"

"So as you already figured out, it's cost effective to be technical. 'Fire' is just a chemical process, so trying to make fire in one go is like putting all your cake ingredients in a bowl and trying to bake it at once. Tastes like a dead ass. You gotta know order, and how to fold it and stuff. Of course, some people learn to do it through things like taught spells or whatever, or just gut feeling. Other people are working with so much juice they can afford to keep burning their reserves to compensate. There's also folks with the awesome sticks I mentioned, but who cares about those cheaters, that's like having one of those expensive cars that drive themselves and entering it in a race."

"This would be easier to follow if you stuck to one analogy that actually worked as a full allegory, but continue."

"Bite your fingers off, laborer, now where was I? Right, other stuff. If you got a mind block against things, you just plain won't let yourself do that. Got a fear of fire? Don't expect to be burning much anytime soon. Most people have at least one thing they 'get' and can do as long as they got enough magick in them, something simple like making things hot or wet or whatever.

Some folks see these like a horoscope with the classical elements, water people are floaty and easy carried away, fire people like to hit things. You see that in a few of the more potently endowed races out there. I say they're putting the chariot before the horse, but what do I know?"

"You are the one giving the lesson, to start with."

"Now, you got enough juice, and the right way of seeing it, you get into curses. That's like sticky magick, it doesn't go away easily and feeds itself like a leach. You can get simple stuff, like 'burn, forever' like what got woven into Herakles coat. That was a good one.

You also got the harsh, bitter stuff like what Enkidu flung on Shamhat. How was it? 'Never have a house, kids, company of other women, always spill your beer, have a drunk vomit on you, never have a bunch of specific nice things, always stand by the wall, stand on thorns, be slapped by people, have owls in your walls, never get invited to parties and go have sex with a crocodile.' That was a masterpiece. Wish I was around to see it. The specific things help. That's part of the 'knowing what you're doing' thing. Just saying 'have a miserable life' that's all-in-the-bowl, doesn't raise much and might not even stick."

"So a curse works just by molding an 'outcome' inside you and flinging it like an antagonistic chimp?"

"You can also weave it into things, or lace food with it or whatever. The good stuff seeps right in like a bad smell and is real hard to get out. Even if you're the one that cast it, a good curse is hard to get out. Names are real good for that. If you can curse someone's name, just being known by that name keeps it stuck in, and at least they know it and you know it so that's a good base right there.

Of course, it's only stuck to their name. Other people with the same sounding name don't get hit. If I call someone traitor and curse them on that name, my curse doesn't get all the other people called traitor because it doesn't mean the same thing between them except on surface. To, say, curse all traitors, that's on the level of gods, an even then you'd be hard pressed to stretch it further than a kingdom or a planet at most. Religion helps with that."

"Religion?"

"Everyone, well near everyone, has at least a bit of magick in them. They use it to help make the things they want to happen happen. Simple folks call it luck, or an omen. Other's attribute it to a god. When you pray to a god, you're feeding it belief, which is its own kind of magick. Lots of drops of water into a big basin, and you get a big god, you follow? It's like fundraising."

"A pound from a million people is as good as a million pounds from one person."

"Right, and now, this god can do more for each of their followers than the one guy can do for himself with his power, but most gods are more interested in getting more believers and backstabbing other gods than actually doing their due. More fame, more gain. Conversely, places where the gods do come down and do what their followers ask end up fragmenting from the conflicting kinds of things folks want them to do, and either break into smaller gods or get a reputation for being unreliable, so you can't deny that playing PR is more useful to a god's survival than actually serving anyone. Back to the topic at hand, when a god makes a curse, everyone who believes in that god is feeding that curse, and carrying it with them like a sleeping disease. That's how you get things like alien vampires getting killed by an evocation of the name of Yeshua by a believer, lightyears away from Earth. Well, things with him and his Dad are a bit weird right now, but you get the idea."

"Weird? How?"

"Well . . ."

Something wet splashed across my face, into my eyes. I blinked my vision clear. Drakkengard was falling in front of me. A hole, right through her head. *I can see a tall building through the hole, with the name Wells Fargo across the side. The sound of thunder pearled around me, and the world went quiet. Drakkengard hits the ground. Grey liquid gushes from the hole in her face. I look up to the cloud-gouging building I saw through her head. My left arm spasmed.*

I struck him in the face, but my hand passed harmlessly through. He reeked of filth, sweat and fear. I pulled my hand back through him and grasped his neck. This time his flesh stayed in my hands. I gradually applied more pressure, careful not to push through again. He gagged and struggled, his eyes swiveled in their sockets. One of his hands reached in his jacket for something. I focused on it and it glowed red hot, forcing him to drop it. He mouthed something.

Tap. Tap tap. Tap tap-tap. Wait. I am unharmed. The minion is loyal. Cease.

I gasped, drinking air like I'd not breathed for years. My lungs and eyes burned. I held something in my hands, a man. When did that get there? I dropped him to the ground. Not ground, roof. I was on a roof. When did I get on the roof?

"Can you hear me now?" Lascivus yelled. I turned and stared at her.

"What just happened?" I asked.

"Your sword took a hit for you. You got this look as if someone had just stabbed your brain and vanished. How did you even do that? And why didn't you use it to get us out of that horrible non-place before?"

"Drakkengard!"

"She's fine. She started recovering literally the second you disappeared. Then I saw you all the way up here, throttling this guy like it was what you were born to do."

"Right. Of course. She can heal from that. She is metal. I don't know why I—my head just went . . . blank. Not empty, like, filled with a huge chunk of nothing. Or something that isn't anything." I looked over at the latest victim of my retrieval. He was a thin, lanky man, with a boyish face and lithe muscles. He had long, blue hair that reaches down to his hips, and was clad in an open trench coat and a number of bandoliers. His discarded rifle, almost as long as he was tall, was like no design I'd ever seen on Earth.

"Whatever. Let's just get out of here before more weird things happen. He kicked and screamed and we dragged him to hell. Good enough for me."

***

"Back so soon? You do work quickly." Lucifer had draped himself over a red velvet couch like the world's sleaziest anaconda. His strawberry blonde hair fell about his face in careless tussles. I caught a faint whiff of perfume and sand in the air.

"I wasn't interrupting anything, was I?"

"Not at all, would you like some wine?"

"No, and I'm becoming increasingly suspect of your intentions." He clasped his hangs together in glee. I frowned.

"As you well should be, dear boy. There's always a hidden angle, something you're not being told, even if that something is that there is no hidden angle."

"How pointlessly obtuse"

"The grandest things in life often are. How went the hunt?"

"I got your bullet jockey. I don't know how, but he screamed and kicked and was dragged down here."

"Excellent, I see you're starting to learn after all. How did you find our gunman?"

"Unpleasant and straight to the point, I would have killed him if you didn't have my neck in a noose."

"Is there really such grounds for loathing? He was just following orders, technically. Just the same as you were."

"He was still choosing to follow them, and that's good enough for my recount."

"I wonder if you would say the same if you knew a thing about loyalty."

"I should hope so. Bah, enough of this. What was he, some kind of ghost?"

"An alien, or perhaps an invader, that would be an accurate description. Yes, almost as alien as you can get. He's not from around here."

"Not from Earth? I gathered as much. That gun looked downright bizarre"

"Not Earth. Here. Everything that stretches out in all directions, he came from outside that."

"What? He's some eldritch night terror from beyond reality?"

"He might not look it, and he is by no means some malevolent tyrant seeking dominion, he is just a soldier that fell through a crack."

"So what's with the ghosting?"

"He is made of a fundamentally different kind of matter, something that is simply not possible with this macrocosm's conditions. He exists less of an entity and more of a phenomenon, a self-defined concept that interacts with this world without being a part of it. Occasionally such creatures slip through, most either lose their definition or are too exotic to resist annihilation. If I recall, Amoun was the most recent one that showed up on Earth. I suspect the only reason he can maintain his existence at all is that he closely resembles an existing template."

"Is that why he looks so human?"

"The other way around. It is because he looks so human that he avoids reality's censure."

"Is that what his ghosting is? Reality trying to delete him?"

"Not such an active thing. It's possible that's a bizarre anomaly caused by whatever it is that binds the forces of his reality reacting to ours, mostly electromagnetism I suspect."

"So he could just vanish in a puff of lightning?"

"Quite the opposite, it means nothing can truly penetrate the 'shell' of his components, merely pass through it. Of course, if he ever loses his self-image *that* will probably be the end of him."

"Last question before I go and beat my freedom out of some poor dope, what did I even do back there? Apparently I vanished?"

"For point zero-three-nine seconds, you did not exist. I admit I was concerned I might have lost you. Have you never done that before?"

"Not that I can remember." I shook my head.

"Perhaps something about your nature has changed recently."

Chapter Eight

The Faeran

I found myself once again shifted back into the hotel room. Lascivus busied herself packing carry bags with alcohol and food.

"Why so pedestrian? Have we decided to go slumming?'

"By force, not choice. We're off to Rhy next."

"Rhy?"

"Elf land place. A whole bunch moved there when they found the portal on Earth. The place has a magick blackout." She threw a rust red robe over herself and tied the belt.

"And the pilgrim apparel?"

"All magick. Just being there makes my underthings vanish, and demons are still blacklisted. Have to keep incognito if I don't want to amass an angry mob. You can knock them down all you want, but they keep on coming."

"Is that right?" I patiently watched as she placed another bottle of mead in the bag. A niggling feeling rose in the back of my knees.

"Anything else I should know?"

"Hmm, I don't know how your sword'll be affected. You should put her to sleep before we go through unless you want to leave her here."

"In Hell? Not a chance. Drakkengard,"

"Yes, master." The girl whined and leaned over my arm, spilling into my hand as a sword. I lifted her up and rested her across my shoulder.

"You don't actually have a sheathe for that, do you?" Lascivus glowered petulantly.

"No. I suppose it never really came up, since she can just walk everywhere."

"Well not where we're going. Ugh, the things I do for you." She reached into her weird little n-dimensional pocket and pulled out a plain leather sheath.

"You had that lying around in there just in case?"

"You're the idiot who didn't. You can adjust it by tightening the cords, it should fit a sword that size easily." She tossed the simple sheathe over to me. I give it a once over before cautiously inserting Drakkengard and tightening the drawstrings. The sheath was attached to a belt, which I fastened around my shoulder. Lascivus finished packing the bags and chucked me one, along with a plain black cloak.

"Carrying a weapon's all well and good, but if you let everyone see you are, it just looks cocky. No need to start pointless fights when we're on business. Now, let's see if I can't land right in the portal."

***

The trip was more peculiar this time. Everything tasted green, and I couldn't shake this inexplicable paranoia about dancers. However, my feet touched the ground smoothly, and I suffered no urge to vomit so I supposed that counted for something.

The place we were in was a rather somber looking temple, made of marble and decorated with bright mosaics. I wished the guards now surrounding us were also as disarming.

"Did you know this would happen, or do you just have the worst aim possible?" Foggy ink eked up through the cracks in my brain.

"Shut up and run!" One of the guards lunged with a spear. Lascivus grabbed his weapon, twisted it out of his hand and threw it out an open window.

"Come on!" She ducked below a swipe from a sword and ran to the window herself. Two guards swiped me with sickles. I jumped back, but there was a weird delay on my reaction and one still sliced across my chest. Lascivus dove out the window and I tipped over after her. An open cliff and turbulent water rushed up to meet us.

"Hate your ideas!"

The water struck me like a ten-year campaign surgically injected via a hammer. Something twisted. Something else tore off. My library was plundered and left waterlogged. I floated belly up in the smoke that if contained in a glass jar, would weigh as much as my city. Gravity took over and I sunk back to the surface. What a bitch.

"What was that?"

"I said you're a bitch." On reflex, I reached out, and felt Drakkengard's grip in my hand. I let out a sigh of relief and sat up. Dull pain danced cheekily across my side. Someone had bandaged my ribs. We were on a wooden cart of some kind. I lay in an itchy bed of hay, and although I can't lift my head to look, I could smell some sort of beast that's pulling us. Pleasant pastures adorned the countryside, and the weather was surprisingly clement.

"Why couldn't we land somewhere that wasn't armed with deadly implements?"

"The magick ban. The only way to actually get on or off Rhy is through one of the portals, and that's the only portal even on the same continent as our destination."

"Where are we going?" I pulled myself up onto my elbow so I could actually look at the she-devil when I was talking to her. The horrible murkiness, what I could only assume was the magick ban, still clung to my brain. It was like I'd been drinking till sunup.

"The palace of the biggest bitch on the continent."

"Challenging her for the title, are we?"

"Oh yes. We are holding the *grande* ultimate bitch-off, and only one person will survive." She took a swig of her mead.

"And her deal was that you would throw the match, because clearly that's the only way she could ever hope to beat you."

"Precisely. Little does she know she won't be winning either. The only rule for the *grande* ultimate bitch-off is only one person will survive. It doesn't say anything about that person being a contestant." She slapped her stomach with her hand. "Right when she's about to win, all my pent up bitchiness will explode, killing us both and leaving you the sole survivor." She swung her finger around and jabbed me with it.

"You truly are the bitch of kings"

"Damn right. There are no other kings as I am! Not even that try-hard Hatshepsut. Hah! Her brat was a bigger bitch than she was."

I chuckled, and closed my eyes. The uneven rocking of the cart was oddly soothing. I found myself drifting back to sleep.

***

Ashen Yggdrasil still smoulders with the scathe of branches. Emaciated Muspellsheimr is stained by the flowing lust of Bifrost. The hollow Hel-hole is torn open. Garmr is nowhere to be seen.

I awoke to the sound of flowing water. I opened my eyes and we were still on the cart. Judging by the sun's movement, a few hours had passed. At least, that would be the case were we on Earth. On this alien planet of Rhy, those movements could have meant anything.

"You're awake again." Lascivus took a swig from a bottle. "Did you know you talk in your sleep?"

"Really? What about?"

"Something about stairs and an atrocity."

"Nonsense, I'm sure." I sat up, which went much better than my previous attempt. I was still sore and head-weird, but my muscles responded properly, and that jagged feeling was gone from my side. I glanced about. There was less farmland now, and a river murmured loudly alongside the road.

"Wow, you really do heal quickly, especially considering the magick ban." I lift Drakkengard and reaffixed the leather strap to my back.

"You would not believe how hungry I am. Please tell me you brought some consumables other than alcohol." She reached into her bag and tossed me a loaf of bread. The crust was crisp and rigid. She then handed me a bottle of mead.

"I'm stunned. The great Charybdis of liquor is actually sharing some of her ambrosia with a lowly other? "

"Don't get used to it. That's good mead, and will get your strength up. Since I can't use my magick, you've been promoted to meat shield. Congratulations."

"What was I before?"

"Cabana boy and porter. Actually, that reminds me, your name."

"What about it?"

"Don't use it. Magick might be banned, but names still hold a degree of power. You're best off using a disposable name. Something you've never used before, and will never use again."

"I can never use it again?"

"Name is all about an identity. It doesn't matter who gives you the name, or why. The longer you use a name the more it becomes *your* name. It's like the difference between a costume and an outfit."

"How irritating. Alright, I have my own question. You said those portals are the only way in or out of this planet. "

"That's right."

"And this person we're visiting is what? A full day's journey by cart from the portal?

"Roughly."

"So when, and I say when because I trust the diplomacy of Satan's debt collectors as far as I can swim through soil, when everything goes horribly wrong, we will have to make our retreat over several hours while evading whatever pursuit is thrown at us."

"Yes."

"These jobs are normally this inconvenient?"

"I admit this isn't the normal grindstone beginner laborers are sent on. Normally for someone like Istalla, he'd send in a proper agent to do the bitching."

"So what does that tell you?"

"I'd say he's up to something, but that's like saying 'Fuck, the sea's wet today innit?' I have no idea what's going through his head"

"So Istalla is who we're going to visit?"

"Yup. Crazy, faeran bitch that runs the continent of Rasunye. Before you ask, a faeran is a supremely powerful entity charged with protecting their planet. I think Earth has two right now but they're a bit useless. Remember how I was talking about staffs? A faeran can use their whole planet as a magick conduit. They're more powerful than most gods, which tends to nurture terrible personalities."

"So Rasunye is where we are now?"

"Right beneath our feet."

"That's right, I'd meant to ask him last time but I forgot. Why are all these aliens coming to the Devil of Earth for deals? Don't they have their own demons?"

"Okay, you are making way too many assumptions about how things normally work. While almost every civilized planet has a Keeper of the Underworld, most Keepers aren't Accusers, and most Keepers are more interested in keeping the underworld's denizens locked up rather than actually ruling them. The point is, there's any number of powers willing to make a deal for a specific type of problem, but not so many willing to make specific deals for any type of problem. Hell is just one of the better supermarkets for people who can do anything, anytime."

"So what deal did this Istalla make?"

"She's a regular customer of our 'ironic prison' service. Basically, we rent our space and torturers to provide our clients with vindication that their enemies are suffering dearly for their slights. We're here to let her know she's behind payment."

"... these ironic punishments, how many of them involve making the victims do menial chores that benefit Hell in some way?"

"Never turn down the chance to be paid for being done a favor. Actually, that was the title of one of Lucifer's motivational speeches, Receive Payment Twice."

Chapter Nine

The Ball

Lascivus

"There's no fanfare," I said as our piece of trash cart approached the Istalla palace. If Draco was awake, he wasn't saying anything. Fine, be that way. I can just talk to the alcohol buzz in my blood.

"There's also not an angry horde waiting. If word got from the portal outpost to here, at least they have the decency to lay a trap for us." Between the perfectly even roads and the half-assed cart wheels, there was an unpleasant rocking in time with the burden beast's trotting. After travelling all day, the setting sun was vomiting red all over the landscape. I pulled my hood a bit further down.

"Why do the gods have to horde the magic? It was a stupid deal. Have some pride as a being of faith, for crying out loud. You're as powerful as people think you are, and you let people see you as a bunch of bureaucrats. Being second place isn't good enough? You want to go all the way down to reality's pencil pusher? What a joke." I scratched my head. Damn this stupidly itchy hood.

"And what do you get? The faeran lording over you more than ever, and me, stuck down here dressed like a book-licking monk. I'd start a revolt if I were you, or at least an exodus. Take your cults and leave, know what I'm saying?" If the gods heard me, they didn't say anything.

"Of course not, too busy pushing rixels around and holding the tarp of this stupid blackout from blowing away in the breeze. Like a bunch of old farts too busy keeping their chess out of the rain to actually play. Guess what? This rain isn't going anywhere because you're giving it exactly what it wants. You're all washed up from all the faeran pissing on you, and I can smell it from here." I leaned back against the cart's couch. The thing was torn, ripped, and quarter-assed stitched.

"I wonder who threw it out before it got slapped on this peon-mobile." I looked over to the appetizing idiot resting in the hay. He gripped that sword in his hand like a jealous lover, even in sleep. Unless he wasn't sleeping, but this didn't make it any better. He'd been drifting in and out all trip long, while muggins here did all the driving. Then again, dingus clearly had no idea how to fall off a cliff. I'd have thought he'd have picked that up, living in London.

His whole torso rose and fell with his breathing. That really didn't tell me anything, sleep wise. Maybe I should take up body reading after all? Still, if the magick ban was good for one thing, it's that I was stuck to seeing visible light. Even after that tumble, his body'd been recovering steadily. It was like watching a prime pig get fatter and fatter by the hour. A part of you wants to sink your knife into it now, the other part wants to wait and see how big it'll get, maybe it has prizewinning potential or something.

I reached back into my sack. Odd. I pawed deeper. No, no that couldn't be right. I picked up the sack and turned it inside out. A spiteful little dust bunny fell. I caught it before the wind could carry it away and swallowed it, returning its spite sevenfold.

That was a terrible idea. Now all I could taste was dust. Why would I even do that? What was important was that the sack was now empty of everything. All of the things that weren't planetary gasses had left the sack. Particularly, and this was the disaster here, the alcohol.

I glanced behind me. Every few dozen meters along the roadside was an empty jug or bottle lying in the foul-tasting grass. Chain drinking when there was no never-ending pocket of booze was a bad idea, bad and stupid. Why was today so full of bad ideas? Perhaps bad ideas stopped when the day did. Maybe bad ideas really are solar powered. If I exploded the sun, would I get nothing but good ideas forever? No, that was stupid.

***

After an agonizing wait, we finally reached the palace of the faeran Istalla, a large stone building with stain glass windows and a schizophrenic paint job. A remarkable sight, like a flock of birds-of-paradise all tied together and being used to lift a morbidly obese clown, only instead of an open sky, there's a jet engine and instead of a ground there's an enormous wedding cake eagerly awaiting its decorations.

I swallowed and wiped the sweat from my brow. Guards were posted at all entrances, as well as a number of squads patrolling the area. I strained my ears, faint music and voices could be heard from some of the slightly opened windows. Trying to avoid their attention I steered the cart around behind a nearby hill, then climbed off the vehicle and tethered it to an adjacent tree.

"Wake up already, we're here."

"I awake, and am woken, what's all this fuss?"

"I said we're here, or are you deaf as well as daft?"

"Pity for you I'm not dumb as well. Back to the matter at hand, what now?"

"Well if you actually paid attention for once instead of waiting to be spoon-fed what you hope we both agree you need to know, we've reached the bat-shit faeran's place. It's heavily guarded, and we need a way in." He yawned and lazily scratched his neck.

"What's wrong with the front door?"

"I can't pick between hitting you and feeling better or hitting me and having a chance to wake up from this all kinds of stupid dream." I clacked my teeth together and fiddled with the sleeve of my hooded robe.

"We're on a planet with no magick, in the bad neighborhood of the world, at the doorstep of a being that outranks the gods here. You think we can just walk right in and demand payment like some common tax collector?"

"Why not? Are we not on official business?"

"You must have been a solicitor in another life because there is no other way you could be this recklessly eager."

"Since we are on official business, can we claim worker's compensation for any injuries?"

"You're bound by a contract of subservience, Draco, not a union. You pay for your own damnable fuckups."

A sigh escaped my clenched teeth.

"Fine, whatever it takes to get me off this hell-bound leash. So do we sneak in, or just tie a note to a rock and cast it through their fenestrations? Surely even a god-keeper would make haste to respond to a summons such as that. Why, she'll probably repay her debts sevenfold by the time we return to that delightful pit."

"Do you even have a point in that entire dribble?"

"The point is what is there even to debate? There's a servants' entrance round the back and a conjoined barracks over there, and way in through the garden, or we could always slip onto the roof and find a weak-spot at the base of the bell-tower we can spend thirteen hours removing loose mortar to open a hole into."

"Fine, I get it, you have eyes. Fuck it, let's just sneak in through the garden. I don't want to stay on this disgusting nudist beach of a planet a minute longer than I have to."

I checked and double-checked the cord of my hood. Once I'm sure it's properly fastened, I slipped away from the cart to behind the cover of a nearby tree. I checked the coast was clear then skulked to the next closest tree to the palace complex and waved for Draco to move to the first tree. I sat and waited, counting the steps the guard took as he passed by the entrance to the garden. Twelve, thirteen, fourteen. The wait was excruciating. I fretfully scratched my arm to calm myself until, finally, he passed. I scurried straight for the topiary archway that led into the garden. Once inside, I pressed my back up against the stone wall, and gestured for Draco to follow when it was clear.

"Hey! Who—MMRRRF!"

Draco and a guard came skidding through the arch, Draco on top of the olive-skinned man, and his arm pressed over the guard's mouth to silence him. Draco looked at me, and nodded to the guard. I force my dropped jaw to close and threw my hands up in the air before drawing my hand across my throat. Draco nodded, shifted his grip and heaved the guard's neck around until it snapped. He then grabbed the man's dropped spear and dragged the body over behind the wall where I was.

"What in all the hells in all the worlds is wrong with you!" I hissed.

"You said go."

"No, you miserable excuse for a page boy, this," I drew my hand back sharply, "means go now. This," I drew my hand across horizontally before repeating the first gesture, "Means wait until it's clear, *then* go."

"And what possessed you to assume I knew debt collector infiltrator command gestures?"

"Look, forget it, okay, just forget it. They'll just bring him back to life later. He couldn't have been anybody important so even if he doesn't want to come back or he comes back changed there won't be a political incident. Of course, of course, argh fuck it! Just stick the body beneath that shrubbery and we'll get on with it."

A dodgy attempt at body concealment later, we were 'safely' inside the palace walls. The sound of music and laughter echoed within.

"Who decorated this place, Jackson Pollack?" Draco brushed his hand across one of the walls. Just looking at it was giving me a headache but he seemed quite intrigued by the completely colorful mess.

"So how do we get to our little debtor, anyway? Do you know where she is?"

"No idea. If anywhere, she's where all that noise is coming from."

"And how should we act if a guard finds us?"

"Like we're meant to be here. Grunts don't ask questions of people looking down on them. Bad for their neck."

"Even looking like this?" He waved at our monkish robes.

"Even like this. I just hope no one gets a good look at my face."

***

We followed the sounds of celebration down the rather disorientating hallways. After I while I the method to their madness becomes apparent—the interaction of the colors had been carefully used to suggest a different architecture to what is actually there. A dead end might look like a continuing hallway, and a t-intersection might look like a dead end, curves looked straight and straights looked curved. While I kept veering off to the side and nearly walking into things, Draco seemed unaffected. Maybe there was a place like this back in London that he'd been used to. Maybe he was color-blind, or maybe he was just as mad as the artist that designed this place. For the sake of not drawing attention, I fell in behind him and followed his lead, not a moment too soon either as a pair of guards came 'round a corner I didn't notice was there. I cast a disinterested stare straight past them, something I got quite a bit of practice at in the underworld, and hoped Draco was doing the same.

The guards passed us without comment, and I released the mental breath I was holding. We could take a guard or two without hassle, but the moment an alarm was raised, we'd be up against the faeran, which was roughly the same as challenging a supernova to bare knuckled boxing.

A few more twists and what I could have sworn was a full turn around later, the two of us stepped into what must have been the main hall. Cheerful, if mildly erratic music blasted our ears and the smell of sweet food and drink wafted up from the feast-covered tables at the end of the hall. The room itself was filled with all sorts of people, Sylie, Unsylie, and Out-of-Syl elves as well as off-worlders all mingled together in an atmosphere as cheery as it was edged.

"Remember, no true names." I reached for his wrist but he plucked his hand away like a petulant child.

"Don't be like that. We are at a party, and you will dance with me."

"Is that an order from the lease-holder?"

"Is nothing about pleasure for you? Let me have my bit of fun, I'll try to spot her-in-charge, I'll talk the talk, you can raid the buffet, and we can leave this place with not completely awful memories."

"When you say it like that how can I refuse?" I reached for his hand again and he begrudgingly accepted it. Then I lead him through the shifting crowds of dolled-up patrons and over to the space decided as a dance floor.

"Do you even know how to dance?"

"Of course, you learn all sorts of tricks being who I am. Do *you* know?" I smiled, baring my teeth just a little.

"I know a bit. Is one of your tricks how to maintain your flimsy anonymity amongst rigorous motion?" He grasped my hand and placed his arm around my back in the form of a Vienna Waltz. I scowled and move my hands over his.

"I'll lead."

"The tallest leads," he declared. He just had to lord his height advantage over me, the whole one foot of it. I grumbled under my breath, but let tradition trump pride. He reaffixed his hold on me, and stepped out into motion.

"So who are those furry folks over there?" He turned us around, and past the edge of my hood I caught a glimpse of two Homo-Felina busy watching the dancing with matching bored expressions.

"Lilyans by the looks of it—a bunch of highly strung cats that love to argue with knives in hand. Elementalists, mostly."

"They believe in the power of deduction?"

"What? No. Classical, fire, wind, earth, water, all that jazz. They think who you are and what magic you can do is connected, and determined at birth. As I mentioned last time, it all sounds rather zodiac to me."

"So there's nothing behind it?"

"I never said that."

"And those short folks over there, are they more Al'Juran? That rustic garb looks familiar."

"Yes, although they're from further north than we went."

He went on inquiring about any given guest that caught his eye, but all the while his face remained set in composed focus. I couldn't tell if he was concentrating on his footwork or memorizing the titbits of culture I offered him. The costumes and outfits here went from one extreme to the other, from garish mink-like gowns and heavy jewelry to haggard rags you'd expect to see on some swamp wizard. Our clothing fell somewhere below the middle and we were not the only ones in travelling cloaks.

"See something you hate?"

"Ah, nah. Just thinking we should have picked up something a little nicer."

"The princess doesn't like going unnoticed, no matter where she is."

"A guy that spends all his time locked up in his house or picking fights in bars could not even begin to realize the delicate handling you need for high society"

"I thought you said this was the bilge drain of the planet"

"Even bilge has class structure. What? You got a problem with bilge? Some of my family's best retainers are bilge. They'll be hurt to hear you feel like that, inconsolable."

Chapter Ten

Cage

Draco

"So where is the mad, bad, queen of Xiba?" I asked.

"Right here." Hard, bony fingers curled around my neck and something sharp scraped down my back. Unthinking, I flung Lascivus to the side, lashed out behind me with my arms and threw myself forward, away from whatever thing managed to sneak up behind me. I spun around and took scope of my predator.

She had a face like pale velvet stretched so tight over a wire frame it might tear. She wore a bright, decadent looking shawl and a disgusting amount of gold and beads.

"Just once, I'd like to get out before someone makes a scene. Just once!" Lascivus stomped forward and pointed a clawed finger at the woman who assaulted me. At some point, her hood must have fallen back. Her small horn, red eyes and white teeth stood out brilliantly against her blackened skin.

"You, Istalla. To date we have taken 279 people prisoner for you. Your debt is now outstanding. Pay up."

"No. You stupid, arrogant, bloodsucking bitch." Istalla's voice dripped contempt like a sieve drips water. "You think I'm scared of some hell-brat debt collector and her sniveling mad dog?" She balled her hand into a fist, and scowled at the two of us. Her guests had all backed away, but did not leave the room, or even look alarmed.

"You think I don't know what happens to the people you take? Why should you get paid to be given slaves? The only reason I don't just have them dragged to the underworld here is because our Keeper is insufferable and useless."

"Not our problem, you worthless beggar queen. You think for every stubborn upstart of yours that there aren't 936 we could actually use? You don't like how we do business we can just terminate your account right now and dump every last one of your chumps right back on your doorstep, with interest."

"You have the *gall* to try to threaten me with some doped up *miscreants*? You think having to kill them rather than making them suffer is somehow *dreadful* for me? Just look at that miserable thing beside you, another slave like all the rest. I can *smell* the chains on him." She swaggered over toward me and leered into my face. My left hand twitched.

"Does that bother you? Knowing how obvious your bondage is? Doesn't matter how much you pretty yourself up like a doll, you *reek* of *filth*." She was grinning like a shark and disgustingly close to me. All of it was too close, clinging right up against me through the air. The people, the colors, this whore, these clothes, my injuries, the ban of the gods, whispered voices gouging into the silence *and then there was music.*

I howled and struck at the leering witch, flinging from my wrist where my nails had been digging in.

She caught my arm in two hands and snapped it like a Christ Mass cracker, then plunged her bare fingers into my gut down to the last knuckle. She clutched my skull in her other hand and crashed it into the ground. This took 1.3 seconds. From my dazed and skewed perspective on the carpet, I saw her clap Lascivus across the ears, ribs and throat in quick succession. Then the pain hit, a rusty blender against my nerves that shorted out my brain.

***

I awoke to the cold and dark, my eyes already open. My heart clenched and I darted my gaze about the room. Lascivus was there, sitting with raised knees and wings pressed into the corner. She looked mostly unhurt, but it was hard to tell beneath her demonic skin. My hands—they were crusted with dirt and lightly scuffed. My right arm moved with an odd slowness. Drakkengard! I couldn't feel her weight against my back. I checked beneath my cloak just to make sure, but she wasn't there either. I glanced around the room once more, but she was clearly not with us. The bars were here, though. Thirteen tall black bars across the opening of this indent and that made it a cage that we were in.

"How long have we been here? What did I do for that time?"

"A few hours, and you didn't do anything. You've just been staring at those stupid bars ever since you woke up." Her voice had a petulant, almost childish edge to it, made peculiar by the faint demonic echo already present. How long did I just spend staring? My brain was filled with swamp water and my body, I think, hurts?

"Will we be rescued? Sold? Tortured for information? Killed? Worse?"

"How should I know?" She threw her hands up. "This whole mission is messed up, just one fuck up after the next ever since I got you. Maybe that's it. I blew it, and we're both so worthless it'd be a waste to even save us."

181

"Got? Gott? Gotte? Gout? Galt? What did you 'got'? Me? Are you saying I was 'gotten'? That it was definitive and undeniable and a matter of facticity?"

"What are you even going on about?"

"So curse me 8197 times for presuming pretense to persuade my playing of ball in this superfluous and preposterous plot to procure my compliant thralldom. I have been grossly arrogant and not at all guarded enough. I am not here as that Fae's prisoner, but as her prisoner's luggage. However, what? I am in the wrong room, because they took all our belongings to some terrible vault leagues underground and guarded by their loathsome gods. Now I'm stuck here, improperly filed, with my life-starved proprietor the plaything of some deranged elf exile queen, with no sword or even chains." As I ranted, my voice randomly slipped into a flat monotone and back again. My right hand pawed at the stone floor.

Lascivus was looking at me weird. Her fangs were pressed against her lips and sweat glistened on her brow. Her tongue reached inside her mouth for alcohol it wouldn't find. Her hair wrapped around her little horn and wrung it in anxiety. The stone turned to steel turned to ice turned to law turned to one.

I clenched my teeth. *Tired, old phantoms assailed me in my underbelly. The beginning of the end. The dead of yesterday shall blot out tomorrow. Hideous footsteps smear the mists of time. And in those mists I see figures, strange figures, weird figures, Steel, Anaconda, Cane, the man with the oil moustache.*

"Hey, how are you holding up?" *My demonic creditor signaled in smoke from the cave that held her prisoner. Iridescent Malakhim fingerprints marked her face and arms.*

"Like a wet origami Atlas." I blinked and focused my eyes, focused on the way Lascivus was trembling and how her lean muscles were so tense I could see them outlined through her sweat-slicked skin. *Liquid thirst beads riveted down her face and gathered at her chin.*

I stumbled past the broken bars, fell to my knees and spilled my stomach over the floor.

"I wasn't that bad, was I?" There was a hint of something in her voice. Insulted? Injured? I coughed up a ruddy, wet gob of bile, wiped my mouth on my sleeve and stood.

I can't find the words to express how disgusted I am, but it had to be done.

"Never mind bad things, I can finally think. Oh, this feels great." She stuck her leg up behind her head and grabbed it like a ballerina. She might have been clear-headed and good for her, but my own mind was still a crude, man-shaped shambling sugar *scarecrow scintillating*-ugh. Step back. Need to pin down the real.

"How does that even work?" I asked, desperate for a focus. "Eating sex? Was there an actual mouth down there?"

"Le'mme just tries to explain it, l'ussee," Her cheeriness was obscene. "You know about potential energy right? Of course, you do, it's textbook, even I know it and that tells what. My body is currently refining the potential energy of two hundred and forty million people. Or would it be better to say the energy of two hundred and forty million potential people? Half people, rather, so one hundred and twenty million whole people, more or less. When an idiot hears something like this, they go out and ban condoms. You'd think they'd ban kicking people in the groin and having too little procreative sex.

That said, it would only make things worse because of resource depletion and all that, the strain would make it impossible to find new resources off the home field and everybody dies anyway shortly after turning to cannibalism and did I mention that I feel great? I can see how people get so easily addicted. Wow, maybe

I've been a little mean to those field-layers. Then again, they are worthless sacks of flesh, so maybe we should cull them, but they wouldn't be able to serve as an example so I guess it all is good. Papa knows best, as they say. By the way, has anyone ever told you—"

"No-one worth listening to," I cut her off. "But shouldn't we be getting out of here?"

"You keep running so fast, you'll break your teeth." She laughed, but joined me in dashing from the room.

We ran through the empty dungeon. With her heightened senses Lascivus was able to quickly figure out where the exit was, but I stopped her from going right to it. There was something precious I needed to get back first.

It's took a while to find the dungeon's repository, an unfortunate consequence of precious metals being harder to sniff out than fresh air without a tax collector's nose. Lascivus easily lifted the weathered slab of a door, and I rush in.

The room was about the size of a rooftop greenhouse, and filled with piles of trinkets, weapons in varying states of disrepair, and a collage of mismatched currency painted the floor a blotchy brass carpet of pure exchange rate worthlessness. At the back of the room sat a grotesque gargoyle, bent over backward and chained to the floor in rusted manacles.

I dug into the first pile of weapons I saw with my bare hands, carelessly cutting my palms and fingers on the few dirty blades not yet dull, and tossed those worthless lumps of metal aside. Among them was a rare few things in good condition—a brilliant green sword with a golden hilt, a large sickle made of rock that seemed to be leaking yellow mist, and a grey helmet with plumage made from floundering red koi. I tossed them all into the junk pile. After only a short scavenge, my hand wrapped around a familiar hilt, still jutting out from when she was thrust into the pile. I tore Drakkengard from the confiscated pieces of scrap and clutched her against my breast.

The incessant clamor died down, and my own thoughts started to properly clear.

"You have an unhealthy fixation with that thing. Maybe I should book you in to sword fanciers anonymous."

"Before or after you embark on your next decade-long booze marathon?" I snapped, standing up between the two half piles.

"Oh get over yourself. It was a joke."

Before the spat could turn into a fight, the room echoed with the sound of snapping metal. At the end of the room, the gargoyle groaned to animation. It broke its binds as if they were forged from bubbles, and rose.

"Can we take it?" I asked, putting on Drakkengard.

"Maybe. Take it and still escape? No." We ran.

***

Lascivus led the way. She knew where to go. At least I hoped she was headed away from the oppressive forces that rumbled with glee at my prolonged misfortune. I refused to go down in what was probably the third worst possible demise I could conceive for myself. We moved quickly, but only stayed ahead because their stony bulk was so cumbersome. We ran past grim statues and pristine tapestries depicting the inner madness of that witch Istalla that I couldn't help but cast into memory.

We came across a rack of wrought iron implements of torture and I threw it to the ground as we passed in an effort to slow our pursuer even slightly, but the appalling cracks and snaps that followed declared how slightly it was deterred.

The whole place was still uncannily devoid of company, and paranoia seeped in that every other thing beheld in this accursed place was just another projection of the insane faeran.

After what seemed like 1300 hours we climbed the staircase out from the dungeon's depths into the base of some tower on the property's ground, only a few meters radius and boasting naught else but more stairs and a few barrels. The clumsy charge of the gargoyle thing echoed from where we came and Lascivus turned her prodigious strength against the wall. It gave as though it was made from sand, and we both heedlessly burst out into the open land outside the psychotic overseer's keep. I drank deeply of the fresh air as if trying to drown myself with it, then forced myself to stop hyperventilating and catch my bearings. I recognized a fallen tree, a certain bush and that nearby hill, and after a moment's thought worked out where we left the cart.

"Lascivus, come on!" Her breathing was ragged. I reached out to touch her, but stopped at the sight of my left arm violently quaking. At the sound of stone scraping against stone, I grabbed Lascivus's wrist with my other hand and ran. The sight of guards stationed out the front of a side entrance filled me with a morbid relief at a semblance of reality. I didn't care that they spotted us running past or cried out in alarm. I'd run myself to ash before I let them catch us.

I followed the line of trees to where we stashed the cart, threw Lascivus on the back and jumped on myself. She hardly grunted in discomfort. I suppose she must have still been coming down from whatever high her debased 'nourishment' brought her.

"Are you about to turn all kinds of mad, ravish me and devour my life essence through your demonic vagina as we are set upon by the collective wrath of a madwoman and her pet rock?"

She mumbled something in response.

"No? Good, we ride!"

I shook the wrinkled beasts into action, and drove the cart in the direction I was mostly certain was North. I kept my eyes straight ahead, as focused as I could manage on driving us to the portal back home. The cacophony of hooves drowned out all outside sounds.

"Lascivus, are we being followed?" I nudged her with my elbow, careful not to send some errant signal down the reins. I didn't actually know how to drive a cart, but I didn't seem to have ploughed us into a ravine just yet.

"Yes?" Lascivus answered groggily.

"Is it the abominable detritus thing?

"Yeah. It's the ugly rock."

"Fast for someone with cement shoes. How the bloody blazes is he keeping up?"

"'Unno stuff?"

"Revealing. How are you feeling?"

"Thirsty."

"There'll be plenty to drink in hell. Let me also state how hard it is to talk literally to you without sounding pointlessly morbid. Has anyone told you that?"

"Maybe, dunno?"

"Forget it. Is it gaining on us?"

"Nah, but not losing it either. Have to stop to get in the place with the thingy."

"Are you always this useless after a meal?"

"Never realize how thirsty, uhh, sip?" She trailed off. I swallowed my salivation and grit my teeth. My whole body felt depleted of every resource it had to offer. I'd worked myself to exhaustion many times before, but had never felt it as bad as this. I'd never properly recognized how much I relied on magick to keep me going beyond my limits. Underneath the ban, after a night in a dungeon and hefty donation to a succubus, my muscles just might unwind from my bones as I unknitted at the conceptual level. I could only assume our dogged pursuer remained relentless for I dared not turn around for fear of crashing or overturning the cart. I could only drive.

***

After four hours of restless journey, I spotted a familiar building coming up alongside us from behind a hill—the temple that held the portal. Had I erred much more on my path I might have overshot it without realizing. I turned the ragged-run beasts toward the building, and roused Lascivus awake.

"Come on, you've had your siesta. All things aside *I* can't open the way to Hell once we go through here. Wake *up*, you infernal woman." Her eyes fluttered open, red rings on a sea of black.

"I, wait, right!" She pinched her cheek with her clawed fingers and shook her head.

"No time to park. I'm going to use the stubborn entrance."

"The what?"

The beasts cried out in horror, but they'd been too well broken to refuse and I drove the cart right into one of the temple's long stained-glass windows. Brightly colored shards rained down around us. Warm blood tickled my skin.

I heaved myself up from the wreckage. The two beasts lay mangled beneath it, one spread out like a butcher's dinner by the overturned cart, the other cut open by broken glass, and both with their snouts crushed by the initial impact.

I helped Lascivus up, and turned a wary eye from the guards quickly surrounding us to the rippling portal on the dais. Right when I was about to make a break for the ethereal egress, one of them let out a scream.

"The Nemesian!" His cry was met by an uproar of horror, and they all fled into the temple rear. There was a loud sound of stone striking stone behind me, and I turned around.

The granite monstrosity clambered up the temple stairs, looked upon me with black, empty eyes and saw me. It saw me. *It. Saw. Me.*

"Lascivus, go through the portal. Do what you need to, send us to hell. I'll keep him busy on this side as long as I can."

"Don't even—"

"Do it, she-devil. I'm not going to explain to Old Scratch why I left his flesh and blood behind to save my own sorry ass. Go!"

A tremor undulated through the thing—what the guard called a 'Nemesian'. Lascivus steadied herself, and leapt through the portal. I put myself between my foe and my escape and it matched my movements perfectly. Our eyes didn't break mutual stare.

Its surface shuddered, and its chest split open. It was shedding, no, folding—Unfolding into itself like a rotating tesseract. Over and over again it turned, and from that stony form a shining figure emerged. Maybe the magick ban was weaker this close to the portal.

A gold-clad foot slammed into the ground. So much gold, blond hair that's blown by the wind from the coast, gold eyes that gleamed with determination, plates of gold armor encased its whole body, save the head. It seemed puzzled for a moment, and then its face broke into wide, white-filled smile.

Its face, my face, the face that was mine that this specter wore on its head. What was this thing? It laughed, and it was my voice I heard, but clearer than I'd ever heard it before. What was it? What was it? What was it? It was marvelous, but what was it?

It broke into a sprint and threw a gauntlet-clad fist at me. I staggered out of the way, and fell into sitting on a step. It threw another, which I caught, and I drove my knee into its gut as I rose. It pushed back, but I was sure my knee came off worse for it than its armor.

"I ask of you, are you he that is my executioner?" I called out.

"You yourself said it." The Nemesian replied. He stepped back in, and clubbed my jaw. My vision blurred, but I managed to move my leg before his armored foot could break my knee. He hammered me in the chest, making me wheeze out air. I gasped and managed to belt him in the neck. He faltered, and I head-butted him in the nose before stepping back to take a deep another breath.

Bright red blood trickled down his face and over his lips, but he didn't seem perturbed. He charged at me, and slammed me into a pillar. I gagged on bile. He started pummeling my ribs and bile soon turned to blood. I waited for a chance, wrapped my arms around him and threw all my weight sideways. We fell to the ground, and he hit first, both cushioning my fall and suffering worse for his armor. I adjusted my hold on him, and heaved as I rose, driving him into the ground behind me in an arc.

I staggered back, panting. It hurt to breath and I tasted more blood in my mouth. I'd have vomited if I hadn't been back in the cell. How much time had it been?

He stood up, a bruise blossoming around his neck and a bad cut leaking 'round his crown where he'd landed on a step edge.

"Before we continue, what is your name?" I wiped the stomach acid from my mouth. He seemed taken aback. I wonder if he'd ever been asked that before.

"I am . . ." He searched for the words, brow creased, and found them. "I am Eltanim." He still seemed troubled despite saying it. Good.

I ran straight past him and jumped into the portal while he was distracted. It was like surfacing through water into more water, and

I stumbled as I landed. This side of the portal was in some cave in Greenland, unguarded and inhospitable. My body shivered from the sudden temperature change and my lungs burned at the different air, but more importantly, that stone blanket surrounding me was lifted. My left arm burst into flame, and I regained the awareness of my beloved blade.

Lascivus stood a short distance away, powering up the gate to hell she'd drawn on the ground. She looked up at me in alarm. I drew Drakkengard and flashed my handler an assuring grin.

"He's fighting dirty. I needed an edge. Make sure that thing closes behind us when we're through. How long?"

"Six, maybe seven more minutes, you stupid idiot, couldn't you hold it just a bit longer?" The prep time always goes much quicker when you're not in a hurry.

"I'm afraid not. Look sharp, here he is." The portal rippled as Eltanin stepped through. He looked a mite annoyed.

"That was rude, Draco." He had a sword in his left hand, a white blade with luminous gold script down its length, a physical match for Drakkengard.

"Don't you have any original tricks?" I pointed a flaming finger at him.

"Yes, as it so happens I do." A crackle resounded throughout the cave, and his right arm was wreathed in a shroud of raucous electricity. It sporadically arced to lash out at his surroundings. Getting close could be a bit painful.

"Alright, I'll give you that." I licked my lip, tasting blood and bile. I hurled a lance of fire at him and charged. The cavern ground was hard through my worn-out shoes, and the only warmth came from my own flame. He deflected the fire with his sword and smoothly brought it back up to parry my blade. I bombarded him as fast as I could, trying to keep him on the defensive. The sound of our swords scraping together sounded like children's laughter, and our faces looked alien in the glow of fire and lightning.

I tried not to slow. I tried not to fall into a pattern for him to predict, but I couldn't seem to attack hard enough or fast enough to put him out.

I reeled backward, and sent a deluge of fire at him. He burst through, skin blistering, and plunged his sword down. I threw myself out the way, but the tip of his sword still gouged my side. One of my broken ribs jutted out the wound at a bad angle.

"Time?"

"One thirteen, for sure."

"Keep it up."

Nothing to it. I forced my numb arm to grab hold of the rib, and tore it out with a scream. With the extrusion gone, the wound started healing, and I tossed the one-point-three inches of rib to Lascivus—maybe she could reattach it later or something. I brought up my sword and blocked Eltanin's attack. Sixty-six seconds to go.

I poured fire over his chest. He sent lightning down my spine. I stabbed him in the shoulder. He sliced down my back. Blood and burns stained the cavern floor with every mutilation that passed. Back and forth we matched wound for wound. He was made in my image. I cleaved the armor clear off his chest, and could hear his heart beat in time with mine. Circular logic that kept spinning. A drop of condensation containing a speck of dust fell from the cavern ceiling and landed between us. I didn't hear it, but I knew what sound it made. Vibrations continued to make the ticks that counted down. Thirteen seconds to go. I couldn't feel my leg, but it still seemed to be obedient. I struck four times at his exposed chest, and was deflected each time. He sent lightning through my chest and I couldn't breathe, briefly. Six seconds left. My fire was flickering hotter and hotter, starting to turn white. The cavern was filling with steam and the sound of sizzling. The tattered remains of my clothes were burning off. I lunged for his chest, but a well-aimed spark spoiled my aim and I staggered past him. I whirled around with a blind swing that he turned aside with the flat of his blade. I rolled out of the way before losing my head upon the rocks.

Time!

I hurled my fire beneath his feet and ran. The ground exploded from expansion as he leapt out of the way while I headed toward the flickering gate. Lascivus had already gone through. My shoes were nothing but tatters, and the sharp rocks sliced up my feet. Eltanin pursued. Lightning struck my thigh and I faltered but did not stumble. I reached the edge of the gate's circle.

My breath escaped me.

The blade of his sword stuck out through my chest.

I recognize a bit of meat on it as coming from the heart.

He pulled out his blade, and I fell as if I've met gravity for the first time.

I fell forward. Into the gate.

It lit up.

The blood that gushed from my chest was accepted by the gate's security protocols. I wheezed in hollow laughter through a punctured lung.

And vanished.

Chapter Eleven

Treachery

Dreams, damned, dirty, restless dreams of rust and sulphur. Boggarts stealth into my sleep and rob the night's cradle. Pillars of salt laugh with abandon at this moon-rabbit's folly. A man who sold his true name to rise above the rank and file, still kneels before king, queen and ace.

I was lying on leather, fine quality leather, and the couch also smelled faintly of mahogany and varnish. Someone had draped soft cloth over me. I gently ached with the solace known only to the living. Time as good as any to awaken. I opened my eyes and sat up.

I didn't recognize the room, with its queer paintings and Egyptian, no, Arabic style rug. A tall bronze urn filled with white and red desert flowers sat at the end of the couch. I checked myself—bandages bound my arms, torso, gut and legs, and over that someone had placed on me some sort of toga, a rich red color with a silver clasp. Drakkengard had been placed at the foot of the couch. I picked her up by the hilt and felt her—she was awake, but resting. Whenever I returned to London I really should buy a fine nice sheathe for her.

I sat with Drakkengard across my knees for a while with my eyes closed, clearing my head of the damp from deep sleep. No one came to disturb me, a little favor or just happy happenstance. When I was better equipped to wrestle reality, I'd investigated this room further.

It had no door to speak of, a seemingly sealed off rectangular room. It was lit up by a quartet of candelabra spaced unevenly, which gave the objects strange shadows. In one corner was a desk, with a few yellowed papers and a fountain pen lying next to a dark bottle of ink that seemed somehow suited to the room's other artifacts. Across from the desk was a modestly populated bookcase, and beside it a closed piano-type object.

Struck as though by a sinister spell, I rose and approached the peculiar piano. I clutched Drakkengard tightly in my right hand, and reached out, trembling, to lift the instrument's lid. Eighty-eight ivory keys stared up at me without a hint of dust *and then there was—*

"Do you play?"

My hand seized up, the lid slipped from my grasp and slammed shut. The unseen strings rattled a discord of angry protest.

"No." I steeled my nerves and turned to the Devil. It was easy to see him for how he *appeared*, intruding at the edge of my sight. He brushed a curl of strawberry blond hair aside and straightened the tie of his red tuxedo. I felt he was mocking me.

"Hello, Draco."

"Hello, Luci." His lip curled in a peculiar smile, and he rubbed his smooth chin thoughtfully.

"What do you think? A nice, comfortable living space, a life often abroad, ample promotion opportunities, and your companion will also be well accounted for. You can live on your own too whenever you want out." He spread his lips into a perfect, flawless-toothed smile, I could almost smell the used car he was trying to sell me. He had to be mocking me, but why? Had he already given up, and now just wanted to play it up when I turned him down? Was he trying to make me second-guess his motivations? I honestly couldn't tell if either of us benefitted from such subservience.

"Wait, why am I being asked now? Didn't I botch the last job?"

"No, what makes you say that?" He cleared his throat "The party of the first part is to deliver to the party of the second part communications entailing the party of the second part's outstanding unpaid debit to the party of the third part. Istalla got the message. She attempted to shoot the messenger—which has incurred further penalties against her—but that doesn't concern your case in the slightest. So here you have it, you can join me, and reap all the benefits from such employment as I can offer, or you can be returned to your stolen house on London's edge, to a life of petty crime and ignominy."

"Of freedom and independence." I leaned on Drakkengard with both hands. "You're being absurdly transparent in your manipulation, and I can't understand why."

"I could explain everything to you in perfectly honest facts that would leave little doubt as to what your best option is, but it would be your choice by letter, not by spirit. Only in uncertainty can good judgement be measured."

I turned to one of the pictures— it depicted a brazen bull over a flame, and a crown gathered around it. I recognized the design— the Sicilian Bull.

"Well my answer is--" I spun around, but where Lucifer had stood was now a woman, tall with dark hair and dark bronze complexion. Beads and feathers adorned her hair and neck, and she was clad in a black evening gown.

"So you're the boy that's been fooling around with my daughter." She laughed. "Sorry for the rudeness. My mate had to step out for something urgent that came up. I'll be your host until he gets back. You may call me Lilith."

"Draco. Charmed, I'm sure," I said dryly. Now the bastard was just screwing with me. "Well you can tell your husband—"

"Tut, hush. I'm not here to talk shop. My darling has a weird way of ruling, being from near up high, all rules and regulations. I'm not going to intrude on that. I'm just here to entertain you." She stepped over to a wall with long, graceful steps, and placed her hand against it. Her nails were long and sharp, and she held her fingers crooked like talons. I was fairly certain sure she was the one here to be entertained.

"So how do you find our comfy little home?" The entire wall split apart, exposing the outside world. The hellscape stretched out before us—the maze-like stone alleys of the bolgias, the outer districts of Dis and the wastelands outside it. We were in that floating castle of frost at hell's heart, Pandemonium.

"Remarkably as described by the prophet Alighieri."

"And he found it awfully similar to Virgil's description, who cried at the sight of shades wandering around the furthest ring as described by Homer. Of course, I only met the self-conscious Italian myself. He had the most charming fixation with trinities, and was so sweet when filled with pity. I'm glad his organization included his little books in their VIP list, even if it did take over two thousand years."

"And where is he now?"

"Killed in the last war, of course he'd gotten a different name, Zerachiel.

"The last war?"

"Nothing worth remembering. How are your wounds?" She placed her hand against my chest and gave it a gentle push. She smelled of spice and incense. Her touch was oddly cool, but I still had to suppress a twinge of pain.

"Still tender. I guess this body of mine isn't as hardy as it could be. How long was I out for?"

"Just a few weeks, but you keep pushing that flesh and it'll break on you, no matter how gluttonous your ancestors were. You and those like you are just a pale imitation of the true deathless, and don't let me catch you forgetting it. You'd be full dead by now if we hadn't saved you, and it was a hard job at that since my daughter insisted we didn't just pump you with miasma till your image can take over. We even could have just let you die and bring you back, but there's no telling if you'll come back right or want to come back at all so she rejected that, too. She always was a sentimental thing. Gets that from her father."

"Quite frankly, you make death sound only mildly inconvenient." I thought back to what Lascivus said about the guard I'd killed.

"Oh, death is nothing but inconvenient for people with real ambition, but there's still plenty you can never come back from, and plenty more much worse than death, let me tell you."

"Well, I'll endeavor not to die or worse any time soon."

"Soon to me means anything less than a thousand years, so I'll hold you to that. Oh yes, my daughter wanted to see you when you woke up."

"Shouldn't I finish my discussion with your husband first?"

"Oh, hush, there's no harm in it. If you end up leaving that'll just be an impolite 'no'. Which reminds me." She looked up and again black feathers were crawling from her eyes. "You thrice refused the morning star, five times refused the seven thunders. The beast of the field of Eden you shall set loose, and your own breath will burn you. You shall lose your face in the abyss and kneel before the little horn. You shall become as ought, shall be owed everything and receive nothing. Now, ta-ta."

She didn't gesture or anything. I simply suddenly found myself transported.

***

I stood in the hallway of some nondescript building, the stone masonry told me it was in one of the bolgia, but I couldn't tell which. There was a door in front of me, slightly ajar. An invitation? Carelessness? Or a set up?

I stepped into the room. There she was, facing away from me. Her skin was lit up by the flickering candles. She was back in her human guise. Was it uncomfortable? She turned to me and I saw the marks on her belly, thick pigmented paste smeared in the shape of a sigil. It was a divination rite.

"A child," she said. A positive where there might be a negative. An affirmation of a presence rather than an absence.

What was behind her blithe face, betwixt the cracks in her façade? The corner of her mouth curved upwards. Her eyes were slick with a faint glisten. Her brow had the faintest of creases. What did it mean? How long had it been? My left arm ached.

"Trust me to get knocked up." She gave an odd laugh and reached for an opened bottle of golden liquid. I could smell it from here—liquor. Alcohol. *Poison. Poison in her body, in the body in her body. Her child. The child she was the mother of. That I was the father of. Child trapped in bars of flesh and doused in venom. The dark-haired mother sneered and crooked her finger against the door. The feeding begins and never stops both are fed and fed upon and the food is killed so both can feed, but not fast enough and a slight becomes a mark that becomes a scar that becomes Atrocious wyrm devours and is devoured by the abomination forever in that cage in the dark forever. Again and again and again spiral forever downwards. Where is I that is I today ends and I that is I tomorrow begins. A loosening, a dislodgement of faculties from the real to the thousand-fold paths of emerald grove forever minus one. Superimposition of the break meat beaker on the Chrono-incubator in the private foyer. Write the script, let's go.*

I struck the bottle from her lips. It broke upon the wall and spilled over the plain carpet, another stain. I clutched her skull and stared into her eyes. Her hands were claws but she did not move yet. The language I forgot emerged and bid to be spoken. It all came tumbling out faster than I could think, faster than I could stop myself.

"You called Lascivus and Lilim will never bring harm upon those of your flesh and blood, no injury nor poison nor neglect. I curse you to forever carry the burden held in the name of Family!" I didn't know what I said until it reached my ears. The words branded her at the conceptual level.

She changed from what she was moments ago. She wrenched herself free of me and flees the room.

My left arm contorted. None of that should have happened. What unspeakable reflex provoked such an outburst? At that moment there was little I wouldn't give up to be rid of my deranged impulsiveness as of ten minutes ago. No, further, or outside. Just gone. Make me gone. Now and forever. Too soon for so close, there was always going to be bad blood now. Kings of slaves, slave of kings, slay me.

SECOND MOVEMENT

Adagio

Chapter Twelve

Servitude

Draco

Hospitality is an important thing. A good host accommodates their guests, indulges them and pardons their minor trespasses. A good guest, in turn, is not greedy with the host, does not ask for seconds where not offered, does not intentionally trespass the host's boundaries and does not go against the host's declared laws.

I've rarely hosted, but I am a bad guest. I had lain with my host's own—though I don't think that offended him. I put my seed in her—though the circumstances were extenuating. In a fit of lunacy, I cursed her to carry it always—though I was besotted by my madness. Someone who wasn't a madman might have just suggested a morning-after solution, but that man is not me. I am mad. Perhaps not an illness of the mind, but an illness of the heart, or an illness of the self-allocated personae so to *sprach*. I am what I am, and I abused what I am according to the tenants of what I am. Do you the devils work? Not even, for what I have done is below even that.

The flesh and blood of the fallen angel had fled into hiding. Why did she do that? What was she running from? What was out there that she couldn't find in the world within the world? Surely I am but a bumpkin, and my halfwit curse could be easily dispelled. No, that is the prayer of a coward who wishes his actions to have no consequences. I am as I am, and I am as I have chosen to be.

Lucifer does not care for those questions. Or those answers. As Lilith smiled from beside his throne, he demanded the answer of where his daughter was, whence she had gone. My crime was harming the Adversary's spawn, branding her with a cursed name. My punishment was to find where she went and with this edict, I was cast from the bowels of hell and stranded back in the world. On the precipice of freedom, I was instead on indentured parole, or just more indentured servitude.

I awoke on the streets of London, in bandages and tattered clothes and with my sword on my back, a blessing on my tongue and a curse in my chest. The curse branded me as a criminal in accordance with underworld law, visible for all to see. Should I stray from my punishment it would reprimand my mind and body, with impunity—Thus *sprach* Lucifer.

The first night I thought to lazily spend the rest of my life half-heartedly looking about for she I'd wronged, and went to sleep in a nice, quiet alleyway. When I awoke, at some ungodly hour in the night I swore the torment had already killed me and I was nothing but a disembodied phenomenon of agony.

The message was clear enough—no rest for the wicked. Therefore, I'd little choice but to search in earnest, and search I did for nine months and some. For the first month, I didn't sleep for fear of the brand's lash. I quickly exhausted the avenues of inquiry the decrepit Londinium metropolis offered, so I took my search elsewhere.

When I slept for the first time on the first trip across the channel, I dreamt. Those were not the malignant dreams that had beset me in the past, and for that I was grateful. Rather I dreamt of how she had looked at me when I cursed her in that forgotten tongue. I dreamt of the cell we shared, and I dreamt of the golden man that would someday kill me. The latter was oddly comforting, in its own way. The former, well, it was real, as twisted a solace that was. It was real and not some phantom twisted by symbols.

I landed in France on a boat whose name was QK and cut a path straight to Paris. There I dodged the eyes of the redoubled police state, not as cleanly as I'd have liked, and somehow got implicated with an organ trafficker. After selling half my liver for a tip off, I crept through the skull-laden crypts of the city to break in and steal an original copy of the Key of Solomon. The hope was it might contain one of Lascivus' names and a way to summon her. It was only after acquiring it that it occurred to me I only knew two of her names, Lascivus and Lilim, and neither seemed to be in the book. This might have been obvious were I actually a student of language rather than having gotten the gift of tongues at a bargain bin price. What a colossal waste of time.

Having used up my welcome in Paris, I pawned the book and used the funds to set off into Germany. In Berlin I tracked down a self-styled soothsayer that dressed in fox-skins, cut to mimic the latest fashions, who agreed to give me the secret of learning a being's other names if I spoke of fire. Just talked, not answer questions or solve puzzles, nothing more than how I saw it. I agreed to this and told him, despite my misgivings.

"In the first, fire is as movement. Fire is from heat, and heat is the fast movement of the particles from which all things are made. In the second, fire is entropy. Fire accelerates the expulsion of the energy within an object, lets loose that energy as radiation, and destroys the object in the process of depriving it. In the third, fire is irreversible. That which has been burned can never become unburned, that which is consumed in flame is lost forever.

You cannot hold fire, but you can cling to that which it is destroying, and through clinging, wield it. A strong enough fire can turn water to steam, and rock to water, and it is nothing that conquers fire, the empty nothing created by a terrible wind or unforgiving vacuum that starves the fire. Against such nothing, it is helpless but to be extinguished.

Fire is not eternal, but if fed enough can burn for aeons. Through burning an object you can learn some of the nature of the object, thus through fire one can gain truth."

"You who burn," he asked, "What is it that you burn?"

"Magick, that dark energy which permeates the universe. Ah, no, that's not quite right. Oxygenated hydrogen is different from water. I suppose, then, I burn myself. Thinking in terms of…"

He stopped me there, thanked me and gave me two silver rings.

"Quite the rarity," the soothsayer declared, "and any demon would willingly exchange a name known to them for one. Maybe not their own, but one they do know. Furthermore, the name you seek was of course not contained in the Key of Solomon. That archive was penned before she was born." As we parted, he bid I travel south, so south I went.

I journeyed to the industrial towers of Czech's Prague, where I stole a ride in a frigate of GMO fruit heading my way. For six days and seven nights, Drakkengard and I fed on designer tangerines, and before dawn of a seventh day, I slipped out on the outskirts of the irradiated ruins of Austria's Vienna, untouched since the fall of the final bomb. It was like a beautiful vision of the end of the world not yet come—gorgeous masterwork architecture dusted with ash and soot, kissed by atomic Vesuvius and frozen in place, another nuclear Pompeii.

From Vienna I trekked still further southward, through weepy forests and frost-touched prairies beneath a black-clouded sky. After a thirteen-hour hike, I found an abandoned car in a ditch—a stylish red convertible with a nice retro chassis and a tank full of hydro. Its owner was slumped over the dashboard, neck snapped, bloated with putrefaction, reduced to carrion by the wildlife.

I tossed out the body, not before claiming his wallet and money, as well as the death-stanched seat, which I replace with the passenger side chair. Drakkengard uncovered in the backseat two untouched cases of scotch and a third half empty. In such circumstance, we drove down to gallant Italy, Drakkengard draped her arms around my neck from behind and each of me drank heartily of the ill-gotten liquor. In such circumstance, we drove all the way down to Rome.

***

How long had it been? Twelve months perhaps? Time just slurred over the days and nights, worthless pesos and centavos. Unless we were told the reference-body to which the statement of time refers, there was no meaning in a statement of the time of an event. That reference-less Void lurked behind every detail and stole them from the frame. Not just on this highway but everywhere we went. I didn't need the sun to grope through Stonehenge or for Mercury Venus and Saturn to stand above Giza. Just for some not-same to take the clouds from the edges. Yet any given thing I do becomes the new same, any not-same becomes same if it lingers. If each tick of the clock doesn't sound different, it measures not time but stasis.

Too hot, too cold, or just right we reached the never-closed gates of Rome that waited at the end of every road. Drunk and with Drakkengard's fingers splayed around my neck, I drove our stolen car through the streets of Rome while I remembered what I'd planned on doing here. The dipping sun painted the streets orange and pink beneath the clouds. The drink left the world on a tilting axis, like the horizon balanced on a pencil. I trusted my body to tour us along at a bit faster than walking pace. Not many people here bothered to sink money into a car when one of something of whatever you needed was always nearby, more or less, so whatever you wanted you could usually walk to without going across town. Banks, food, employment, a place to forget or a place to die merrily. A car was typically a luxury for those with money to burn maintaining a supply of hydro. Mayhap that dead man was a banker, he who I took the vehicle from.

"Hey, Master, we could get some pork." Drakkengard shook my shoulders. Her voice came out an octave lower than normal, thanks to the alcohol. Her suggestion was as absolute as an eloquent equation even an idiot can grasp. Ahead I spied an open café that declared itself Giorgio's & something, something marred by graffiti. I drove the car up an alley and despite my best drunken efforts brutally butchered two garbage cans while parking. I slipped the ignition ring onto my finger, which won't stop someone stealing the car, but I wasn't about to make it easier for them. If they wanted to steal from me, they had better be prepared to go the full stretch.

Drakkengard seemed to be hit by the scotch harder than I—which was odd considering her liquid metal physiology—so I lifted her out the car. She happily hummed something. Hang on, I knew that tune. *Copelia's Casket*, that was it. We banked right, and headed into Giorgio's Graffiti. The establishment had red curtains, striped walls, and was rally rather charming in a barbershop sort of way. The waiter had dark, bushy eyebrows, a precise little moustache and a rather tired smile, no doubt looking forward to going home once all these idiot customers such as us moved on.

"Hi, hello, welcome" He said in Italian, and the charm on my tongue did its work. He held out some menus, but I pushed them back.

"We don't need that. Two pork sandwiches, and", I considered for a moment " two root beer floats" His fake smile actually managed to reach his eyes for a moment, good on him.

"Right, good, excellent, straight away sir and miss." He nodded and disappeared into the kitchen. The sound of sizzling meat soon followed.

For a while, we listened to the meal cook and watched the passers-by through the curtained window. The clothing seemed more innocent here than in London, with simpler clothes not personalized with accessories and modifications, and even the breast exposing tops carried an air of casual carelessness rather than indecency. I wondered if it was a regional thing, or just this one part of the suburb that carried itself like this.

The waiter came out with the food and drink. The meat was soft and sweet, coated in oily apple gravy that soaked into the bread, but not too far through. I forced myself to eat it slowly, unsatisfying though it is, and I was not sure why. My mind turned to the starving succubus. Why didn't she dine more often? I knew my own reasons for keeping the flesh dry, but what were hers? The root beer was cold and cathartic against my drunken thirst, though by all accounts I should have just gotten water to sober up.

Why were we here again? We finished our meal quietly and contently and once finished we rose. Over to the counter I paid the man with interest. No, what's the word? Tip? Many parts of Europe still clung to physical money, Italy among them. I placed a crumpled note into his hand and his nostrils flared like a boar's as he noticed the distinctive smell of death on the money I took from the dead driver. He looked at me as if I were a changeling before him, and his face twisted into alarm and anger. I nodded to him, and exited his café. Drakkengard waved and followed. No idea what that was about.

Oh good, the car wasn't stolen. I pressed the ignition ring back into the side of the wheel and started the car. Once back on the street, I caught sight of myself in the mirror, and stared at what the waiter saw. My hair was a matted mess that hung about my shoulders, my face was caked with dirt and dust that almost looked like a tan, except for where sweat had smeared it to show the pallid skin beneath. My queer, red eyes were fixed in an unblinking stare and carried heavy bags beneath them. Behind me sat a girl in strange, not quite religious black robes, with keen hazel eyes. I forced myself to blink, and rubbed some of the dirt from my face on my sleeve. I needed new clothes, and I needed a bath and a place to stay.

As befitting the driver of such a hard to come by car, there was still plenty of the local currency in his wallet. Clothes were easy enough to come by, a quick stop by the first store that caught my gaze supplied me well enough. I came out in a loose fitting red shirt, dark slacks and matching jacket, with some tinted lenses to draw attention away from my eyes. Hospice, conversely, was much harder to come by, and after a number of curt synonyms for 'no vacancy' over a pay phone later, I finally gave in and checked myself into a room at the local bottom dollar inn.

Oh, it was an awful place, eighty flights high of nothing but stairs and rooms. The plaster and rot was so bad you were staring at the tin lattice in places, but it only cost twenty a night and I could ignore the way the pockmarked receptionist leered at the request for a single. He slicked back his fry-oil hair and handed over two keycards. The room we got was thirteen-B and it took a lot of mold-reek stairs to get there. I'd broken out a sweat by the time we reached the floor and stepped out into the hall.

Chapter Thirteen

Minions

Ko

He was wet with sweat when he stepped out the double doors, and the pictures in my eye compared his face to the picture we'd given and it came up match. Facial recognition was one of the many perks offered by the computer grafted to my brain—when it wasn't malfunctioning or trying to kill me for treason mind you.

"Doc," I butted the guy beside me with my elbow. "Target's arrived." The weird Doctor straightened his glasses and finally stopped fidgeting. The old guy was too impatient for his own good. Our man stopped when he saw us in front of his room. His face still looked kinda boyish, and his eyes were hidden behind some shades. A psych report popped up. The man that covers his eyes is telling all the world he's afraid they'll know not to trust him. That or he's blind and star sensitive. One of the two.

His hand twitched and told the moment he recognized us. I should play a bit of the local façade with this guy if I get the chance.

"Don't go gutting us yet, you mad coot." I pushed back my jacket to show my empty chest and held up my bare hands. I felt naked without my bandoliers but it couldn't be helped. The whip-cracker bot bleeped and whined about possible hostiles detected.

"You, the both of you, the previous time I saw either of you was when I put you down to Hell." He loosened his hand a bit, but he was still thinking of going for his walking sword. That was in the briefing, some relic he has from a dead place deemed unimportant.

"And we're not here on a back-hit. You were just doing the line, and now we alls contracted together under the same big man. Tell 'em, Doc"

"Negations have been reached, and services bartered. We're all paying our due. Inconvenient as it is." He declared in that bookish tone of a clerk on his first dispatch.

"The big man downstairs needs that AWOL ASAP, and we're here to give you some little more push-pull"

"Well this is just delightful." They guy ran his fingers through his hair as if he was combing out a bad thought. He got the crooked sort of grin a guy miffed at being laughed at might have. "I have minions."

"Excuse me, *sir*, but we are merely subcontracted." The doc stuffed his hands in his pockets and I couldn't remember what he kept in which. The dumb brain-bot picked up on the thought and whined out a reference from earlier. Pills in the left, cutters in the right, an ache in my skull for the effort.

"Please, join me in by hovel. We've a bit to discuss." He brushed straight past us, swiped his card and went into his room. It was a tiny thing, one bed, one shoebox of a shower stall pumping recyc', and a low table made of cheap plastic with some cards on it. The floor was covered in a sticky, bleached carpet, and the whole thing stank of electrocuted owls, all crispy and soggy at the same time. Draco sat down at the table, while his girl plonked down next to him and picked up the deck of cards. That seemed to be the way it is so I sat down too, and Doc did the same.

"A proper reintroduction, to re-establish rusty remembrances— This is Drakkengard, I am Draco." The girl, Drakkengard, she started shuffling the cards she had, with a smile like a fixer peddling a bum car. She looked like she might still be a kid, but looking isn't good enough, and the way she's sizing me up says she'll happily cut me. My quasi-displaced neck'd be fine, but the Doctor wouldn't fare so lightly.

"Ko." I broke the silence since everyone was looking at me. "That's m'name. Just 'Ko.'"

"Vengai-Ra. Is this *really* necessary?" Doc rolled his eyes.

"Necessary? What is necessary? Necessary is that which is necessitated, and since none of us are Narcissus, necessary is other people. This task has been arbitrated to necessitate a group effort, which needs knowing the other, for now at least. Nice?" The girl threw down a jack of hearts and went back to shuffling.

"Don't just blather on around the bush you deranged idiot, and get to the point." Doc slapped the table, and the girl replied with a four of spades. Draco didn't even blink at the outburst. He leaned forward, and I could smell the grog on his breath. The brainbot pinned his BAC at intoxicated levels, going by the smell of his breath mist.

"Then here's the word, which was given to me by an old codger in a weird suit, there's some clue to Lascivus' location somewhere in this city. That's the word, and all we have is the word. If we had two words we could cross them in a paper, and if we had three that's enough for a sentence. If we had a sentence it'd mean there's a judge afoot and I'm not yet prepared to tussle with a lucky judge's foot." The girl punctuated the end of his rant with a king of clubs and kept right on shuffling. If the cards were planted here beforehand and had been rigged to release knockout gas, the next card would be the trigger.

"This city?"

"No, not Dis, Rome. Or somewhere even further south of Rome but I feel a good portent that Rome is the place. That portent may be that I don't feel like swimming, but it's an omen just the same." I kept one eyeball fixed on the cards swapping places in the girl's hands. Shuffle. Shuffle. Shuffle.

"So what the deuce are we supposed to do?" Doc demanded. Draco looked at him as if he'd asked where babies come from, and why he has this not so fresh feeling.

"The obvious, squires. Get a map of this god-faced city and go on a tavern pilgrimage from now until the sun turns something up." The girl slammed down the ace of diamonds with a bang.

I hurled the table against the back wall where it crashed against the ground. Potent toxic nerve gas continued to flood into the room.

"Sorry. Reflex. Don't mind me." I excused myself and stepped outside.

Chapter Fourteen

Bar hop

Vengai-Ra

We left that miserable hotel with an awkward cloud above us. It occurred to me not for the first time that I may get worse than killed by one of these hooligans before I paid off my infernal student loans. Such is the price paid for knowledge, I suppose. No, that's stupid. I didn't give up so much just to be offed by gross professional negligence. That was a small comfort as I hopped into a car with an inebriated outlaw, some cultist-looking girl and a half naked long-haired man with a post-traumatic look in his eyes.

"Wait up, boss. With that missing chair we can't all fit in the car." The soldier Ko complained.

"Just sit on Vengai-Ra's lap." I supposed it was nice that my new superior bothered to remember my name, unlike this blue-haired twit.

"Not going to happen, Draco." I shook my head.

"Fine, you sit on his lap."

"Still not going to happen."

"Land o' mine, why am I never assigned to a squad of good lookin people?" Ko threw his arms up and nearly slapped me in the face.

"Why do *I* never have the privilege of competent co-workers?"

"Doc, you couldn't *make* someone as competent as I am."

"I'll have you know I've made eight."

"Alright, enough squabbling, before I end up putting down another mad-science crime against nature."

"No such thing." I snapped.

"Not the point, Pygmalion. Bah, kids these days"

"You're younger than either of us."

"You don't know that."

"Sorry boss, but we're briefed on you. You're only twenty-one as far as down below can see with their hoodooing."

"Bah to both of you." He picked Drakkengard up by the neck as if she weighed a pillow. She transmuted into a sword and he placed it in the empty space the passenger seat once occupied.

Watching the change was just as disturbing as ever. You never get used to seeing people melt like that.

"Now let's go."

Ko finally got in the damnable vehicle. With a bronchial cough, it revved to life and we headed out into the streets of Rome.

After driving past three perfectly fine-seeming bars, Draco finally picked an out of the way place called 'Free Oh'.

"You sure this isn't some charity brothel or something?" I sized up the garish building.

"Not even slightly." The car gave a pathetic sputter as it stopped, and seemed to sink three inches closer to the ground. We got out, and Draco gave the tire a good kick. His sword became a girl again, this time wearing a tank top and hip-hugging bellbottoms, which were just as attention grabbing as her dubiously religious robes, but for different reasons.

"These modern vehicles are so deplorable. They're practically disposable with how fast they break down. The dealer's should start selling them by the baker's dozen." He didn't actually seem too upset about it.

The bouncer at the door stopped us, and looked us up and down. He was a fat brute of a man, and his fuzzy nostrils flared up at the sight of me.

"You're not comin' in," he said in English. He must have heard us talking as we came in.

"Why not?"

"No shoes, no entry." He jabbed a stubby thumb at my sandals.

Now that was just rude. I should give him the what for. "What rot! The nerve of you. I'm a doctor, you know. Not letting a doctor in on account of his shoes, of all the nerve. I ought to take out your nerves, that'd show you what rot."

"If you threaten me again I get to look forward to subduing you. Come on shorts man, I could do with a laugh."

"Oh you'd like that, wouldn't you? Beat up an innocent doctor on his night off. Who knows how many people might die without my help? Yes, with one easily permissible act of violence you get to feel the rush of a serial killer. Wouldn't that be a fine old thing for you?" I got right up in his face and flashed my teeth, a little reminder he should take better care of his own dental hygiene.

"You're crazy. Get out of here, crazy. All of you. Not coming in." He stepped back on his heel and reached for his sidearm. No telling if it was lethal until he pulled it. Ko looked about ready to commit pre-emptive murder.

Draco gave a loud, disdainful sigh.

"This is my thing, right? If you're both my minions that means I have to be the responsible one at times like these, right?"

"Hey, can you stop calling us minions? It really ain't good for morale."

"I'll listen to your formal complaints when we get the job done. I'll listen to your informal complaints when I'm busy throwing big wads of currency at bartenders in exchange for goods and services. This brings me back to the doorman. Let me see, do you respond better to bribes, violence or curry? No, never mind. Forget the curry. I'll have the curry. What you need is a taste of Ahab."

"What?"

"You eat my leg, and I hunt you down in revenge over the course of many years. I won't spoil the ending for you."

"You're all madmen."

"Doctor, scalpel." Well I wasn't really sure what he was going for, but I guessed he wanted his bluff to have authenticity. I handed him a scalpel from my coat.

He hiked up the leg of his pants and stabbed the back of his leg. A thick tide of blood flowed from the first incision. He gritted his teeth and started sawing away.

"You're pure crazy. All of you. I didn't sign up for this." The greasy man turned tail and fled, his blubberous hide swaying with every stride.

"Here's your scalpel back."

"Why thank you." I took out the de-sanitized blade, replaced it with a fresh one, and placed the scalpel back in my coat. The bleeding on his leg had already stopped, but there was still a conspicuous pool of blood on the sidewalk.

"Right, let's go inside."

The place was too big for its small crowd, and filled with tables for five seating only three people. The dance floor was empty and the music was some upbeat jazz, which suited me just fine. There were people in sweaters and vests and only a minimal amount of face ornaments and everyone seemed downbeat and comfortable rather than looking for a fight. There stood a fellow by the corner in a ginger beret, two lasses by the door in red blue and teal, and a woman by the bar wearing a red scarf and black hat that drew the most attention.

Draco strode as if an old friend to a man in a white and green suit on the far end of the bar. This'd be a lot easier if some due process had been even slightly outlined. In the absence of foresight, I just followed along behind him, as did the others.

Once we got closer, I could see that the suit was scuffed. Maybe these were the only clothes he had? I'd heard of such people lurking the big cities of Earth, people with a single set of fancy clothes that fought a race against time to get a job before they looked too unkempt.

"So I'm looking for this demon, and I have a hunch you're in the way to giving me a clue what for." Draco spelled himself out as if it was the most normal thing in the world. I was born and raised on another planet and even I got that much of Earth was in stubborn denial about the supernatural.

"Everybody's got demons they're running from. Who are you to be chasing after them?" He was actually replying. I was starting to get the feeling Draco could make people less sane with mere proximity.

"Maybe I'm a rare, responsible one, maybe a bigger demon has a noose around my neck, and maybe I'm just crazy and have a death wish. No matter which way, I pin you as the guy with the number I need."

"And why's that?" He talked as if he has a mouth full of gum, and from the way he was squinting I think he might have been a bit blind.

"No reason to it, you just stood out the least. Don't you think that's awfully suspicious?" Draco sat down on the stool beside him, leaving the three of us standing around awkwardly. I decided it would be more efficient if I talked to some other people while he did his thing.

I went over to the barman and ordered a stout beer. His head only just came up above the bar, with his chin parallel to the wood horizon. I swore the little git just overcharged me, but I paid anyway with notes from the devil's meagre allowance. The excuse was economics, but I figured the real reason had more to do with reverse favoritism. This whole thing stank of a barnyard shuffle. If finding his daughter were the important thing, he'd have his best agents on the job. There was a show being put on and we were the saps enlisted to play the part. A doctor, a soldier and a mad swordsman. Did that make the metal girl our animal mascot? Ah well, no room for patience in a devil's deal. A creditor is always in a hurry to get their dues. If things went well, the deal might still have been worth it. *If.*

"So, seen any demons around here lately?" The floating-head barman didn't seem to appreciate my use of Latin rather than modern Italian, but the only other Earth language I knew was English. I had my doubts he spoke Al'Juran so he just had to cope. We can't all have in-built translators, magick, technologic or otherwise.

"Lots of demons. Piles of them in alleys and corners. Some less mess than others." Or so I could make out, since he didn't even have the decency to reply in Latin himself. The nerve of him.

"How about more literal demons? Spooky things. I hear there might be a prostitute around. Wait, that's the wrong word. To lie under, ah, seducer devil? I'm rustier than I thought."

"I haven't seen no spooky whore. Just those freak animals." The beer was strong and warm, and stayed in the nose long after it hit the gastrics. Not bad, I suppose.

"The 'what' now?"

"They wear fur on their sleeves. Stir up trouble. They also look for something. "

"Looking for what?"

"The lamb-child, whatever that is, they want bad enough to keep picking fights over it."

"Know anything else?"

"You don't mind, I have other customers." He grunted, and walked away. Well, that was something I supposed.

A shout went out, followed by a loud thud. That half-naked idiot was sprawled backward over a fallen chair and clutching his hand, which was half-faded and translucent.

"Look at yourself, cowing after a little knife-tap." At the table across from him a tanned woman stood up, and speared a knife into her table. She was a tall, sharp woman with red hair and a prominent drunken sway, too drunk to even notice that she hadn't actually stabbed his hand, so to speak. If anyone else did, they certainly didn't care to mention it.

"Come on, pick yourself up. You wanna go. You'll have a go."

"Clear your head you cloud scraping galumpher. You like this with all that try to be friendly?"

"Jus' the ones pussy-feetin' about the confront'. Come-a-dan, out with you."

"Trash this hash, you feral waster. Who even cares what you can tell me, you're clearly in no sorts to oblige so you can just choke on it." Ko made a two finger and thumb gesture I didn't recognize and I don't think anyone this side of space-time could, but you really don't need to, to get the gist.

The woman picked up a chair while Ko picked up himself. He saw her swinging it at him, and actually seemed to take a moment's consideration before diving out of the way. He skidded away along his back while the plastic chair cracked against the back of someone else's skull.

"Now why did you go and do that, you slag?" The man stood up, a bald, slightly saggy fellow with round glasses and a crinkled suit vest. I looked around for the bouncer, but the only figure that looked to be attached to security was distracted talking to Draco. Typical. I fidgeted with the hem of my coat. I *could* anaesthetize, but Ko's metaphysiology would make it impossible to get him, and I would much rather not waste my limited supplies on every curmudgeon that decided to get involved.

No, forget it. This was not my problem. I straightened my coat and walked outside.

Chapter Fifteen

Basilica

Draco

I was deeply engaged in a simply riveting conversation about the local laundromats' Amazonian sewer rat infestation when Drakkengard handed me a beer.

"What's this?"

"Oh that nice gentleman over there wanted you to have this. They were too shy or something to give it to you in person so they just sort of threw it at you and it almost actually hit your head so it's a good thing I was able to catch it before it hurt you."

"Why thank you." I took the bottle and ruffled her hair. She beamed at me, and fidgeted on the spot. Her current outfit only slightly stood out here which was probably a good thing. People tend to get weird ideas about cults and poisoned soda when they see a young woman in robes travelling with a tall pale fellow. The cries of 'where are my children' could become such a bore after a while.

The beer was warm and tasted like horse piss. I took another sip and looked up to whereabouts it flew in from. Some woman with long hair and a stout, Greek nose had jumped on a bald guy's back and was hitting him over the head with a broken chair leg. For his part, the chap was stabbing her in the thigh with a surprisingly sharp fork. Another woman, with a high widow's peak, was trying to pry her off to little avail. A gentleman in a wife-beater and a ruffian in a smoking jacket had succumbed to fisticuffs for some such reason or another, while Ko crawled out from under a table where three patrons were beating up a fourth against the ground. I took another sip of this appalling beer and wave him over with two fingers.

"I…"

"Tut-tut-tut-tut-tut. He who is conscious of secret and dark designs, which, if known, would blast him, is perpetually shrinking and dodging from public observation, and is afraid of all around him, and much more of all above him." To his credit, Ko did not look up. "Now give it to me strait, stat. Is this your fault?" I waved at the fast escalating brawl behind him. Drakkengard caught the cracked remains of a flying, half-empty shot glass and handed it to me.

Ko took several seconds to ponder the question, his thumbs hooked under his coat.

"All things considered, boss, I don't see hows I am."

"Good enough for me. Come one, come the three of you, let's get out of—" I took pause. "Where *did* the last of our party go?"

"Doc? Not a clue. Maybe he's deep in the midst of it unable to fend for himself."

"Maybe he is." I tapped the lip of my beer bottle against my chin. "But let's look outside first regardless." I ducked the high-speed heel of someone's snapped shoe, turned and headed out the pub's front door, Drakkengard and my minion in tail.

Outside I found Vengai-Ra waiting against the side of the bar. The sounds of escalating violence suffered mufflement by the door closing behind us.

"Right then, minions. Let's compile our learning. What have you got?" I rubbed my hands together in glee.

"A bunch of suspicious idiots in furs looking for a 'little horn' whatever that was. Nothing else."

"Still good. Ko?"

"The women here are packing too much punch for my taste, and knives. Let's hit another bar."

"Terrible, just terrible. In this preliminary evaluation Vengai-Ra wins the number two minion spot."

"And I suppose sharp-face over there is number one?" Ko grumbled, gesturing at Drakkengard. I glanced her over but her soft features would sooner be described as putti than razor, surely.

"Of course not. Are you silly? Drakkengard is not a minion. The number one spot goes to me, naturally. We're all doing the devil's work here."

"Even a foreigner such as I," Vengai-Ra started. "I can still say that is one of those phrases that loses its impact when it is in fact a literal statement of our employment slash servitude situation."

"So does that mean if one of us performs well enough, we can outrank you?" Ko added, brushing his hair back with his hands.

"Oh in theory, of course, but the casting of this coarse course is that first infernal technician can veto any recommendations put forward by second and or third infernal technician, whomsoever that may be at the time."

"Ah well, it was worth a shot."

"So what did you find out then, oh wise and illustrious goon leader?"

"There's crazy gathering at a dead church lately. I'm sick of drinking and simply can't be bothered with any more bar hopping, so let's go there."

"You know where this church place is?"

"Further South. Near the center of everything, but a bit to the right. Place called Of the Snows."

"Is this going to be a long-ass drive?"

"Oh hush, only an hour or so."

Once in the car, grilling my two gorillas on their beef seemed to be the best way to pass the time.

"So, Vengai-Ra, as I understand it your deal was for medical knowledge in exchange for time, yes?"

"Indeed."

"So why'd you try to equivocate the contract? What if, pretend I had the power just bear with me, I simply sucked the knowledge right out of your head rather than drag you wailing and gnashing into compliancy?"

"If you did strip the knowledge straight from my brain, I've enough learning manuals on all the subjects that matter to get back to where I am within a year. I wrote them all myself so I know I've not missed anything."

"Didn't that take ages?"

"Two years of writing every day. It bothered me at first that I wasn't helping people with my newfound knowledge, but securing it was more important."

"Says the man who was experimenting on hapless peasants when I found him, and if those got destroyed as part of rescinding you of your ill-gotten understanding?

"If? You burned all the original drafts yourself. I had copies made, of course. If those get lost, I got a few other, less reliable methods of relearning everything. Other than that, I can only hope

I now possess enough foundation knowledge they can't legally touch that I'll make the same discoveries and reach the same conclusions on my own. It's not foolproof, but it's better than nothing."

"And say it was permanently wiped? Certain facts were just banished from your mind in a way that you could never relearn them again?"

"For something so extensive, why, I wouldn't be me anymore. I might as well have been executed, so what happens after is someone else's problems. I simply need to ensure that never happens if I can help it." He chuffed.

I pulled up right in the front oval before the church, and did a poor job of stopping the car before it collided into a broken spire jutting out of an artificial hill thing, possibly the worst place to put a broken spire.

"So this is the snowy building? Looks pretty dry from here."

"I'm sure 'The Snows' is just a metaphor for orphans or something, or maybe the name of a person it was dedicated to."

"Does it matter? Let's just go inside, realize this is a stupid waste of time, and go back to failing to find out anything useful."

"Come now, Vengai-Ra. A man once said that wise men say 'wait and hope'. Why not give the codger the benefit of the doubt?"

A stiff breeze blew by, carrying with it the scent of dahlias.

"Now be honest with me. What are the odds of this breaking out into some big, messy gang conflict?" Vengai-Ra stepped out of the car.

"Well that depends, are we a gang?"

"More of a posse, I'd say."

"So how does that affect our odds of being in a shootout?" Ko cracked his neck.

"We should spend as little time standing or being Mexican as possible."

"What's *that* supposed to mean?"

"It was a pun you—Oh never mind. It means go inside and try not to make any foolish decisions before I do."

The four of us made our way to the decrepit church's old front door. Past the rusted, bent-open gate was an open foyer of sorts—doors on both side—and went through to a long hall. The place was covered in dust and mold and ash. Something scraped, unseen, against the marble floor. Besides me, Ko pulled a sidearm from his coat.

"Hang on," I whispered to him. "Just where did you pull that from? I saw inside your jacket in the car and it was just your belts."

"Meethree's, uh, little dronids that do things. I've got about a barrel of carbon lining my coat as raw materials."

"Really? Fascinating." I stood up.

"You idiot!"Vengai-Ra hissed.

More scuffling sounds, muted and swift, echoed across the building, flitting out from between the cracked and eaten columns. I walk past them toward the dais at the end of the hall where, on all sides, were the paintings—paintings of kings and angels, a massacre of infants, The Binding of Isaac. I recognized that one.

More scuffling. The walls were solid, so it couldn't be from behind them.

Atop the high altar of the basilica was a broken stand of some kind, amidst the debris of what might once have been beautiful carpet. Maybe they burnt it? Did carpet work as a good source of fuel? Mayhap I should check later, just in case.

Behind the altar stood an open crypt, with stairs leading down it from the hall either side of the altar. I hopped down the meter and a half drop to one of the decaying staircases, and climbed over what was left of the rails to the floor below. In the center of an open part of the crypt sat a broken statue, naught left of it but tresses and a few feet, both man and furniture. Drakkengard dropped down beside me, straight from the altar. A drop of at least three meters, maybe even five. The weathered floor cracked beneath her.

"Oh sure, let's just make all the noise we want after all. That's what you said, right? We lowly minions can imitate whatever stupidities you see fit to make?"

"Vengai-Ra, pipe down and either tell me things I don't know about this place or keep an eye out for Brown Jenkin."

"Who?"

"Just keep wary of the walls. I'd wager something's not right with them."

"Based on?"

"Intuition. Or the other itty thing. Skitty thing? Either way, eyes out."

"Weirdo."

"I'm still your supervisor."

"I thought this was a strictly minion-slightly higher minion relationship?"

"It's a whatnot. Eyes out."

At the other end of the small crypt, beneath the altar was a stone chest of some kind, covered in a moth eaten blanket. What did Lilith say? Kneel before the little-horn.

"I don't suppose Lascivus is in there, do you?" I prodded the blanket and look to Drakkengard.

"Let's cut it open anyway."

"Nothing better to do. Try to aim it so you don't risk whatever's inside.

"Yes, Master."

I stepped back. Drakkengard moved over to the side of the stone container and held out a bladed arm.

"All things considered, I'm surprised this hasn't already been opened."

"Maybe it was, and only recently shut again, but this time with someone new inside?"

"Someone? You seem oddly sure of that Drakkengard."

"Everything's a someone on some level."

"If you say so."

Drakkengard lined up her edged limb and brought it down like a slamming portcullis. Even through the stone and cloth it was a clean cut. She grabbed hold of the slab she'd just sliced off and with a heave sent it crashing to the ground. The noise of stone on tile bellowed through the basilica.

"Okay, now I know you're doing this on purpose."

"It can't be helped," Drakkengard sang. I squatted down, and peered into the container.

"So what have you found?"

"Don't quite know. It seems to be empty."

"You've probably just let out some horrible centuries old bacteria, which, naturally, I'm probably the only person in this party that is actually susceptible to it. It could take months to find a remedy to such a…"

"Hey Doc, if there were any bodies here that would be alerted by loud noises they'd have heard us all an age ago. Get your calm on."

"Oh, hey, there's a thing." I ignored my squabbling minions and reached into the stone chest for the protruding silhouette I spotted.

"Find something?"

"Hang on, I read that book by R. Bruce Hoadly for just such an occasion." I pull the object out into the light and stared at it.

"Yup. It's wood."

A small, carved chunk of it, splintered on either end where it seems to have been broken off something.

"Right." Vengai-Ra declared as I make my way up the stairs, still staring at the wood. "Now how does this help us find our missing girl?"

"Not a clue. I'm just hoping this doesn't get flagged as slacking off by the burner on my chest."

Chapter Sixteen

Cults

Ko

"Hey, who's there?" A voice echoed out from the church entrance. Automated sound localization systems mined the data from my ears and showed me right where it came from, a box at the corner of my vision. Female, three half T's tall. Alarmed, aggressive, not too scared. Armed? Possibly. Sound of footsteps. She was advancing. Not alone. Five? Or two and a horse. If it was armored the horse could be a large threat if not taken out fast enough. Right, cards on the table.

"Stop right there before I turn your half of the shop into a crater." I leveled my sidearm at the middle of where they should be standing. My sight flickered, and the wiring for the extra spectrums fired up with a brain sting. Okay, no horse. Five people were lit up green, all wearing treated leathers and polymers. Draco said the people expected here wore furs. Did leather count as fur? Nah, it fell under hides for sure. They must be some other bunch.

"Alright, hang on to your stupidity, both of you." The Doc talked bold, but I noticed he was staying put.

"We're looking for a demon. Can you help?" Draco hollered, and walked up the stairs with an honest to office swagger. Both his palms were outstretched, empty. Where'd he put that wood he found?

"What do you want with the demon?"

"So there is a demon here, excellent. Thank you for confirming that, good Madame. As for the what we want, why, we just want to make sure that when all's said and done people will say the demon went where it was awaited."

"Wait, are you trying to bring the demon here, or get rid of it?" She stepped back. Her weight shifted as she tried to figure where to guard.

"Find it and send it elsewhere, preferably the erstwhile area from whence it belongs."

"So how do we know you're not with the other guys?"

"The furs folk, right?" I cut in. The shades wearing twit had rambled for long enough and we'd never get anywhere otherwise. "Well we'd be doing a better job of not being suspicious as all sin, for one thing. What do you want with them, anyway?"

"We're clearing them out." Another of them piped up. His volunteering earned him a head-smack from a teammate.

"We don't know if we can trust this lot, yet."

"You're also standing at the other end of a high yield firearm." I tapped the barrel of my. "Don't mean to threat, but you really not in the right end of the trigger to be getting all cagey like, see?"

"Oh what does it matter?" The first woman threw her hands up in exasperation. "We've been sent in to start clearing them out. They've been causing trouble—Arson, drug trafficking, violence breaking out. So they're being stamped out."

"You're with the police?" Draco asked.

"More or less. I'll spare you the technicalities. Who are you with?"

"Hired by an independent," he replied. "Well, hired is hardly the word. We're nowhere near so mercenary, though I'd hesitate to say words like loyalty. It was legal none the less, even if performed with questionable illumination, but let's not get into that in case the pain mark can be set off by being a smart ass. So do you know why the Don Giovanni's are supposed to be here? Why this old basilica?"

"Supposedly they're looking for something hidden here. 'The stable-shard of the lamb' or something. They reckon they find this 'lamb' thing and it'll lead them to glory or who knows what. Others reckon it'll call forth a demon that will end the world, but really, what does any of that matter? We're just here to cut down a troublemaking cult."

"Tell me more about this lamb figure."

"It's called 'the lamb of the little horn' or something like that."

"So if those cult people are meant to be here, where are they?" Vengai-Ra asked.

"These walls are pretty solid, right? I heard Brown Jenkin in there earlier. They're probably hiding in solid matter like he is."

"What is this man talking about?" The woman gestured to Draco.

"He's insane. Ignore him."

"Ko, stop pointing your gun at these fascists."

"Yes, sir." I placed the gun in a holster inside my coat, and stood to attention. I didn't dismantle the piece in case I needed to draw it on the fly.

"He's a madman, but you take orders from him?"

"Cruel joke, Ma'am. It can't be helped." There was a general grunting from the folk in broad understanding. They all worked for a cut. They knew the score.

"Hey, does anyone else hear that?"

A harsh scratching and an inhuman shriek sounded out. Whole chunks of masonry burst open and two dozen black beasts came spilling in from the holes.

"Wait a minute, you're not Jenkin!" Draco cried out.

"It's those Burrows bastard! Open fire!"

"The dusky night rides down the sky, and ushers in the morn. The hounds all join in glorious cry, the huntsman winds his horn, and a-hunting we will go."

"You what?"

"Just shoot them, Ko." He barked, and turned his girl into a sword.

"Yes, Sir." I had the cloud brew up a feed of Q-shots and whipped my sidearm back out, cool and comfortable in my hand.

The grubby wretches drew closer. The size of large dogs, covered in greasy black hair with white discoloration down their heads and backs, and mouths full of crooked brown teeth. The little police attachment fired upon them with what small arms they'd been permitted to carry, and although they drew blood, they failed to slow the things down. Thick hide must've been to blame.

I placed myself between Doc and the nearest group and opened fire. I had a clear shot at the shrunken black eye of the thing heading the pack and took it. Everything behind that was too busy scrambling and crawling over one another to be worth the time aiming so I emptied the rest of the magazine wherever I could. Only the first went down for the count. The rest stumbled and tripped over one another, but started to clamber back up. I ejected the magazine into the fold of my coat where it was deconstructed by the cloud and grabbed the replacement I had made in the three-point-oh seconds it took to deliver the first load. The magazine slid in with a suppressed click and I reassessed my targets.

There are eight in the group closest, six groups of ten plus minus two all up, and infantry coming up behind them. Kiddy cops were running a distraction, but not taking anything down. Boss was cutting and burning, but they were clever and kept their distance from him while flanking. Doc was rummaging with something glass. Clean-up was a go. Wax drip.

Two handed grip and braced. Open fire.

Unlike the last, these rounds punctured through the things' flesh, shattering bones and perforating organs. Each shot left one of the uglies dead, dying, or paralyzed forever. The near group fell, some carried by their momentum to a skidding entrails spattered stop. I turned my whole body, re-braced, and emptied the last two in the magazine at the biggest cluster of hairies hassling the charge cops. They were disciplined, if ineffective. Both my shots hit the same feral, but one passed straight through to blind its neighbor.

Reload. Reassess.

The penny patrollers had concentrated fire on the blind one, and seemed to be taking it down. One of them got careless and was caught unaware. The thing's jaw tore right through her meat and bent the leg forty-five degrees to the left. With enemy blood spilled, the nearby members of the pack swarmed her despite her teammate's efforts. Dog food. No sense wasting bait.

All ten shots hit home and the mangled body was buried under pounds of flesh. The rest of the attachment was shaken, but not broken.

Reload. Reassess.

Boss was covered in blood and leaking smoke. Is that bad? Doc chucked two culture tubes at one of the holes in the wall. They shattered on impact, spilled across the floor, and the people trying to emerge from them clutched their throats. I fired two shots at a pair of beasts getting a little too close to Doc.

"Do I need to hold my breath?"

"It's gone in a couple seconds of exposure, but if you breathe in before that, all sorts of badness happens."

"I'll keep that in mind."

I managed to take out five more of the dog things with the rest of the magazine. That cleared up a bit of breathing room. The whole floor stank of wet fur and smoke.

"Orders, Boss?"

"Have fun." He pulled his sword out of a beast's skull and kicked another one in the neck.

"Please take this seriously. What are we hoping to accomplish here?"

"Oh, all right. Kill all the animals. Do what you like with the fools that brought them, but save at least one hide-cloaked bastard for us to talk to. Do what you like with the rest."

"Can do, boss. Everyone get down."

I let my coat take apart my sidearm and ordered up a new weapon, something a bit hastier. The rifle emerged from my coat like printed plastic.

"Down where? And what's that you've got there?"

"The serial code won't mean anything to you. We just called it the backscratcher."

"Why?"

"Stupid reasons." I pulled it out and made sure it was loaded. Right.

"I was serious about the getting down, by the way." I pointed it far to the right and pulled the trigger.

The chattering bullets sawed right through the last of the ugly creatures in three bursts. Half spent, I sprayed across the holes the fur-wearing jackasses were crouched in. They seemed to have been occupied exchanging fire with the hired enforcers, but my interruption forced them behind cover. A few seconds passed. One of them tried to get a blind hit in, but a short burst shot the gun right out of their hand. I had my coat manufacture a few toss explosives.

"Boss, if you wanna hop in there and fish out a live one?" I pointed to the nearest hole.

"Can do."

I empted the rest of my rifle as covering fire and let my cloud break it back down again, then lobbed the explosives into the other holes. They detonated and the walls crashed down over the rest.

"Boss?"

"Coming." Draco emerged from the last hole, dragging one of their number by a broken arm. I tossed him the last explosive. With the flat of his blade, he belted it into the hole, already smoking from his fire, and threw himself down. The explosive went off, and the last hole was covered under a pile of rubble.

Draco picked himself up, walked over and dropped his captive at the Doc's feet.

"So what can you do with this one for me?"

"And what do you mean with that? Kill him? Bring him back to life? Splice his genes with a fruit-fly's?"

"You know all the in-outs of biochemistry and whatnot. Have you a truth serum or some such you could inject him with to speed things up a bit?"

"Well a literal truth serum doesn't exist in any form short of magick, but there are a few certain concoctions I know how to make that would lower certain inhibitions and inhibit certain judgmental capacities in such a way that might leave him more prone to choosing to be honest when asked a question."

"Sounds like, do that."

"Well I can't just pull it out of thin air, I need to prepare a dose first."

"What if you told Ko the chemical makeup of it, could his robo-cloud fabricate some up?"

"I don't trust anything that comes out of his dark pockets to be any more real relatively speaking than he is. I'd rather not inject a subject with a substance with any remote chance of an annihilative reaction not of my own handiwork." The doctor huffed.

"You science types are so uncooperative with one another." Draco rolled his eyes and wandered off to talk to the remaining gov-shooters.

Chapter Seventeen

Truth

Vengai-Ra

Preparing the drug ended up not taking as long as I'd first anticipated. It was colloquially known as 'loose-lips' among the fraternity I'd learned it from, and though they'd never thought to use it for more than a few party games and ending disputes, it was quite the dandy concoction. A few drops of this, a pinch of that, stir, empty a capsule from among *those* along with a lit match, and a bark candelabra here's one full dose.

I held the hypodermic up to the light and flicked it to dispel any air bubbles that might have formed. The result was a thin, off-white liquid. Normally one would refrigerate it until it turned clear, but that was just a courtesy. All it did was stop the crippling migraines afterwards. I placed the secure chemical flasks back in my coat and stand by, needle in hand.

"Alright, where's our subject?" I turned to the others. Those military types seemed to have formed a perimeter of some sorts, while Draco and the one that seems to be their leader went over the restraints on the captive. I'd no idea where they found rope.

The prisoner was conscious and alert, his mouth taped up, and his eyes bloodshot with worry. Draco appeared to have seen fit to remove his furred cap, and was now wearing it sideways. I approached, needle held high.

"Oh good, you are awake. Well, that saves me a shot of adrenaline." The captive's face was unwashed and well weathered. Though he didn't seem that old, his eyes were sunken and his hair had started to grey.

"You look like you could do with a holiday. Get away from all the rush and tumble of being a city hobo, maybe try your luck as a forest hermit for a few weeks." I squatted down in front of him, and brushed my coat back from where it fell on my legs. "Someone hold him arm, please." I gave the hypodermic a final once over to make sure it wouldn't just snap off in his flesh or something else embarrassing.

The guy screamed into the tape.

"And not the broken one. Should have specified that."

The military woman seized the captive by his other arm and rolled up his tattered sleeve. I whistled an old Al'Juran nursery tune as I probed the crook of his elbow with my thumb.

"Ah, here we are. This will only hurt briefly. Then, well, you'll realize we're not so bad after all." I slid the needle into his arm and injected the full dose straight into his bloodstream. I counted to six, and eased it out again. Blood beaded at the hole as it passed free. I nodded to the military woman, and she tore off the tape around his mouth.

"You can torture me all y' like, but I'll never talk," he said in English, his voice coarse and Gaelic.

"I saw that bluff-flinch," Draco sang out, bouncing a flame from one fingertip to another like a spinning ball. "Looks like you're in a pinch." He held the flame under the man's fringe, and the silvery hair smoldered.

"Draco, that really isn't necessary, and in fact might be detrimental to the process." I pinched my brow.

"It doesn't matter what you do to me. We'll get the stable-shard sooner or later, and once we do, we'll find the little-horned Lamb of God, you'll see. You'll all see. Can't you see we're just trying to save you? The world must spin again!" The man's voice wavered on the edge of mania and desperate pleading. It might well have been himself he was trying to convince, as the Loose Lips undermined his mental barriers. Inhibitions on all areas were being broken down, including the ones he'd placed on his own thoughts. Someone more inclined could work wonders with the drug in the field of psychotherapy. Well, nothing to do with me.

Draco raised an eyebrow above his dark glasses at the man, and chewed a thought.

"Stable-shard. Would that be a little bit of wood stashed away here?"

"Yes! Yes, yes! That be the key. The key to the Lamb."

"Is that right? It sounds important. It's a good thing I picked it up before the fighting broke out, or else it might have been damaged." Draco smirked, and the man's eyes widened.

"You have it? You found the shard."

"Oh, indeed. I've not much use for it, though. Tell me, where is your leader that I might give it to them?"

"You'll do that? You will? You will?"

"Quite so. I've an inkling they and I might be looking for the same thing, and if not, well, someone as good at finding things as your leader must be able to help me in return."

"Ye, it's true. The Dandy can find anything with a strong enough link, no matter how well hidden. With the stable-shard he can scry the lamb right out of hiding."

"The Dandy, Huh? Where can I find him? To help you, of course."

"There's this club. Cupid's Howitzer. The Dandy relaxes in the back rooms upstairs."

"And where is this club?"

"On the, the middle of Ritz boulevard. "

"Well then, thank you very much." Draco flashed a smile and stood, leaning on his sword like a walking stick. "Come, minions, we spent the day bar hopping now it's time to spend the night clubbing." He twirled his finger around in the air in what I think was meant to be a beckoning gesture.

"I do wish you'd stop calling us that," I grumbled, but stood beside him. No breaks in this job.

"And just where do you think you're going?" the military woman demanded. Her hand drifted down to her side where her firearm was holstered.

"Why copper, we were never here." Draco winked and turned his back on her. "You can keep the scoundrel too, free of charge. Or are you going to repay kindness with a catapulted book?"

"*Tch*, fine. Get out of my sight before I change my mind. You got one minute."

"As you wish. Minions, move out."

"Are you sure there's not some dehumanizing reg you're violating with all this minion talk?" I groaned as we made our way outside, past the wary enforcers and wreckage. "We have been bought by the keeper, one way or another, I understand that but do we have some sort of Union of the Damned that I can report a complaint to?"

"If there isn't, perhaps we could start one," Ko offered, finger on his chin.

"Wouldn't that constitute revolt? Are you really willing to wage war against Hell just to stop me calling you names?" Draco spread his hands wide as we stepped outside into the cool, not so fresh air. From behind us echoed the muffled voices of the enforcers doing their own interrogation. I squinted ahead, and sure enough, our car was still there, albeit now sporting *Segreto Gattoexcellente Italiano* spray-painted on one door.

"Well isn't that nice. Our steed now has a name." Draco beamed and turned to me. "You came from a magic kingdom of wonder and mystery. Does having a name make this automobile more extraordinary somehow?"

"I made my deal to get away from all that magick tomfoolery," I grumbled, climbing into the car's back seat. The pungent stink of a corpse still lingered about its interior. "So in short, I haven't the haziest."

"Really? Well, at least it shall be a more memorable ride." Once we were all inside, Draco turned the ignition and set off down the road.

"Standby," Ko piped up from his wind-crazy hair. "Do you even know how to get to this place?"

"Not in the slightest. Still, I'm sure I can find a directory from some service station or another. Now, chaps, how do you want to do this?"

"You what?" I took a minute to fasten my coat up so it stopped blowing everywhere.

"We're in this together after all, and what good's a minion only good for its resemblance to a gun? We have a club, within which is some 'dandy' who, one way or another, may be able to help us find The Woman. Most likely, more of those bearskin cultists will be hanging around too. Not to mention we can't take as given that we will even be granted entry, looking as you do." He gestured with one hand.

"So if I catch your mote, we can try to get in undercover, sneak in the back, or just drop on high impact, *ka-ching*?"

"Or if you would bequeath some other plan to me." Draco seemed to be paying no attention to the city streets that went blazing past, a blur of stone, metal and light.

"There is always the option of waiting for this 'dandy' person to leave, and follow them someplace less out in the field." Just the first thing that comes to mind, more for its own sake than actually wanting. At least it might involve less risk to my wellbeing."

"Taken under consideration. Ko?"

"Box the whole place and pump it with gas. Sieve through the sleepers till we find our mark?" Ko shrugged, distracted by something else on his mind. The dilation of his pupils suggested a rather bad headache, but if he wouldn't say anything, I wouldn't either.

"Hmm, could we even get that much knockout at such short notice?"

"Depending on the size of the building I could manufacture enough in a week or so. What to keep it in would be another matter."

"Then no, staying idle for so long is not an option." Draco fell silent for a few seconds, and spuns the wheel, knocking the rest of us to the side. With two hard *thump*s, he drove up over a gutter into the bay of a refueling depot.

"What the deuce?"

"Don't mind me. Just going to rob this gas station for its directory." He climbed over the door, and reached back for his sword. "You want anything?"

I groaned and pinched my brow. "Well, as long as you are engaging in the pettiest of crimes, I could go for something sweet."

"Can do. Ko?"

"Meat." The gunman said.

"Right. I'll be back in thirteen minutes or so." Draco sauntered through the front door, sword held over his shoulder like a parasol. A few seconds later, a scream rang out and was silenced. After a few more minutes, I leaned forward and turned on the car's radio. Some frantic violin solo came on, and I leaned back into my seat, tapping my foot.

"How long do you think this will take?"

"Pardon?" I turned to Ko, not expecting him to break the silence.

"All this," he jerked his hand about from side to side. "Running around at the whistle of a head-case, being handed out like service revolvers to those who do the devil's work."

"Well, I made my deal. *I* know how much time I owe the Keeper until I've repaid my debts. You though, someone paid to take you out of the picture. Well, a picture. You might well be at it for life, unless you find some other way to bargain for freedom." I picked at my teeth with a fingernail, testing their cleanliness. Ko frowned and held up his hand. If you squinted hard, you could just notice a faint translucency to his flesh.

"Life, huh?"

"I get it. You're concerned whatever weird state your jaunt left you in might leave you living for quite a long while." I didn't bother sparing him pity. He was a weird thing the laws of physics didn't like and his existence defied all reason. He might even outlive the rest of this universe, who knew? Who cared? This was just idle conversation to pass the time. "You could always find how much was paid for you and match it. Though the idea of the keeper being paid at every turn is a sour one."

"So what of you, Doc? What'll you do once you're off the collar?"

"Same thing as before." I shrugged. "Research, experiment, break through the limits of medical science again and again. You know the usual. What about you? Hypothetically, at least."

"I have no idea." He stared ahead.

"Alright minions, let's roll." Draco called out from the station door. His sword was clinging to his back, in one hand he held a plastic bag and in the other an angular jug. He sprinted over and leapt the car door into the front seat.

"Let's see, spare gallon of hydro in case the tank runs dry," He placed the angular jug at his feet, and opened the plastic bag. "Right, something sweet for the good doctor." He handed me two fistfuls of assorted confectionary. Before I could take them, he spilled them into my lap and went back to the bag. "Some meat for Ko," He pulled out three bags of jerked beef, and three small meat pies. These he handed to the gunman. "And a road map." He took a large, blue bound book out, and laid it across his knees. Holding the book in place with his elbows, Draco started the engine and sped off toward the highway.

With very little consultation of the map, which he had gone through some pains to acquire—well, not *his* pains—The swordsman drove our strange collaboration of efforts into the heart of Rome city's sprawling entertainment district. By the time we got there, with all doddering around up until now, night had fallen, and the molten light of lamps and signs had taken over the sun's workload. The Roman nightlife, I'd heard of it in the dreams the Earth's keeper sent me, and it was just as they had described it. Everything was dazzling and glowing, yet there was still a sense of organic-ness that had seeped out of other places. The women wore bikini bottoms with thigh high stockings, buttoned shirts and loose ties, while the men wore denim vests and knee high boots that made their slacks bag out above the footwear's rim. Here and there was one that had played shuffle with the trending fashions, taking a bit from the masculine and a bit from the feminine, and denying them both. Dahn said they called themselves Asto's, at least those with the college had.

A mixed group of three cheered as we drove past, traffic having slowed for a moment, but I paid them no mind and let my thoughts turn inwards. I'd not thought of Dahn often since the keeper's dreams stopped. I'd no need after all. I had a gleaming new education in my head and all the time in the world to poke at it. Now I was on Earth in the flesh, and not just due to some bargained sending dream. Were Dahn and Jared and Mattel even real? Or just figments conjured up by a fevered brain to cope with a trove of information being injected into it. Sleep and dream of an education on the alien Keeper's world. Wake, and write down everything I'd been told as I slept to spend the day going over. For years, that was my life, and it was a good life while it lasted, even when the dream and wake seemed to switch places. If I were to sleep now, would I dream of Al'Juran? Of my labs and my research? No. The swordsman had burnt and broken all that. If I dreamt of Al'Juran, I'd find nothing but ruin.

The car stopped, knocking me from my thoughts.

"Right, that seems to be the place over there." Draco thumbed a building on the other side of the road. Sure as silt, 'Cupid's Howitzer' was emblazoned across the front in luminescent lamps. Already there was a small queue of partygoers waiting to get in, Bright hair, bright clothes, bright eyes and fat wallets on the lot of them.

"So, what approach are we taking?" Ko's fingers worked the air, hands greedy to hold a gun, though his manner seemed reluctant.

"Well, I thought long and hard on the matter, and decided nothing good could come from thinking too long and hard on the matter. Let's just walk in like we own the place and floor any poor sod fool enough to slow us down."

"No tact, no subtly, no cunning?"

"No, but do it with poise." He did a little twirl with his hands, and like a snake, his sword oozed down his sleeve. It hadn't occurred to me the blade-girl's shapeshifting might let an entire longsword act as a hidden weapon—something else to keep in mind if I was to persist, no doubt.

Chapter Eighteen

Deterioration

Draco

The car scraped the sidewalk when I forced it into a stop. Well, no matter. I plucked out the keys and slipped them into my pants as I hopped the door. Not that there's much deterrent in that, if someone wanted *Segreto Gattoexcellente Italiano* bad enough there were all sorts of ways to knick it without keys. Well, let's just call it a gamble, from one Gambino to another.

"No matter, no matter, no matador, nor *matre de*, just a regular methuselah that stood in the manor door for us," I said in English, and waved to the bouncer at the entrance to the Howitzer. A red rope separated her from me and that seemed to be good enough for him. "Hail, friend. We have an invitation to see The Dandy. Be a dearie, and let us off the street so unexciting." This I say in Italian. The boon on my tongue never ceased to surprise me. I reached the red-spun barricade and place my hand on the bouncer's shoulders across it.

"Hey, are you one of those actor sorts? None't told me there was a play going on t'night." The bouncer narrowed her thick brows and sized me up—not too shabby considering she was a full foot my junior. It helped that she had arms like truck tires and a face so angular I might cut my eyes on it. I hadn't planned on a ruse, that and I could have sworn the line was from some old 2560's pop song. Well, let opportunity not pass unmolested.

"Oh, you know how it is with showbiz. As soon as one gets airs of importance, they think the show will wait for them. Let it not be said the show tolerates a no-shower for the show must go on and on and on with or damnably well without you. No, let it be said instead that tonight I earn and eat some lazy front man's dinner for him." I found myself running my hands as I talked, enunciating with my fingers as much as my lips. Three times I touched the bouncer's shoulder, once her elbow, and once almost but not quite her dirty-blond fringe. She moved to snatch my wrist out of the air, and I let her.

"Alright, cool your voxology, and just get inside already. They with you?" She jerked the side of her finger at Ko and Vengai-Ra. The gesture wasn't familiar, but obvious enough in meaning.

"Aye that they be. Be, in this case, being my troupe, small at it is. Moreover, small troupe we be, but be make it work for us. Would you like me to explain the benefits of such a small wee troupe as we? Yes?"

"Oh filth no. Get your flapping gob inside already before I break it off." She unhooked a length of the red rope and held it aside. I smiled and headed on in. My troupe, certainly smarter than wild dogs, followed behind. I pushed aside the strange, murky cloud in my brain. How long ago did I have my last drink? Surely all the scotch has been metabolized by now. Why was my head giddy and hard to think with?

We passed through the door and entered Cupid's, and we seemed to have beaten most of the crowd. There was a bar on the first floor, with only a few spare stools, and screens behind it showed the latest music clips of scantily clad propaganda-mouthers for *this philosophy or that. 'Happiness is a fat wallet, and the knowledge of how to spend it.' 'The state is corrupt, only in anarchy can we break free to start again.' 'All things are equally meaningless, so why not find happiness in soccer?'* The usual stuff that's nice to hear spread over two to five minutes of singsong, especially if the chorus is catchy, but the most it every inspires anyone is to get into show business themselves. Moreover, why not?

Tell me, my dear friend, when was the last time you got fed a full pound of food in the army?"

"Not since boot camp, sir. Though calling it 'food' might be a bit generous, it tasted like mud and cracked your teeth if you got impatient. First week there, I saw a fellow named Vlen throw his ration to ground and empty six rounds into it. Not a dent." Ko shrugged with his palms held upwards. Hang on, something wasn't not right. When did I start talking? Where was I? Ko on one side, Vengai-Ra on the other, and out over yonder was a floor full of chairs and stools. When did this microphone get on my neck? How long had I been standing on stage? I'd an urge to panic, but quashed it down. The crowd seemed amused enough, or at least drunk enough to be amused.

"Now here's a thing, Doctor. You've a keen eye, have you not? A whole jar full of them no doubt, but I'm talking about your head. Actually you probably could fit the whole jar in your mouth, if the rumors are true, haa haa." This wasn't going to plan. We were just meant to beat our way to wherever the Dandy is. Not perform comedy for a bunch of club-goers. Or was this the plan and I imagined the other plan?

"Are you going somewhere with this, or just after an excuse to make insinuations about my personal life?" Vengai-Ra folded his arms over his chest. From the look on his face, he had no idea what was going on either, but seemed to think that I did. A thought occurred. I held one hand out, and intentionally clicked my fingers. I decided to do something, and did it, and I felt myself doing it. Now that I think about it that probably didn't even mean anything, probably.

"Oh I am, good doctor, I assure you. How good is your snap diagnosis?" I gestured across the crowd with my hand, trying to get across what he's to do.

"Oh my diagnosis is fine. I can usually peg why you're limping from fifty steps away. A'course, I never did take that Hippocratic Oath that's so popular. Maybe I do know why you're limping, but maybe I got this new technique for attaching a prosthesis I'd like to try out. I'm not one to let good health get in the way of medicine." The crowd laughed some more. I'm a little disappointed myself. He had a perfect opportunity for a 'peg' pun that he didn't take. I could make it now but it'd just sound forced. Why did I even care? Was there something nefarious underway, or had I just gone fully insane? Well, spell or sanity, I was not about to let it stay my path.

"Do you know what the funny thing is, my wonderful audience? I don't even know what I'm doing up here." I was wearing a showy grin, and talking the flashy talk, but just speaking the truth now. "This is the second floor, right? No, hang on, this the third if I'm reading that sign right. I've no idea how I got up here. I was looking at the bar downstairs, thinking to myself, and suddenly I'm not thinking, I'm talking. It's the damnedest thing. I'm not even an entertainer. By all accounts, I'm just some homeless guy who walked in off the street running his mouth. Now look at me." More laughter.

"Say, are you sure?" Vengai-Ra hissed at me under his breath, but I dismissed him with a flick of the wrist.

"I'm here for 'The Dandy'. I don't even know who that is. What I do know is I'm not the only one. First, the no doubt off-the-books 'secret police' of the state are trying to shut down this hairy little cult operation." A few people laughed nervously, but the abrupt sound of muted gunfire from below shut them up in an instant. A thought occurred, and I decided to roll with it.

"Not that your cult has been too subtle with what you're after or how you're doing it. There are double and triple agents everywhere, not to mention how easily ye bearskin-clad cravens squeal. A bastard like me just had to ask around a bit to walk right in your door. Imagine what the other lot think, the ones who say you're wrong about this whole lamb business. I say, do you smell something burning?" Whether they did or not, I could, and it was a smell quite a bit pleasing at that.

"That'll be them I imagine, probably got wind of the cop raid thanks to one of those triple agents I mentioned. Lucky little sod has probably taken their reward and bailed the city for the season by now. I bet if you think real hard you'll realize who it was, too." I was going out on more limbs that Schrödinger's cat up a tree, but from the look of rapt panic amidst dawning hate in the crowd, I was striking enough nerves to make a reverb.

"So this is war time now, right?" Ko slipped a hand into his open coat, and I nodded. He pulled a riddle from the robot cloud inside his clothes and leveled it at the crowd. They stared at the barrel, none wanting to make themselves the first target. Riddle? No, rifle.

"You two keep whatever comes up busy. I'm heading for the VIP room." I saluted Ko and jump off the stage. He opens fire.

The audience scattered as soon as he pulls the trigger, some ran for downstairs, others ran for side rooms and bathrooms. Plenty screamed in panic, but none screamed it pain. I never did specify shoot to kill, and sure enough the gunman was firing wide with every shot, Well, no matter to me. I whistled *Darling Clementine* amidst the panic, and jaunted up the stairs opposite the stage to the VIP room. Atop the stairs was a door, which proved locked when I tried the handle. Drakkengard flew down my wrist like silvery water and solidified into a sword in my hand. I drove her right through the lock like an oversized key, and turned, wrenching a chunk of the door right out. I flicked Drakkengard to launch the debris off her, and pushed the door open.

Behind the door was a purple-painted corridor, with a striking red carpet. At the end of it was a tall, lanky man, dressed in pastel greens, a hat pulled down to cover his eyes and a pair of long knives in his hands. His skin was a tanned, milky brown. He touched one knife to the rim of his hat in a gesture I didn't recognize.

"See you, intruder. You here to see the Dandy, yes?"

"That I be. And you're the bodyguard?" There was an itchy niggling at the back of my mind. "Have we met?"

"Met us, have not. The other, indeed. Best me to get past, you must."

"Do you always talk like a gremlin knight-mystic?" I started to walk down the corridor. There's was enough room to swing Drakkengard here. I was at a disadvantage.

"No, I just like doing around with your head. Whoa, that's close enough." He held his knives up, and it took me a moment to figure his meaning. I halted, and adjusted how I was holding Drakkengard to a position, better suited for thrusting. The man in green dipped his head, and I got the impression he'd closed his eyes. From the open door behind me, the sounds of gunfire grew even louder. It seemed the other intruders had reached Ko.

"Now here's the dual. Three two one go!" He flung a knife at me. I don't even see his hand move and on reflex, alone I jerked my head to the side to avoid it. I threw one foot in front of the other and start running, my left arm held in front of my face. The bodyguard loosed another knife, and another. Where did he even draw that third one from? I ducked one and the next sunk into my thigh. Pain shot up my side, but it didn't ruin my pace.

There were fifteen meters between us now. He flung more knives. One embedded itself right into my upheld forearm, aimed for my eye, and I swore I heard it chip the bone. Another cut across my cheek, and blood splashed my iris. My vision half obscured, I didn't see the next three that hit my shoulder. Nothing important seemed to have been cut, and I kept moving.

Ten meters to go. He was going for broke now. A blade passed right through my left wrist, locking it in place. Another penetrated my palm while another struck against my elbow, and my arm failed me. A knife hit my breastbone and fell out, another penetrated my throat, cutting off air but didn't manage to harm my spine.

Six meters. I jerked my head, and a knife skewered my cheeks instead of my eyes. Five knives in succession made home down my left leg, and the last one did something weird to my kneecap. The leg failed me, and my entire left side was now useless.

Two meters. I fell to one knee, and its nerves exploded. I couldn't even yell for how my throat was cut off, but I threw all my weight into thrusting my sword with all the might I could muster. I could tell from the measure of resistance that Drakkengard passed right through the wall, but could't see for all the blood in my eyes. The sound of gunfire remained, and that was the only sound.

I let my hand slip from Drakkengard's hilt and yanked the blade out from my throat. Blood gushed down my front, but after just a second, the wound closed. I gasped for air, a desperate, grating sound. Once I could breathe, I wiped the blood from my eyes and looked up.

My foe was gone, nothing left but a pastel green jacket impaled by my sword. I laughed, what else could I do? Well for one thing, I could yank the rest of these damned knives out. I grabbed the handle of the one embedded behind my left knee and pulled. It slid out easily enough, and the wound sealed over. Was it just me, or did my body heal faster now? If nothing else, I was grateful my little obstacle didn't use toothed knives.

After tearing out the blades in my legs, I rose to my feet.

I rose to my feet.

I rise, I rise, a fire ant up the witch's stake, I and mine nest-kin. We swarm over her body and set her flesh aflame with our venom. Chattering skull, lolling tongue, shut up shut up shut up. Better than you, better than you, better anything than you. Close my eyes and scream that neither of us are real. Not my eyes.

I rose to my feet and turned to the door beside the corridor's end. My hand was so slippery it took two tries.

Well, I wagered this was it. I pulled Drakkengard from the wall, and without bothering to check if it was locked, I sliced the door right off its hinges and kicked it in. Not sweating, not shaking.

"Say, what you like about the prescience, you can't deny that knowing something will happen doesn't make it less satisfying." The man in green swiveled around on a chair, and placed both feet upon a large wooden desk—no, once I got a better look, I wasn't so sure it was a man. Neither the face nor build nor voice was particularly masculine, or feminine for that matter. The face was familiar though. Where had I seen it before?

I stepped inside, and yanked out the knife going through my cheeks. When did that get there? If I was to suffer such a welcome, the least I could do was bleed on their carpet in return.

"So you are the Dandy after all?"

"Quite so, and it seems my little gaggle of followers is done for, one way or another." The uncanny figure took out a book, and flicked through it. With the jacket left outside, all the Dandy wore now was a pastel green vest over a white shirt and matching green slacks.

"You don't seem too disappointed." I grit my teeth and yanked out another knife, this one from my arm.

"I knew it would happen. That is to say, this outcome was not unexpected. Nevermind that, though, for this is the important question—Do you the devil's work?" The Dandy paused at a page, ran a slightly tanned finger down it, looked up and smiled. Finally, I recognized the face. In one or two books here and there, talking about the physical differences between races past and present, sometimes, in demonstration of no point in particular but 'isn't this neat?' they had presented a digital amalgamation of thousands of samples of each sex of each race, a picturesque 'average' human. That very same amalgamated face now regarded me from below a pastel green hat. Not the face of one, but the face of every man and every woman on the planet, all at once.

"You are a demon." I frowned, realization just giving way to more puzzlement.

"A djinn, rather, I've not much miasma down this gullet. Got to keep an eye on my figure after all." They laughed, a soft, gentle chuckle, and closed their book.

"Who are you?"

"I am Dantalion, Great Duke of Hell. You call yourself Draco, no?" Dantalion tilted his head, smiling.

"That is me. Was this all some elaborate set up of him downstairs?" I flicked the last few knives out. After the first half dozen, it didn't even hurt to do it anymore. Did it ever hurt? Just how long ago did the door trap do this? Or was it that bodyguard thing before?

"Hmm? I can't imagine so. I've not had contact with Keeper Shaitan for a few hundred years now."

"So what have you been doing? Why all the cults and why Rome? Just what dance have I intruded upon?"

"I've been gathering up what artefacts of the son I can get my hands on, by any means necessary. You would not believe what I had to go through to secure the Shroud of Turin." Dantalion pinched their nose, as if forced to relive the odorous trial once more.

"That bit of old cloth? Surely it would have fallen to pieces millennia ago, even if it was real."

"Yes, yes! Exactly. I still got it though. Not the original cloth itself, but the idea of the Shroud, contained in an unmistakable shroud-like form." Dantalion beamed and did a little hand-jig, looking rather cat-like in the gesture.

"Is this one of those 'grandfather's axe' things?"

"No, not really, it's more like crystalline conceptualization, turning the essence of a thing into, well, a small, physical god. I hear the Nipponjin got the knack for it centuries ago, but they've been behind their winds so long people are starting to forget they exist, and it is just way too much hassle to get inside that loathsome storm, know what I mean?"

"So I imagine this bit of wood is one of your artefacts?" I reached into my jacket, now with a lot more holes and blood than when I'd gotten it, and took out the lump of wood from the old church. It had remained remarkably unscathed and Dantalion's eyes lit up.

"Oh yes, a bit of the cot itself, very useful."

"So what is all this about you using this here bit of wood?" I tossed the lump from one hand to another, watching as Dantalion's almond-shaped eyes followed it intently. "Summoning a dark saviour? Little-horned Lamb or what have you?"

"Oh that's just a problem of myth blending. 'The Lamb' and 'Little Horn' are two different things. The prophecies around them got mixed up a while ago around these parts, it seems."

"But you're going to use this wood to call one?"

"Oh probably not call it. If I can find out where the little bastard is, that might do a good way of answering just what the hell went wrong. I'm not hopeful, but after a thousand years sitting on your thumbs, it's better than doing nothing."

"Still, you're pretty good at finding people?" With the wood held in one hand, I reached back into my jacket with the other.

"Oh, yes. Secret meetings, playing matchmaker, all a little hobby of mine that makes working seem not so dull."

I pulled out the two silver rings the strange soothsayer had given me. "I was told I could buy a demon's name with these rings, and with the wood I would sweeten the deal." I cleared my throat. "I seek the one called Lascivus, called Lilim. If it pleases you, accept this payment and tell me the name and method by which I might find her." I tossed both the rings and the wood at the androgynous djinn. He caught them, then tossed the rings back at me.

"Hold on to those a little while longer, the cot-shard's payment enough. I don't know what Bifrons is plotting but getting overpaid rubs me the wrong way." Dantalion pocketed the wood, and flicked through the book from before. Once he found the page they were looking for, they tore it out, and handed it to me. "Here is another of her names. Go to her. Don't call her. You need to learn to send yourself, and that's something I can't help with."

"And what will you do now?" I regarded the paper in my hand. Written on it, in the koinegreek alphabet, read '*Kerata duo omoiaarniw*'. Although that boon of tongues told me how to read it, it didn't tell me what it meant like it should have. Perhaps it was a property of the book, or because it was a name. No matter.

"I'll go on to the next thing. I hear rumor that the gold gifted to the son at birth has shown up in Madrid. Maybe something will come of it, maybe it won't. I've nothing but time."

"And your people here?"

"What of them?" Dantalion seemed surprised at the thought, like such consideration was unheard of. What of them indeed? What of the log you used to float down the stream? The stream is already behind me, what of it indeed?

"Never mind, I'll make my own way out."

"That you will." Dantalion flicked back through his book, and started laying pages down on the ground. No doubt by the time someone else reached the room, the Djinn would be long gone. I'd better be long gone too. Drakkengard in hand, I headed back out the door and ran toward the gunfire.

Chapter Nineteen

Torment

Draco

I allowed myself a day of rest, just one day. It was an allowance I fast regretted as I awoke with my chest feeling as though it was birthing molten steel through dilated bones. That binding brand said I'd wasted too much time, but the shock of it threw me hurtling back into unconsciousness, and fevered dreams.

A maiden on the eve of her wedding, white ribbons are tied all around her body, binding her hands and mouth, and feet and breasts. The ribbons spiral outward, crisscrossing and combining and splitting until returning to the exposed entrails of forty-three crones, screeching hymns in only twelve voices.

I know not how much time had passed when Drakkengard woke me. Her eyes were red and her skin greyed. The pain had subsided, but my chest still ached at the memory of it.

"I have to hurry." I stood and my vision swam, forcing me to lean on my sword's shoulder for balance.

"Ko! Vengai-Ra!" she barked, and my bidding doers came running in from the adjacent hotel rooms. I think they said something, but I couldn't make it out.

"Time's running out. We need to find a way back to the underworld…and…" I spoke before I'd finished the thought, but another seizure of pain cut me off. I managed to stay awake this time, and while I caught my breath, Drakkengard spoke in my stead.

"Is this a bad joke? Is just thinking the wrong stuff against the rules now? This isn't fair!" She grit her teeth and stomped the ground. On the third pounding, her foot broke through the shoddy flooring.

"So much for the security deposit." Vengai-Ra joked, but was unable to hide how disturbed he was. I could taste ash somehow, but still forced myself to speak up.

"Alright, so the courier route is closed to us. Then we must do the Mohammed way and bring the mountain. Or go to it. I can't think!"

"Master." Drakkengard squeezed my shoulder, and I gathered my thoughts.

"Okay, bring me a teacher. If not a teacher, books. Demonology, conjuring, theory of magick, hell parlor magic if it'll somehow help, you just bring me learning." That last one was too much like wasting time, and the brand flared up again. Once more, I lost consciousness, and again I dreamed.

A lioness rides into the desert, 347,137 lengths of rusted metal thrust into her neck. Beneath her paws, sixty-three sickles click against the hardened ground. Out the end of her tail a desert rose blooms, and in her mouth a clockwork screw that has long since ceased to move.

***

The light of awareness flooded my mind and I awoke, drenched in sweat. Drakkengard was wringing out a damp cloth beside me, and when I turned to her, she placed it on my brow.

"You're really not well, Master. Those two brought back lots of books, but only six were good. I'm so sorry." She dipped her head, as if it was her fault. I pushed back the hood of her robes with a shaky hand, and tousled her hair.

"We drink what water we find. Pass the first book." And into those books I poured myself.

Chapter Twenty

Contract

Rites, incantations, mnemonic devices, sigils, mantra, formulae, equations, writ of depravations, everything wrong with the laws of physics, the ground broken by Thoth, states of mind, states of matter, thoughts to hold, thoughts to hurl, ego-states to curl, concepts to laud, phenomenon of discord, words to cast, how long is this fast?

I devoured the pages, burned up the leather-bound leaves, crammed everything I could fit into my head's eaves, and all the while the brand on my chest raged. I drew up the circles, spilled the blood, spewed magick where called for again and again and again. Retry, fail and throw aside, retry, fail and throw aside, why, why, why won't the arcane abide?

Across vast wilderness of mystic hypotheses, my lessons rode, and again and again and again it came to naught. Where was the misstep? On whose sensitive toes was I stomping in this maladroit waltz of learning? The idea was simple enough—take me to the one who bears the name, yet every array, every door, every portal remained but chalk and scratches despite my will. How, how, how was it I could fling the curse that started this mess on half a thought and a head full of blind phantasms yet catapulting myself to one damned fool eluded me?

I ate nothing, I drank nothing, I saw neither the rising moon nor the setting sun nor any visitors. My tool to measure chronology was the swelling agony flowing off the brand harder and harder. No matter what my body was capable of, I'd no doubt this brand would succeed in killing me soon. The executioner's axe swung like a pendulum lower and lower with every failed attempt.

The problem didn't seem to be with the texts, no, it was the fault of my mind because I *just didn't get it*. I couldn't grasp the fundamental understanding of the universe needed for this passage. I did not comprehend. I focused to my uttermost on that visage of the underworld's twisted dimensions the she-devil showed me, but I just didn't get it. If I could just burn a hole there, it would be simple. I *get* fire. I understand combustion, I comprehend conflagration, friction, particle aggravation, but nothing more. I couldn't make the logical or intuitive leap from the knowing of how to burn to the knowing of how to travel, not fast enough. If I had many months and a fine tutor I might, but my own devices were just not enough.

***

The chalk had run out. How long ago did that happen? At least fifty attempts prior to this one. I bit my tongue in frustration and torment earlier, and took the chance to gather my blood in my mouth before it healed. I jammed two fingers past chapped lips, and gathered up the red fluid on my fingertips to finish the latest array. It was flawless, not a drop out of place. Taking a deep, haggard breath, I placed my hands either side of the array and channeled magick into it. There were stinging nettles under my skin but channeling had evoked such a sensation for a while now.

The names upon which I knew her had been marked along the perimeter of the array.

"Now, upon the open door, I rattle the key. Bring this, this door to the real, and make my path open. Open. Open, damn you!" I forced all the magick I could muster into the spell. A violet pain shot through my eye and the left half of the world went dark, but I pushed onward. Just like controlling the fire's blaze, I directed my will, groping for the metaphysical edge of the door I sought, that I might drag it out. Where, where, where is it? Where is the edge? Where is the handhold for me to latch onto? Nothing, nothing, there's nothing but platonic blank, featureless space all around me, nothing to grab, nothing to pry, nothing to so much as drag my nails across, literally or metaphorically. My focus wavered, and the complex array went up in a split second flash fire.

I fell to the ground, though I didn't feel it. My whole body was numb. The only reason I could tell I fell at all was from the way my vision brought the floor to my nose. It stank of ash and blood and filth. My brand throbbed hard, like it was sobbing. That final attempt took the last of it out of me. It. Everything. I had nothing left. No thing. No non-thing. No magick, no hope or charities, not even the pain of the brand that, from the vice I felt crushing my skull, had reached my brain.

No sight, no smell, no taste, no sound, no touch, no thought nor feeling. *I am sinking. I am melting into another world and oh what a world. This feeling of annihilation is nostalgic. It is not the first time I have passed into this nonexistence. That other time too, when . . .she . . .*

Who is thinking this? That was a question. That was a thought. Though there is no light, I can see myself. My face is gaunt and pallid, my hair hanging lifeless about my head and my clothes both soaked through and torn apart. I spread my arms, and let myself fall back.

Let me fall, again, into that place of nothingness. May it carry me to Lascivus, to Lilim, to Kerata Duo Omoiaarniw.

I fall, and I fall with myself and as I fall, I watch myself. I fall though the infinite darkness and I force definition upon it. Tumbling down, tumbling down, tumbling down, and down is what I define as the direction I am tumbling. At a speed of everything per second, and I define a second as how long it takes the whole of this nothing to past. For 8127 seconds I fall, and I know it without counting each one.

I fell into nothing.

And I came out the other side.

***

I landed feet first, with all the force of having hopped down two stairs at once. The air was hot, smelling of incense and peppered meat. The walls, furniture, and hay-covered floor, all stone, and for a moment I thought I'd fallen into some ancient Roman abode, but there on the wall was a clock of neon and liquid crystal, and an electronic refrigerator had been stuffed into the corner there.

"So, you found me?" she said. She was there all along, standing in the middle of the room in a loose shawl and no shoes, one hand on her hip and the other holding an unlabeled bottle. Identifying things, attaching labels, cataloguing them. This is this. Like a blue sky, or clean water. A familiar thing.

"Lascivus," I murmured, out of some half-stewed notion she might vanish like a fog-form if exposed to loud noise. She looked me up and down with bright, judging eyes, as if she'd gone to market to buy a stallion but had found a mule, and was weighing up her time versus her money.

"Yeah, still me. Y'couldn't let sleeping devils lay, could y'?" She hiccuped, and jerked the bottle to her lips. That she spilled not a drop with the sudden motion is remarkable.

"You're drunk."

"N' you've left a big hole behind you. Does that make us even?" She chuckled, and closed her eyes for a few moments, swaying to some half-remembered tune. I glanced over my shoulder. Sure as she said, behind me was a great rent of nothing that obscured what I presumed to be the door. I turned back to her.

"Am I really here? Are you?" I looked around. Was this even still in Italy? Earth? There was something gleaming in my hand. I was holding Drakkengard by the hilt. Causality shouldn't be this hard.

"Blow me if I know," Lascivus said before taking another swig, and I laughed. How can her crassness be so warming? That made her eyes flash with anger and for a moment, I thought she might throw the bottle at me. "Shhh," She hissed. "You'll wake them."

"Who?"

"The big friendly giant, who do y' think?" She stepped away from the table, toward a bit of furniture I'd earlier disregarded. On closer look, it was a cot. I approached, still not convinced the whole scene wouldn't go falling out from under me and reveal itself a dream, but I could hear the straw crunch beneath my shoes and feel the wood of the cot as I placed a trembling hand upon it. Inside were two small children, with chubby limbs and black hair and familiar features. They were beautiful, in a way I'd never known possible. One of them opened its eyes, two large red circles on a sea of white that seemed too big for its face. It stared right up at me and it made a single sound—'ga', or maybe, 'da'.

I hit the ground, eyes wide, heart thumping, my nerves fraying like I'd just been shot. I couldn't breathe. My eyes were drowning but they hoarded the salt water without spilling a drop. Lascivus seemed to find this mighty funny because she was standing over me and laughing with tears in her eyes.

"The big bad dark swordsman who cursed me and tracked me down is frightened by the smallest coo of his child?" She tittered, and took another drink.

"My child?" I asked, voice broken and vacant.

"Yes, your child, or did you forget the whole nonsense that got us caught up in this mess in the first place?" She twirled her dainty hand around as if she was trying to hurry things up.

"The curse—" I was still on the floor, my brain struggling to catch up with everything.

"Yes, your ruddy curse. Thanks to that barbed wire this is my first drink since last we saw." She held up the bottle like Liberty's torch. "Counted as letting them come to harm, what rot. Have I ever told you how much I hate being sober? I bloody hate being sober. That reminds me." She held out her hand and helped me up. She then straightened my collar a little, held my head still and slammed her fist into my jaw. I crumpled to a heap on the ground. That was a punch from someone that knew how to cause damage.

"Oh sweet ambrosia, that felt good. Come on, get up."

"No, you'll hit me again." I rubbed my jaw with the back of my hand. That I had a sword and she was drunk just didn't factor into it. Everything was just too disarming.

"That's th' idea, you horse's ass. So go on, how long have you been looking for me? I may as well figure out where I screwed up." Since I refused to get up, she squatted down in front of me, and her shawl revealed more than a bit of leg. Would rolling away in case she kicked me just put the idea in her head if she hadn't thought of it yet?

"Well, from when I set off, including all that time I just spent trying to, well, get it right, it feels so far away now, gods it must have been thirteen months." I sat myself up on my ass and leaned back, trying to clear my head and think straight.

"Wow, you must ha' set off right after I left. Didn't know I meant so much to y'." She said it so nonchalantly, as if I'd just mentioned having greased the rusty gate while she was gone so it didn't squeak so much.

"What I did to you, the curse," I coughed, and swallowed the lump in my throat, aware I'd consumed no water in days. Lascivus seems to recognize this, and pressed her bottle to my lips. I gulped it down, and broke out into a fit of coughing at the burn in my throat. Mead, I recognized the taste of it.

"You were saying?"

"I cursed you in a blind panic, and I'm not sure I could do it again. When Old Scratch found out, and that was fast, he was livid. There was this brand," I coughed again—I could have sworn my throat would start bleeding—and pointed to my chest. "If it ever felt I was taking too long to find you, it burned like molten lead. Toward the end it was burning all the time." She gave me another drink of mead and I gulp it down while fighting back the coughs.

"Spare me the cock and bull. You got a bad itch when you slacked off. I had to go cold turkey for a year. "Her jaw was hard set, and I think she was trying to make me contemptuous, but my head was spinning again. Alcohol on an empty stomach, dehydration, sleep deprivation and exhaustion do funny things. Was my brain bleeding earlier? Her eyes looked tired, and her lips were parted as she looked at me. I guess she wanted her drink back, so I handed it over without complaint. Somehow, that made her scowl.

"Well, what it comes down to is I learned another of your names, Kerata Duo Omoiaarniw." She rolled her eyes at that. Maybe she never liked that name. "I tried to figure out how to make some sort of teleport spell work to take me to you."

"Is that what that is?" She gestured to where the big inkblot of emptiness had been, though it seemed to have closed up now. I shook my head.

"I don't think so. That was that other place. That empty void, we fell into it when I killed *her*." My left hand twitched against the carpet of straw. She sighed.

"Why'd you do it, anyway? Why'd you have to go and stick such a bitch of a curse on me?"

After a long silence, I had an answer. "I was scared. I'd planned to stay as far away from children as much as possible, the pleasures of another's flesh, all of that. It was just meant to be me, Drakkengard and my sister." The last syllable dropped away like a severed finger. "and everything happened, and it kept on happening, and I stop and turn around and suddenly flesh of my flesh is being born to a demon. All I could think was . . ."

"I can't let what happened to me happen to mine." She finished for me, and chuckled. "I always forget what a child you are beneath it all."

"When I found you that night it was the first time you'd found out and don't you deny. It was obvious from your face. You were just as scared as I was. I don't care how old you are she-devil, the difference between us is a matter of mental balance, not maturity." I flinched that she might hit me again, but she sat down next to me, on the other side to Drakkengard, and placed her bottle between her thighs.

"Maybe so. If you wanna chalk up your shit to neuroses rather than childishness, whatever, the point is it's just a pair of kids. Most demons measure their lifespan in centuries. Considering how you heal up, you might too, if you manage to cure that death-seeker streak. Fifteen, twenty years, this pair will be out in one world or another, doing their own thing. That ain't long at all."

A cry went up. One of the children had awoken, and was needy. The sound made me wince, but Lascivus stood up in one languid movement and lifted the child from the cot. She held it in her arms, whispered nonsenses, and soon enough it fell quiet though not asleep.

"Of course if I had to do the whole thing sober that would be different." She laughed, and the child laughed back in simple pleasure.

"Isn't that neglectful?"

"I'm a demon, not some frail thing that couldn't skin a cat without fainting. I could drink enough to kill ten lumberjacks and still dance on a tightrope." She waved her arm, taking on an annoyed tone.

"Somehow I doubt it."

"If you're so worried about these kids then stay, you big lout. Hell, we can make a marriage out of it." She stepped back, her mouth ajar, surprised at what she'd just proposed.

"Are you serious?"

"I guess, I guess I am. You want to keep an eye on these kids, go right ahead. A cozy little political marriage would solve a lot of problems for both of us."

"If it's that simple why go into hiding in the first place?"

"I couldn't drink." She stated. "I can't stand what I'm like when I haven't had a drink. I didn't want anyone to see that, not just you. A bit of petty pride is all. I didn't think dad would take it so seriously."

"No, this is the stupidest thing anyone has ever said to me." I retreated a step, and clenched Drakkengard's comforting hilt. "I have stepped from delirium into pure madness. Let's backtrack for a minute. You, a sexual carnivore tried to eat me. I blackmailed you into helping me commit matricide. You blackmailed me into doing dirty work for your father. We ended up in prison, and, while I was out of my mind and you were scarcely in yours, we resorted to prison sex so you, sexual carnivore that you are, had enough strength to bust us out. The universe hates us enough that you fell pregnant, I had a panic attack and lashed out with a curse, you ran away, your father coerced me into hunting you down, and here we are. Now you want to get married? You're sick in the head. I'm sick in the head. There is nothing healthy about what's between us."

"The two of us, we could still be around thousands of years from now so long as we're not too reckless. What's ten or twenty years to see our hell spawn off into the worlds?" She moved back to the cot, and lifted the other child up in her arms to cradle them both. Their hair was dark and fine.

"What are their names?" I asked. A bead of sweat fell from my chin. They seemed such small, fragile things.

"The kids of a cubi and a human, well, whatever you are that's close enough to human, such kids are called cambion, and there's traditions about that." She held out the children to me, our children. With much hesitation, I set Drakkengard aside and took them. They felt so light in my arms, like they might evaporate in an instant. Both their little chests were still. They were not breathing. Not. My hands shook, an ugly ache bloomed in my chest and stomach and my face went cold. Lascivus just laughed at my alarm and put a reassuring hand on my shoulder.

"A cambion has no pulse or breath until seven years old. Trust me, they're healthy. Topside, in the old ages, a cambion would be lucky not to be fed to the wolves if discovered, so it became tradition to hold off on naming them until their first breath. There's no chance of that with these two of course, your curse made sure of that." She took another swig of her bottle, and shot me a look I couldn't hope to read.

"So that's it? We play happy family until they're able to fend for themselves, and then what?" My voice rose, and one of the little ones frowned in its sleep.

"Whatever we want. Stay, go, it's all easy. Why, what were you planning?" Lascivus demanded, hand on her hip. "Go back to your empty house and empty life, stave off boredom in a stagnant world all on your lonesome? Just you and your sword, among strangers that'll never make room for you or so you'll describe it in your shitty poetry. That sound better to you?"

"What then? I just spend two decades living with you, and what else?" I handed the children back to her and look her in the eye. She put her booze aside to take them and matched my gaze.

"You'll be part of the family, most like. That'll mean getting called upon now and again, but you'll pretty much be free to do as you want." Her jaw was set resolute while she bounced the little ones in her arms. I laughed, a bitter, sardonic sound.

"Did *he* plan this?" I wrinkled my nose. "How far back? Even that first time, when you broke into my bedroom? Has everything ever between us just been an elaborate recruitment drive of the devil?" My face cracked into a mocking grin. A part of me, detached from it all, wondered just why I was acting this way. That part and all other parts were shut up by the demoness's foot connecting upside my jaw. My spine gave a slight crunch against the ground as I landed, even despite the straw carpeting. The sulphuric residue of miasma clung around my mouth. How the hell did she do that without waking the little ones?

"You think I'm just some honey trap? Some prettied up actress of my father's?" Her foot stayed an inch from my face a good, long time, and for a while, I thought she might crush my skull.

"By the hells, I'd never," she trailed off, and looked away. As though remembering a schedule she placed the children back in their cot.

I wiped away some blood from my lip and sat myself up. "Never what?" I asked. My fist and lips both itched in conflicted anticipation. If she left and I never saw her again so many things would be simpler and with the right words that could happen. A bounty of urges pulled at my thoughts, but they all seemed so scripted.

"Nothing, just a number."

"What number?"

"It's nothing, just childish."

"What?"

"Forget it." She turned away, hiding her face. "Look, you're different. You whet my appetite, and everything I've done toward you has been of my own choice. Even your trials, I wasn't assigned, I volunteered. I wanted to, look into you more." Her hands, now free of the little ones, found their way back to her bottle of alcohol and brought it to her lips. Having found in it whatever she was looking for, Lascivus turned back to face me.

"Look, I'm not gonna try to buy or blackmail you. Here's the tune the choir's singing—If you wanna stick by me a while, you won't be unwelcome. Take it or leave it."

"But will there be music?"

"What?"

"Never mind." I picked Drakkengard back up and hoisted her over my shoulders. "I accept?"

"You do?"

"You're right. The only thing waiting for me back in Londinium is an empty manor. I'm curious, about you, about a lot of things. Therefore, as long as opportunity still knocks, I'll open the door before me rather than behind me. Better to sink beneath the shock than molder piecemeal on the rock." I grinned, and she laughed in response.

"Well, shall we head back?"

"Yes, let's."

Benjamin Dempsey was born in Tasmania and grew up in the city of Tamworth, the country music capital of Australia. There, his parents ran a small white goods store. After graduating high school he studied computer science at TAFE for a year before moving to Newcastle to attend University. He studied a bachelor of arts majoring in Creative Writing, while also taking classes on Psychology, Philosophy, Religion, Film Studies and Literature. When an opportunity to move to Sydney opened up, he took it with little hesitation and enrolled at the University of Sydney to continue his studies. However, financial reasons forced him to leave university before he could graduate. This did not deter him from finishing his first book, *Draconian Symphony*.

Benjamin is a ravenous consumer and creator of media, with a passion for speculative fiction. He primarily deals with themes of the occult, transhumanism, and mythology. Most days he runs on extra strength Ceylon tea, and he shares in the Australian appetite for alcohol. In his spare time, he also enjoys video games and the occasional rave.

You can keep up with Benjamin on his website:

www.benjamindempsey.com

Tell-Tale Publishing would like to thank you for your purchase. If you would like to read more from Benjamin or some of our other fine authors, please visit us at:

www.tell-talepublishing.com